BAYAMUS & CARDINAL PÖLÄTÜO

Bayamus

and The Theatre of
Semantic Poetry
and
The Life of

Cardinal Pölätüo

with Notes on His Writings
His Times and His Contemporaries

Two Novels by
Stefan Themerson

Introduction by Keith Waldrop

Exact Change Boston 1997

Bayamus ©1945, 1949, 1965 Stefan Themerson/Gaberbocchus Press
Cardinal Pölätüo ©1954 Stefan Themerson/Gaberbocchus Press

This Edition ©1997 Exact Change
All Rights Reserved
ISBN 1-878972-21-9

Cover illustration: Augustus Pugin's Theatre of Anatomy
Illustrations on frontispiece and p. xi by Franciszka Themerson,
from the first edition of *Bayamus* (Editions Poetry London, 1949)
Illustration on p. 236 by Stefan Themerson, from the first edition
of *Cardinal Pölätüo* (Gaberbocchus Press, 1961)

All illustrations courtesy of Jasia Reichardt and the Themerson Archive,
12 Belsize Park Gardens, London NW3 4LD

Exact Change books are edited by Damon Krukowski
and designed by Naomi Yang

Exact Change
P.O. Box 1917
Boston, MA 02205

Printed on acid-free recycled paper

INTRODUCTION BY KEITH WALDROP VII

BAYAMUS

CHAPTER 1	THEATRUM ANATOMICUM.	1
CHAPTER 2	STILL LIFE WITH A BLACK SHOE.	3
CHAPTER 3	FINGER IN THE MOUTH.	8
CHAPTER 4	THIRD LEG.	12
CHAPTER 5	BAYAMUS' STORY.	16
CHAPTER 6	ROLLER SKATE.	20
CHAPTER 7	MUTATIONS.	24
CHAPTER 8	HOUSE WITH BLACK COLUMNS.	27
CHAPTER 9	JE SÈME À TOUT VENT.	31
	My translation of the Quartier Latin French song sung by the woman knitting the sky-blue woollen yarn	
CHAPTER 10	RHODODENDRON.	44
CHAPTER 11	THEATRE OF SEMANTIC POETRY.	49
	My S.P. translation of the Chinese Poem: 'Drinking under the Moon' By Li Po	
	My S.P. translation of the opening words of a Russian Ballade: 'Haida Troika, the Snow's Downy…'	
	The S.P. translation of the Praise of Created Things which Saint Francis made when the Lord certified him of his Kingdom	
	The S.P. translation of a Polish Popular Song 'Taffy was a Welshman'	
CHAPTER 11	(CONTINUED).	72
CHAPTER 11	(CONTINUED).	77
CHAPTER 11	(CONCLUDED).	79
CHAPTER 12	BOTTLE PARTY.	80

CARDINAL PÖLÄTÜO

PART ONE..99
PART TWO...156
PART THREE...198
CODA...213
DICTIONARY OF TRAUMATIC SIGNS..........................215
ENVOY..233
NOTE...235
THE CARDINAL'S LETTER TO THE TIMES.....................236

Introduction

by Keith Waldrop

*

Stefan Themerson was born in 1910, in Poland (that is, as Jarry would have it, Nowhere) and went with his parents to weather out the First World War in Russia — not, one would think, an ideal climate.[1] After the Revolution, the family returned to resurrected Poland and in due time he went to study in Warsaw, considering a program in physics and architecture. From this wise aim he was somehow deflected into writing, photography, and film and, by 1938, was well known among the Polish avant-garde, particularly for his films, made in collaboration with Franciszka Themerson (née Weinles) whom he married in 1931. (All their Polish films except *The Adventure of a Good Citizen* seem to be lost for good, but this one remains a masterpiece.)

In 1937 the couple moved to Paris but were soon separated by another war, Stefan joining the Polish army and Franciszka having escaped to England where, in 1942, they were reunited. During these years of separation, he wrote his first novel, *Professor Mmaa's Lecture* — in Polish, but it came out in English (presumably his own) in 1953, with an introduction by Bertrand Russell. All the characters are termites.

---

[1] Actually, his home town Plock (on the Vistula) was, in 1910, part of Russia. The Britannica from that time gives it a population of twenty-seven thousand, a twelfth-century cathedral, and the tombs of two medieval Polish kings.

INTRODUCTION

The Themersons settled in England, made two more films and, in 1948, created a small press, Gaberbocchus, one of the most important (big or little) publishing houses of the period, printing Jarry, Queneau, Grabbe — all in Barbara Wright's translation; printing C.H. Sisson, Stevie Smith, David Miller, and a great (but still unrecognised) poet, Patrick Fetherston;[2] printing the work of the exiled Kurt Schwitters; and many others. Printing also the drawings of Franciszka and the texts of Stefan. The books are beautifully designed.

Before *Professor Mmaa's Lecture* was published, Themerson was turning out more fiction[3] and, along with novels and novellas, a number of "philosophical" works. But it is not among the philosophers that he belongs, rather with those writers we used to call moralists, Swift rather than Hume. His essays proceed by parable (*factor T* [1956]), or by Socratic narrative (*Special Branch* [1972]), while his novels often move more discursively.

Themerson's ethic has two basic premises. The first is that we should know what we are talking about. If we fail to know what we are talking about, we fall, not into error — which would be correctable — but into *belief*, from which there is no escape.[4]

Bayamus (1949), his funniest, maddest book (Russell declared it "nearly as mad as the world") is central to Themerson's work, since it introduces the antidote to belief, which is *semantic poetry*.

To define semantic poetry here would be pointless, since the novel you are about to read does so exquisitely and at length, but one may note its rela-

---

[2] *Three Days After Blasphemies* (1967).

[3] In English — one thinks immediately of Conrad, and also of Ruth Prawer Jhabvala (like Themerson, a Jew), though these three wonderful English-writing Poles have little else in common.

[4] The distinction between knowing and believing is discussed in the second section of the pamphlet *factor T* (in which — by the way — Cardinal Pölätüo already makes an appearance): "I can *know*... that if I turn on a switch the bulb will give light; and I can *believe* that if I turn on a switch the bulb will give light. If I *know*, and then it happens that the bulb doesn't give light, I shall call an electrician. If I *believed*, I should go down on my knees... and pray forgiveness from the bulb..."

tion to "Logical Atomism"[5] or, more broadly, to the realization — essential to the thought of the last hundred years — that false beliefs are often simply misleading linguistic constructions. Themerson, in his chapters on the "Theatre of Semantic Poetry," deals with this in the lightest way imaginable, and then, at the "Bottle Party" which follows, manages to introduce the gravest ethical consequences — without becoming grave.

His other moral principle he labeled "Decency of Means," and sometimes presented it, more eccentrically:

> Axioms are mortal,
> politics is mortal,
> poetry is mortal,—
> good manners are immortal[6]

which perhaps says little more than that ends do not justify means, but that is worth saying — and resaying.

After *Bayamus*, he produced a series of fictions loosely connected by recurring characters. These are

Wooff Wooff or Who Killed Richard Wagner? (1951)
Cardinal Pölätüo (1961)
Tom Harris (1967)
General Piesc or The Case of the Forgotten Mission (1976)
The Mystery of the Sardine (1986)
Hobson's Island (1988)

There is no particular order in which they should be read. They are all parts of a comprehensive satire.[7]

---

[5] Russell's revolutionary notion: "Every proposition which we can understand must be composed wholly of constituents with which we are acquainted."

[6] Exordium to his novel *The Mystery of the Sardine*, the punch line also appears elsewhere in his work.

[7] Russell had said, in his preface to *Professor Mmaa's Lecture*, that Themerson "parodies so

INTRODUCTION

Cardinal Pölätüo begins in the year 1862 and stretches into the year 2022. In the former, the Cardinal begets the poet Guillaume Apollinaire, who is, however, carried in his mother's womb until 1880. (The historical Apollinaire did not know who his father was and, so, felt that he could take his pick. He chose — sometimes, anyway — to be an offspring of the Bishop of Monaco.)[8]

The Cardinal is a philosopher, founder of the philosophy of Pölätüomism, and — like an earlier, more celebrated thinker — he wishes, for the sake of his system, to get rid of the poets (which in this case means eliminating his son) because they are the "true heretics." After all, they know what they are talking about and therefore do not "believe." (What happens in the novel, I must add, cannot possibly be predicted from this basic situation.)

Themerson wrote twelve books for children,[9] a brief account of Kurt Schwitters in England (1958), and an opera — both words and music — about Francis of Assisi, in which the Saint opens a canned meat factory and himself becomes the icon (trade mark) for "Brother Francis' Lamb Chops."[10]

Franciszka and Stefan Themerson died in 1988, she in June, he in September.

---

many points of view that the reader is left in doubt as to what, if anything, wins the author's assent. Perhaps this is as well. The world contains too many people believing too many things, and it may be that the ultimate wisdom is contained in the precept that the less we believe, the less harm we shall do."

[8] In 1880, there was no Bishop of Monaco, but the first person to have that position (in 1886) was in fact suspected of amorous relations with Apollinaire's mother. Themerson, by the way, (or at least Pölätüo) thought the poet was born in Monaco (where he spent some time as a child). Actually, he was born in Rome.

9 So I am told. Having seen only the remarkable *Adventures of Peddy Bottom* (1951), I assume most of his children's books are hidden in Polish.

[10] *St. Francis and the Wolf of Gubbio* (1972).

Chapter I

Theatrum Anatomicum

*

'And now, which do you want to see, the Theatre of Anatomy or the Theatre of Semantic Poetry?' said he.

'Both,' said I.

'Well,' said he, 'the Theatre of Anatomy is in 1815.'

'I don't mind,' said I.

'That's O.K. then,' said he, 'let's go.'

And we went to the Theatre of Anatomy.

The Theatre of Anatomy was a separate apartment divided off from all other apartments and passages by a single wall of nearly circular outline reaching from floor to ceiling; the ceiling had the shape of a hemisphere, and the floor consisted of a circular space (in the centre) surrounded by four circular platforms rising tier upon tier. Each platform was protected by a handrail supported by bars painted black and white. On the upper platform there was a young man who had his body and limbs placed in such a position that the weight of the body rested, and was balanced, upon the feet, the legs being straightened. His back was a little out of the vertical and his head erect. Both his hands rested on the handrail, but in the right one he held his black top-hat, the inner surface of which was covered with yellow lustrous fabric that had been woven from the fibrous thread spun from the fine strong filament produced by the caterpillars of the moth *Bombyx mori,* to form their cocoons.

On the circular space in the centre of the floor there was a table. On it stood two large transparent vessels. The first contained a pair of infant human beings joined together by a fleshy ligature; the second — just a normal female foetus in the womb, in an advanced stage of development. The part of the ceiling directly above the table consisted of a hundred and twenty translucent sheets of a hard and brittle substance made by fusing silicate with some other materials, put together in suitable order and position. Midway between the hemisphere and the table the bony framework of a human body from which all the soft tissues had decayed or had been removed, hung on a thick strong cord of intertwined fibres of flax. This cord passed over a small grooved wheel contained in a block fixed in the centre of the translucent hemisphere. The other end wound round a small wooden cylinder with a short handle, fastened to the pilaster near the door. A man in white trousers and a blue jacket, with a yellow cravat at his neck, appeared at the doorway. He seized the short handle and turned it. The cylinder paid out the thick strong cord which passed over the small grooved wheel, and the bony framework of a human body from which all the soft tissues had decayed or had been removed passed silently through space, down to the level of the table.

'Are you satisfied?' asked Bayamus.

I looked at the skeleton. It was beautifully made.

'Yes,' I said, 'certainly I am.'

'Well,' he said, 'I am very glad to hear it,' he said. 'And now let's go to the Theatre of Semantic Poetry.'

Chapter 2

Still Life with a Black Shoe

*

The road we took from the Theatre of Anatomy to the Theatre of Semantic Poetry was urbanised to the utmost extent. *Urbanised* does not mean here that it was designed to perform a regular function as a city street. It means only that there was not a trace of rural character in it. There was no line at which the sky and the surface of the earth appeared to meet, since there was not a trace of sky above and not a trace of earth beneath. Underfoot there was a mixture of a kind of inflammable pitch with sand, gravel, etc.; overhead there was a ceiling supported on a continuous series of arches converting the vertical pressure of the weight of construction above into horizontal thrust, which could serve as evidence that the architect's intellect was so defective as to be incapable of rational judgment and action, since the whole work had been made not of stones or of bricks bound together with a mixture of lime, sand, and water, but of concrete strengthened by an iron framework embodied in it, which ought to have imposed a new form of architecture instead of forcing the reinforced concrete to ape the style of building of the XIIth century.

A little farther on there was no more XIIth century architecture. Here, some plastic composition of lime, sand, and water, rendered cohesive by the admixture of hair, and dried hard, pretended to be a marble fluted column with four spiral scrolls of the Ionic order.

'Do you know that gentleman?' asked Bayamus. 'He is making signs to you.'

Near the Ionic column, at one of the Regent Street, w.1. Café Royal pieces of household furniture, consisting of a flat horizontal surface of wood supported on legs and used for eating at, sat Karl Mayer; old, short, frail, white-haired Karl Mayer, author of the scenario of the expressionist film: *The Cabinet of Dr Caligari*. I was startled. I knew that he had died in 1943. Admittedly I wasn't present at his funeral, but I read about his death in a newspaper: DEATH OF MAN WHO DROVE CAMERA IN PERAMBULATOR. And here he was gaily making signs to us.

'My dear friends!' he said as we approached, 'I've been waiting for you!' And shifting a heap of papers, magazines and stills from the long bench covered with black leather, he invited us to sit down.

'How are you?' I asked. 'Very busy?' — I knew that in 1943, not long before his death, he had at last got a job in Ω Studios as supervisor to an act of turning certain raw materials (sensitized films) into economically useful and marketable goods, (size: width 35 mm., length 2,000,000 mm.), connected with the business of buying and selling.

'Oh, yes, my dear friend. At 8 each morning I'm already in the train,' and he shouted, waving that part of his body which formed the extremity of the forearm below the wrist-joint, and consisted of a white palm, knuckles, fingers and thumb, 'Waiter!'

And when Philippe Guibillon (né 1889 à Bordeaux; British nationality 1925; previous nationality French; married; three children: first: F/Lt. R.A.F.; second: in sanatorium for the special treatment of patients suffering from tuberculosis; third: a girl studying economics at Cambridge) came, Karl Mayer ordered:

'More coffee for my friends, please, and cigarettes, 555 STATE EXPRESS.'

I knew that he had been in hospital before he got the job at Ω Studios, that his bodily well-being had been very poor, and his personal means insufficient to support his life in ease or comfort.

'And how is your health now?' I asked.

'Oh, my dear friend, my health is reaching the highest possible level of excellence!' said he. And he allowed his features to assume an expression somewhat resembling that in laughter, unaccompanied by any vocal sounds, his pale lips being closed and curved upwards at the corners, and his facial muscles relaxed, especially those round his black and sparkling eyes.

But I still had in mind that headline announcing Karl Mayer's death.

'Excuse me,' I said, 'is it true that when you started making films you used to move the camera in a perambulator?'

'My dear friend,' he replied, 'of course I did. Is there any ambitious, independent young film-man who didn't do that sort of thing? Didn't you?'

'Yes,' said I, flattered, 'I did.'

'Then you see for yourself, my dear friend,' he said. And after a very brief space of time: 'When I started my cinematography, not a single film-man, I mean no creator, no one who counted, had yet died. All of them were still young fellows.' He combed his white hair with his white parchment hands which seemed to allow light rays to pass through them. 'You know, my dear friend, I was the first person who started to clap your film. And I was also the first person who started to clap Cenkalski's film. Please tell him that when you see him.'

'I will certainly,' said I. 'And do you know that...'

But he interrupted me:

'Tell him, please do!'

'Yes, I'll tell him,' I said.

And then he said:

'But you wanted to say something....'

'Well,' said I '... and do you know that many years ago Cenkalski and I were the first people to start clapping your *Cabinet of Dr. Caligari* at a private show in Warsaw?'

'That's wonderful,' he said. 'Generally it is very painful for an artist if nobody breaks the silence when the words THE END come on the screen.'

Suddenly:

'I don't mind,' said Kurt Schwitters, *dada*ist and inventor of *Merz* art, who had approached our table. 'I'm used to it. People always bawl when I'm reciting *dada*. But I don't mind.'

'Bawling is better than silence,' said Karl Mayer. 'And it's very often better than applause,' he added and put his foot on the white, figured, finely woven strip of linen which covered the Café Royal table. It was an extraordinary picture, that white square of linen with an empty coffee-cup, a green ash-tray made of synthetic resin of the phenol-aldehyde group, and between them the black leather casing which covered Karl Mayer's foot, reaching over his ankle and fastened by means of laces which passed through eyelet holes.

At that moment Philippe Guibillon came with more coffee and 555 STATE EXPRESS cigarettes; he glanced at the table but did not seem to take any notice of what I mentally called: STILL LIFE WITH A BLACK SHOE.

'Look, my friends,' said Karl Mayer, 'here is my new invention. An interchangeable heel! I already have the exclusive rights, granted by Authority, to make and sell this device. They say it's a great thing for the Army. Look how smoothly it works...' — and without any effort he detached the heel from his boot, found another one in his pocket, and put it in place. 'Production is not possible for the duration, because there is no rubber, but nevertheless don't you agree it's an ingenious contraption?'

'Yes,' said I.

But all the time Kurt Schwitters was gazing at the box of 555 STATE EXPRESS.

'Excuse me, Mr. Mayer,' he said now, 'may I take just this one side of this cigarette box? What a beautiful yellow colour it is! I shall stick it on one of my collage-pictures. I always take everything I find interesting. When I was on my way to the Pen-Club conference called to celebrate the tercentenary of the publication of Milton's "Areopagitica", I found near the Institut Français a piece of wire from a house which had been bombed two hours before, and during Mr. Forster's speech I made a space-sculpture out of it. One always finds beautiful things lying around. You don't mind my taking it, do you?'

Bayamus glanced at the small device worked by a coiled spring enclosed in a flat round silver case which was attached to a band he wore round his wrist, and which served for measuring time.

'Are you in a hurry? Where are you going, my friends?' asked Karl Mayer.

'We intend to go to the Theatre of Semantic Poetry,' said I.

'What's that?' he asked.

'I don't quite know yet. That's why I'm going. But I imagine it ought to be something like painting by means of colours taken directly as they are supplied by Messrs. Rowney, or Messrs. Winsor & Newton, or Messrs. Lefranc. Without mixing them on the palette. It must be a kind of writing of poetry, with words skinned of every associational aureola, taken directly as they are supplied by the common dictionary.'

'My dear friend,' said Karl Mayer, 'I think I'm not too old for that idea. But I can't possibly go with you now, I'm so very busy.'

Bayamus was already on his feet. In the hall he took his black, hard, round hat from the cloak-room attendant, and we went out through a mechanical device consisting of a heavy revolving gate so constructed that only one person could pass at a time.

Chapter 3

Finger in the Mouth

*

'...It is a highly complicated question, Bayamus,' said I, trying to find an answer. 'Well,' I repeated. 'Suppose you are Nature; Suppose you are the sum of forces and agencies at work in the physical, external world; the sum of physical processes, of causes and effects which underlie and produce all existing phenomena; And suppose your finger is an artist; Suppose one of the five separate members forming the extremity of your hand practises the application of skill, dexterity, knowledge, and taste to the aesthetic expression of feeling and emotion, or the production of beauty through the medium of colour, form, words, musical sounds, &c., as a profession; Now, suppose you put your finger into your mouth; Suppose you put it into the orifice protected by the lips in your head; suppose you put it into the cavity into which the orifice leads, containing the tongue, teeth, etc., and serving as the means both of transmitting sounds, of masticating food and of stimulating sexual responses; And now suppose you try to bite your finger; Suppose you use your teeth upon it, suppose you augment the force exerted by your teeth on your finger, suppose you increase the PRESSURE. What then? Well, from among several different events which may follow that cause I will select two:

'1st, your teeth impress your finger,

'2nd, your finger presses on your teeth.

'What is interesting to examine in the first case is the finger; to be precise, the IMPRESSION made on it by your teeth. The greater the sensitivity of your finger, and its power of yielding to external stimuli, the deeper and more beautiful is the impression.

'What is interesting to examine in the second case, is your dentition, and the extent to which your tooth was EXPRESSED out of it by your finger.

'And now, if you are Nature, as we have supposed, and if your finger is an artist, then in the first case he would be an IMPRESSIONIST, and in the second an EXPRESSIONIST.'

Bayamus put his finger into his mouth.

'It's rather difficult to bite one's own finger,' said he.

He took his finger out of his mouth, but I begged him to put it in again for a moment.

'Don't press it too hard with your teeth,' said I, 'just a little. And now try to move it out and in, once more, please. Can you feel its shape?'

'Yes,' said he.

I took his finger out of his mouth and showed it to him.

'You see,' said I, 'you have made it wet and very smooth and it is paler than it was. It is really a very academic finger. Do you recognise it at all?'

He looked at it.

'Well,' said he, 'Canova and his *Sleeping Nymph?*'

'Quite,' said I, 'and now, please, put it into your mouth again and try to bite it a bit harder.'

He did so.

'I'm sure,' said I, 'that there is already a very beautiful impression of your teeth on your finger, a Claude Monet, eh?!; kindly try a little more, please, just enough to feel the bone…Cézanne? isn't it?; now, if the hard ivory-like objects which are in your gums cut the skin and the muscular tissues of your finger, and reach that hard structure which composes your skeleton, your finger becomes a cubist.'

His face was distorted, but his head made a short, sharp downward movement as a sign of assent.

'Well,' I said, 'but don't you now feel the pain not only in your finger but also in those firm tissues in the upper and lower jaws in which your teeth are set?'

He nodded: 'Yes.'

'Do you know what's going on there, in your gums?'

He shook his head: 'No!'

'*The Cabinet of Dr. Caligari,* Karl Mayer's expressionist film. And that is the answer to your question.'

He got his finger out of his mouth. It was badly cut. I took a handkerchief out of my pocket and tried to bind it up.

'And,' he said, 'do you think that pressure is to be measured in pounds to the square inch, or in kilogrammes to the square centimetre?'

'Do you mean the pressure of your teeth on your finger?' I asked.

'Not exactly,' he said. 'What I mean is the pressure of the sum of forces and agencies at work in the physical external world, the sum of physical processes, of causes and effects which underlie and produce all existing phenomena, — exerted on that part of it which practises the application of skill, dexterity, knowledge, and taste, to the aesthetic expression of feeling and emotion, or the production of beauty, through the medium of colour, form, words, musical sounds, etc., as a profession.'

'Well,' said I, 'I'm not sure about pounds and square inches, or kilogrammes and square centimetres, but....'

'Look,' he interrupted, 'then you have nothing more to measure with but seconds. All that can be measured can be measured in pounds, inches and seconds, or it can't be measured at all.'

'I don't agree with you,' said I, 'you can also measure by counting. By counting the number of forces and agencies at work in the physical, external world, and by counting individuals. You can say, for instance: Under the pressure of such and such a number of rainy days, and of such and such a number of umbrellas available on the market, — there was such and such a number of individuals called impressionists; and under the pressure of such and such a number of objects having a new shape, and produced since the industrial revolution, and of such and such a number of wage-packets lower than a certain amount of money, — there was such and such a number of individuals called expressionists.'

'And do you think that one can find a law in that way?'

'I don't think that one cannot. But I'm not sure that it would be possible to verify such a law by experiment.'

He didn't answer. And it was only then that I realised I hardly knew him. I walked by his side wondering how to put a question which would give me some information about him, when, suddenly, he stopped, grasped a button on my jacket and said:

'Look here,' he said, 'Who, actually, are you?'

Chapter 4

Third Leg

*

'Oh,' said I, 'that's just the question I wanted to ask you.'

'You wanted to ask me who you are?' said he.

'No,' said I, 'I wanted to ask you who *you* are.'

'I put the question first,' said he.

'That's correct,' said I, 'but really and truly I haven't much to say about myself. Just an ordinary man, that's what I am.'

'Well,' said he, 'so am I.'

But this obviously was contrary to the evidence.

'You are not going to tell me,' said I, 'that you are just an ordinary man.'

'Why not?' said he. 'What the deuce is there in me to make you doubt it?'

'Well…' said I, letting the flaps of tissue which protect my eyes slide down gradually to their full length.

'Well?' said he.

'Well…' repeated I, glancing down at his third leg.

He did have three legs. A left, a right, and a central one. His central leg was quite an ordinary leg with the very slight difference that it was perfectly symmetrical. I hadn't seen it naked, but the two sides of the black shoe he wore showed such a correspondence that they conveyed the impression of a beautiful foot composed of five toes, a big toe in the middle and small ones at either side. This central leg served Bayamus as support when standing, and for progression, like his other two legs. Sometimes he bent his left and right knees and stood up on his central leg, ready to make a speech. Sometimes he propelled himself suddenly into the air with his central foot and then landed on his left and right. Sometimes, when he wanted to keep step with me, he bent his central knee and walked on his left and right feet.

He caught me glancing at his leg.

'Well,' he said, 'is that what you find so remarkable, so noteworthy, so strange, that it arrests your attention, and excludes me from the class of ordinary men?'

'I can't deny it,' I confessed.

He uttered a series of inarticulate sounds expressing the emotion of having his mind affected by interesting or mirthful ideas.

'Well,' he said finally, 'there is such a number of really extraordinary phenomena in this world that it seems to me that there must be something funny about your mind to concern itself with my third leg.'

'Really extraordinary phenomena? For instance?' I asked.

'For instance,' he said, 'all the men with only one leg.'

'Bayamus,' said I, 'aren't you talking nonsense? There are many people with only one leg. Thousands and thousands of them. My own uncle, for example.'

'Well,' said he, 'and didn't it seem strange to you?'

'No,' said I, 'it didn't.'

'Well,' said he, 'and was he born a uniped?'

'Who?' said I.

'This uncle of yours,' said he.

'No,' said I, 'he was born a biped.'

'Well,' said he, 'and how did he lose one leg?'

I saw the subject was of great interest to him.

'Well,' said I, 'he fell from a tram, and the steel concentric disc with rotary motion, used to facilitate the movement of the tram on the pair of steel lines laid parallel to each other and fixed into the road, cut off his left leg.'

'The left one?' asked Bayamus.

'The left one,' I said.

'Well, he became asymmetrical then,' said he.

'That's right,' said I, 'but he would also have become asymmetrical if it had been his right leg.'

'Quite true,' said he. 'And why did he fall out?'

'You see,' said I, 'he was a Jew.'

'Well,' said he, 'when did it happen?'

'Oh,' said I, 'about 1924, or maybe, '26.'

'But,' said he, 'Hitler wasn't in power at that time.'

'No, he wasn't,' said I.

'Well… ?' said he.

'Well,' said I, 'there were in that tram some persons engaged in the acquisition of knowledge at Warsaw University, and some persons engaged in a course of study at Warsaw Polytechnic.'

'Well… ?' said he.

'Well,' said I, 'they said to him: "you sheeny, you mangy yid, go back to Palestine!"'

'Well?' said he.

'Well,' said I, 'he told them he had been living in Poland for 890 years, and he told them something about their attitude not being in line with the teachings of either the University or Christ.'

'And then?' said he.

'And then,' said I, 'they pushed him out of the tram and you know what happened then.'

'Well,' said he, 'and you dare to say that your uncle's single leg is not a more extraordinary phenomenon than my third one?'

'I do,' said I. 'I don't see anything extraordinary in my uncle's one-leggedness.'

'You don't?' he asked.

'No.'

'Why?' said he.

'Well,' said I, 'I found it quite natural. Quite in accordance with the ordinary, observed processes of nature; quite in accordance with logical notions of cause and effect. If somebody who was a Jew set himself against a baptised person engaged in the acquisition of knowledge at Warsaw University or engaged in a course of study at Warsaw Polytechnic, then he got thrown out of trams. That was quite ordinary and quite normal. Quite in accordance with the body of rules, usages, or principles, with the procedure, action and behaviour recognised by custom and usage as correct. I knew that under suitable conditions nothing could prevent the inherent latent capacity for exerting energy from exerting it in the direction of cutting legs off, and I knew that under suitable conditions nothing could prevent the hidden, unexerted powers of intellectual or spiritual action from constructing an argument to justify such a powerful wish to enjoy leg-cutting, or to obtain shoes by that method. It wouldn't surprise me if you were to show me ten thousand unipeds. Because I know the mathematical probabilities of having one leg cut off.'

'Well,' said he, 'but you know also that there are mathematical probabilities of having an extra leg, and in spite of that it seems extraordinary to you!'

'Well…' said I, 'I know deformities occur, if you will excuse the word, deformities due to environment before or after birth, but I've never seen anything like….'

'It's not a question of environment,' he said, firmly, 'it's a question of mutation. It's nothing extraordinary if after such a huge number of generations, a new gene appears.'

'Well,' said I, 'if it's a new gene then it will be inheritable!'

'Well,' said he, 'and what's extraordinary in that?'

He jumped on his central leg, then retracted it, and walked in step with me with his side feet.

'Well,' he said, 'I see I shall have to tell you my story.'

Chapter 5

Bayamus' Story

*

'I never saw my parents' he said, 'but a few years ago I managed to get a photograph of them. It was taken some time before my birth. It is a wedding photograph: Father is obviously in his Sunday best, mother in white Alençon lace. They lived near Alençon, Normandy, in a small village on the River Sarthe. They were peasants, and cultivated a small plot which they held on lease from a marquis. I learned all this from Dr. Roux, a general practitioner of Alençon. Well, I was born 25 April, 1909.'

'What a coincidence,' I interrupted. 'That's approximately the day when a certain union of two gametes and of their nuclei and chromosomes took place and gave rise to me.'

'Very pleased to hear it,' said Bayamus. And he continued: 'I imagine my mother must have undergone terrible pain that day, for my father and the neighbours to send for a doctor. It was Dr. Roux from Alençon they sent for. At that time there were no motor cars. They sent over a heavy cart used for carrying farm produce, and by the time Dr. Roux arrived I had already been born and he found the village in a state of revolt. They were all talking about the devil. The parson said he would never baptise such a creature even if the Pope himself were to ask him, and they seriously wanted to kill the poor girl.'

'I beg your pardon...' said I, 'did you say: "girl"?'

'Is there anything extraordinary,' said he, 'in being born a girl?'

'Well...' said I.

'I was born a girl,' said he. 'Nevertheless, that wasn't why they wanted to kill me; but because I was born with three legs. Dr. Roux was in an awkward and dangerous situation. They wanted him to kill me.'

'And did he?' I said, realising at the same moment the stupidity of my question.

'No,' said Bayamus.

He took out of his portable, flat, shallow, oblong case of yellow fibre an iron device consisting of a kind of sole and of four small solid wheels with ball-bearings, fastened it to his central foot, and kicking off from the pavement with both his side feet, he moved quickly forward on its smooth, hard surface.

When I caught him up —

'Dr. Roux' he said, 'was convinced he had no right to interfere with Nature. He was convinced that I might not be a freak of nature, but a Mutant, an individual who would breed a new variation.'

'Well,' I interrupted, 'but what do you mean by not interfering with Nature? Dr. Roux was himself a part of Nature. Nothing he could do would be interfering with Nature!'

'Well,' said Bayamus, 'let us say then that the idea of not interfering with Nature, which was in Dr. Roux's mind, was the means Nature took to protect the new individual.'

We were continuing our walk; Bayamus on his roller-skate, and I trying to keep pace with him.

'And what happened then?' I asked.

'Does it really interest you?' he said.

'Yes,' I said, 'and I'm sorry I interrupted you.'

'Oh!' he said. And after a pause: 'Dr. Roux used a trick. He gave 20 francs to my parents and 20 francs to the old witch who was playing at midwife, and he told them he would cut my body up, but it would have to be done in the Theatre of Anatomy at Alençon. Then he wrapped me in a shawl and brown paper, wrote out a death certificate, told the crowd surrounding the poor dwelling that I had just died, and took me to his house in Alençon.

'Dr. Roux was not a rich man, and afraid of losing his practice he hid me in a back room in his house, where nobody would find me. But after a few months people began to talk. They knew something queer was going on in Dr. Roux's home. Then he bound all my three legs together and introduced me to his friends as a poor niece afflicted with paralysis. The sympathy of all the town was now with him, but the trick could not continue for long because I couldn't very well grow up with my legs bound. So he took me across the Channel, where he found an oldish, very rich and lonely lady who was only too pleased to act as foster-mother. Over there, I mean: on this side of the Channel, nobody pointed their finger at me, and I lived a normal life, like other children.

'Dr. Roux used to come to see me every year. What interested him most was the development of my sexual organs, because he still had in his mind the idea that I would breed a new generation of tripeds. Poor Dr. Roux! I know now that in the end he fell in love with me. He wanted to wait till I was seventeen and then marry me. But when he came to see me in 1923, when I was fourteen, he suddenly discovered that I had developed into a male. I remember well that he wept. He shed tears like a little injured boy. Then he performed a minor operation on me which consisted in changing the position of my testicles, after which he had a long, friendly and very serious talk with me. "Bayamus," he said, "because you are no longer Bayama. Bayamus, that is your name. The first and only known specimen of the Homo triped. That is what you are. And your mission is to have sexual intercourse with women and to cause them to give birth to a new variation, the new variation of tripeds. That is your mission!" That's more or less what he said. I've not seen him since.'

'And have you any children?' I asked.

'Well,' he said, 'I don't know. I can't give you any assurance. You see, after this talk with Dr. Roux, I lived with this old lady who had brought me up. I was a child. I didn't realise that she was too old to conceive my offspring. She was already over sixty. And then... well, you see... biped women have their prejudices. And social relations are also... It's a very difficult task for Nature to start something new in so-called civilised society. What about you, if you were a woman, would you object to marrying me?'

I had the feeling as if something inside me turned violently against that suggestion. But after a short moment of reflection I realised that the feeling was due not to Bayamus being triped, but to his being male.

'Well,' I said, 'I wouldn't mind if you were female.'

'I'm afraid,' he said, 'you don't understand what I mean. It isn't only the question of sexual intercourse. It is the question of having children. Women I knew showed a great interest in my person and were quite happy and satisfied with me. But they insisted on using all those contraceptive thingummies, thingumajigs and thingumbobs. And look. I'm already 36 and I still don't know whether I've started a race of tripeds or not.'

'That is sad,' I said, 'but now, tell me, why do you persist so firmly and so obstinately in starting this new race or species or variation? Will these new men be happier than we are? What will they gain, what will they win with their third leg?'

'Oh!' he exclaimed in astonishment, 'how absurdly you talk! How can you even ask?! Look at this... Roller-skate!'

And kicking off from the pavement with both his side feet, he moved quickly forward on the iron device consisting of 4 small, solid wheels with ball-bearings, and of a kind of sole which was fastened to his central foot.

Chapter 6

Roller Skate

*

'Now, now,' I said, 'personally I cannot find in myself any tendency, inclination or disposition to see the bright or hopeful side of these roller-skates. I don't expect great things of them. You see, during those active international hostilities carried on by force of arms which began a series of open conflicts between nations much exceeding in any dimension the average or ordinary example of its kind, and to which was given the name of the First Great War, I was in Russia. You see, my father was a doctor, and he had been mobilised by the Russian army. When the front was moving towards the East we were travelling to the East also, in order to be on the same side of the firing-line as he was. *We* means his family. I was 4 when the war started, and 8 when the armistice was signed. Well, then we came back to my native town, to our old home, which I didn't remember very well. There I found my brother's pre-war roller-skate in a lidless box, with a handle at one side, made to slide in and out of a wooden framework in a huge, gigantic piece of those theoretically movable articles of household requirement, including divisions for hanging clothes. You see, the roller-skate was to hand. But I couldn't use it on the roadway because it was covered with hard, large, round cat's-head sized stones; I couldn't use it on the trottoirs, pavements, sidewalks for pedestrians, at the sides of the roads, because they were for people walking on foot; and I couldn't use it on the esplanade stretching high up alongside the river, because the surface there consisted of wet, pulpy earth which stuck to the iron wheels. In addition there were two psychological or social reasons as well. The first was that my roller-skate was unique in the town (I've no idea who gave it to my brother), and people pointed at me with their fingers, just like the people in Alençon would point at you if you were there now, — and I didn't like being pointed at; the second reason was, that for many of my colleagues the roller-skate was as unattainable as a bicycle was for me, as a motor car was unattainable for those who owned a bicycle, and as a private vehicle with four wheels, drawn by two or four horses, for conveying persons, was unattainable for those who owned a motor car, as at that particular point of the time-space continuum a carriage driven by horses was still higher on the ladder of social hierarchy than a vehicle driven by a compact, powerful engine in which energy supplied by burning fuel is directly transformed into mechanical energy by causing an explosion of the fuel in a cylinder behind a piston; and I didn't like to possess something that provoked feelings of envy, because that gave me feelings of guilt, and in such a state of mind it is rather difficult to ride on roller-skates. But even if we put aside these two psycho-sociological reasons, the only surface smooth enough for a roller-skate was that of the floor of our flat. But there was plenty of furniture around the place and altogether you see the nonsense of skating in a room, don't you? The surface of our Earth is anything but smooth, even, or glossy; it has irregularities and projections; it is shaggy and rugged; it has alternate depressions and elevations; it is rough. I'm sorry, but I don't see the place for a roller-skate on it.'

'You are a funny fellow!' said Bayamus. 'You don't see that all you have just said is the very reason why our biological roller-skate is still undeveloped. However, the surface of the earth is now becoming smoother and smoother. We level it, we remove its roughness and projections, we smooth the roads and paths. And now Nature is free to develop a biological roller-skate under man's sole. She has already given me my third foot, which is perfectly predestined for that purpose.'

'Now,' said I, 'you can't have a roller-skate without wheels, can you? And there's simply nothing in Nature remotely like a wheel.'

'And,' said he, 'the Earth itself? And the Moon? Aren't they sort of wheels which turn as they move through space?'

'Well,' said I, 'let's say then that there's nothing like that on the surface of the Earth.'

'And,' said he, 'roller-skates, and bicycles, and cars, and....'

'Well,' said I, 'they're produced by man.'

'And the snail's shell,' said he, 'isn't that produced by the snail? Where's the difference?'

'Well,' said I, 'the snail can't help producing its shell, while a bird, for instance, can refrain from building its nest, if it wants to.'

'That's not true,' said he, 'under certain conditions, for instance, calcium deficiency, the snail can stop producing its shell, and under certain conditions) for instance, if it is about to lay its eggs, the bird cannot refrain from building its nest.'

'Well,' said I, 'what I'm talking about is the difference in method. The shell develops, increases in size by the formation of new tissues, while the nest is built by putting and fitting together separate objects, elements, materials.'

'Then,' said he, 'what you mean is that Nature, while she can build wheels via the mediation of man, cannot grow them.'

'Yes,' said I.

'But why not?' said he.

'Look, said I, 'what's a wheel? A disk capable of rotating about its own axle. But if so, then it can't be connected with that axle. Neither by connective or muscular or nervous tissue. How can it grow then?'

'That's very simple,' said Bayamus. 'Imagine a kind of corn growing under the sole of your foot. Just like a nail or tooth growth. It takes the shape of an axle. Then, on particular points round the axle excrescences are formed. I suppose all this will be done in the womb, or in very early childhood. But then the axle hardens like bone, and the excrescences harden like hooves. The axle, however, hardens a little more quickly than the excrescences, and the excrescences, which have the shape of small wheels, become looser and looser, and finally you can rotate them as much as you like.'

'Well,' I said, 'but don't forget friction. You would need a small receptacle attached to them for holding lubricating oil.'

'Now, now,' he said, 'and what about our oil-glands, that excrete waste products which would oil the bearings, and what about our sweat glands, excreting water which by evaporation would prevent undue rise of temperature?'.

Chapter 7

Mutations

*

'Maybe you are right,' I said.

But he suddenly stopped.

'Wait a minute,' he said, 'where have we to go now?'

'Have you already forgotten!' said I. 'We are going to the Theatre of Semantic Poetry.'

'No,' he said, 'I didn't forget *that*. How could I? All the time I was telling you my story I was thinking about the Problem of Semantic Poetry!'

'I'm sorry, but I don't see the connection.'

'Don't you?'

'No.'

'Look,' he said. 'You might beget a child in the womb of a biped woman, but that child would be only a re-arrangement of genes. But if I beget her a child it would be real progress. Because I am a Mutant! And the same with art. You might cross a Titian with a Rubens… their offspring would be only a rearrangement of genes. But cross a Schwitters with one of them and you would have a real progression of Picassos. Because Schwitters is also a Mutant! And so is Semantic Poetry! Third Leg! Roller-skate!'

'Well,' said I, 'I agree that the differences in pictures or poems which bring about the "fit" and "unfit" state which natural selection and eventually the evolution of art can act upon, are not due directly to past and present environment but to revolutionary jump-like divergencies from type, to dadaistic roller-skates, or to Semantic Poetry Third Legs. But don't you realise that, in art at least, those very divergencies, those sudden jumps, are not spontaneous; that *they* themselves are due to environment, and that therefore they are not what are called: mutants.'

'Fallacy!' said Bayamus. 'Even in living beings, certain mutations can be induced by environment, namely: by bombarding cells with X-rays or by poisoning them with colchicine. And they breed true, that's to say, their descendants will inherit the new character according to Mendelian rules. Not the degree of spontaneity, not the cause of spontaneity, but the fact of transferring the new characteristics down to posterity, — that's what really matters.

'True, Dada-Roller-Skate, Semantic Poetry, Third Leg, etc., became what they are because their cells were bombarded with Class-Struggle-X-Rays, because they were poisoned with Society-Colchicine. But then they behave like Mutants. They breed true, i.e. they are perfectly capable of being inherited. They make what we call: progress. We ought to protect them!'

'Why?' I said. 'Why should we protect them? Why should we interfere with the struggles which arise between them and the original type? If they are "fit" they'll be all right, if they are "unfit" they'll have to go.'

'How cruel you are!' he exclaimed. Then he meditated for a while and said: 'Their "fitness" or "unfitness" does not exist in itself. In one environment they are "fit" and survive, in another environment they are "unfit" and are eliminated. But: the environment — is also: you. Are you really satisfied enough with your own type to use it as a standard for all newcomers and to make judgments: that one "fits" with me, so it can remain, that one does not "fit" with me, so it must go? Wouldn't it be better for yourself and for "progress" if you were less cruel and arrogant and more broad-minded and meek?'

'Well...' I began. But then I recalled his first question. We were still standing on the corner of the street, and I still held him by the small portion of flattened, rounded horn which was attached to his coat and passed through a slit in a corresponding place on the opposite side of it. 'I say,' said I, 'why did you ask: "Where have we to go now?" if you haven't forgotten that we're going to the Theatre of Semantic Poetry?'

'Because I've forgotten the way,' he said simply.

That part of my body which forms the extremity of the forearm performed the act of moving in the direction of the back of that part of my body which is situated on top of my spinal column, and the nails and tips of my fingers and thumb started lightly to rub the skin, with its sebaceous glands, hair follicles, etc.

CHAPTER 8

HOUSE WITH BLACK COLUMNS

*

'Shall we ask?' said I.

He looked very unhappy.

'Whom?'

I showed him a very tall, pink-faced policeman standing at a point where three streets intersected, forming a letter Y.

He thought a moment, and then —

'O.K. let's try!' he said.

'Excuse me, please,' I said to the policeman when we approached him, 'could you tell me the way to the Theatre of Semantic Poetry?'

'What?' he said.

'... the way to the Theatre of Semantic Poetry,' I repeated.

'Oh, yes,' he said, 'take that street to your left, go up to the end, and ask the policeman there, on the corner. You can't miss him.'

'Thank you!' I said. But at that moment a short, lively French *agent de circulation,* whom I hadn't noticed before, came forward and said cheerfully:

'*Excusez-moi!* Why go such a long way to a Theatre? There is a very good film in the *cinéma du quartier,* very near here. I went there yesterday with my girl-friend. Go there!'

'It's a pity,' said Bayamus, 'but my girl-friend has already seen it.'

'*Ah, bon!*' said the *agent,* 'then go with your niece.'

'I haven't got one,' said Bayamus.

'If I may suggest,' said the tall pink-faced policeman shyly, 'why not go with this nice looking gentleman?' — and he pointed at me.

'Sorry,' said I, 'but I have to go to the Theatre of Semantic Poetry.'

'Well,' said the policeman somewhat coldly, 'I've already told you the way.'

But Bayamus suddenly exclaimed:

'I remember the way now! We have to take that street on the right, and then....'

'I say!' the policeman said suspiciously. 'How is it that you remember it now?'

'Because of that house over there!' said Bayamus.

'Now, then,' said the policeman, 'you are not going to tell me that you recognise that house!'

'Why not?' asked Bayamus.

'Because they're all so like one another. That's bloody private enterprise which built family houses and whole streets in series. I wouldn't recognise my own house if I hadn't put a small pre-war Woolworth-Buddha in the ground floor window. And some upper-class people still think they'll frighten us with their talk of the monotony of a socialised world!'

'Are you a socialist?' I asked.

'Before the General Strike I was in the Labour Party, but since then, I've been in the Fabian Society.'

'Fabian Society or not, I recognise the house all the same,' said Bayamus. 'It has two columns painted black like cemetery tombstones.'

'Now, now,' said the pink-faced policeman, 'in that street on the left you have thirteen houses with black columns like cemetery tombstones.'

'Yes,' said Bayamus, 'but in this particular house there is a brothel.'

'That's definitely not true!' said the policeman.

'How isn't it true?' said Bayamus, 'I was there myself yesterday!'

'Maybe you were there, but it isn't the thing you say it is.'

'How isn't it the thing I say it is?' said Bayamus. 'I was there yesterday. On the second floor. There were three girls.'

'Maybe you were there yesterday, maybe on the second floor, maybe there were three girls, but it isn't the thing you say it is,' said the policeman.

'Oh, come now,' said Bayamus, 'I drank beer with them, and….'

'Maybe you drank beer with them,' interrupted the policeman, 'but it isn't the thing you say it is.'

'How isn't it?' asked Bayamus. 'I drank beer with them, and then I took one of them to the adjoining room, where there was a bed all prepared for making love….'

'Well,' said the policeman, 'maybe you took one of them to the adjoining room, maybe the bed was all prepared for making love, but it isn't the thing you say it is.'

'But I made love to her,' cried Bayamus, 'and I gave her two pounds, and I gave the old witch there half-a-crown, and I went away.'

'Maybe you made love to her,' said the policeman, 'maybe you gave her two pounds, and half-a-crown to the old witch there, maybe you went away, but it isn't a brothel.'

'And what is it then?' asked Bayamus.

'Just a house,' said the tall pink-faced policeman.

'Well,' said Bayamus, 'then could you tell me what a brothel is?'

'Yes,' said the policeman, 'brothel is a word used by translators for describing the French word: *bordel,* Italian: *bordello,* Spanish and Polish: *burdel.* But there is no such thing in this country.'

'I see…' said Bayamus. But then he looked enquiringly at the policeman and asked:

'I say! Why did you tell us to take that street on the left? I know now we ought to take the one on the right!'

The tall, pink-faced policeman blushed like a girl.

'I'm sorry, sir,' said he, 'but I've no idea what Semantic Poetry is. I preferred to be inaccurate rather than discourteous.'

'That's all right,' said Bayamus. 'Thanks!' And making a sign to me to proceed, he turned to the right.

But the short, lively French *agent de circulation* held on to me familiarly by my coat, and drawing me aside, inquired:

'That friend of yours, *hein?* could you tell me where he got his *drôle de scooter?* Can one buy that sort of thing?'

I was rather embarrassed.

'I don't think so,' I said, 'you see, it's an American device. You won't be able to get it until the shipping is all right again.'

'That's a pity,' he said, '*Dites,* can one sit on it as well? If so, it will be a grand thing for *nous autres,* us policemen!'

Chapter 9

Je Sème à Tout Vent

*

When we were passing the house with black painted columns, Bayamus said:

'And what if we drop in for a moment?'

'Bayamus!' said I. 'What's the matter with you?'

'Didn't I tell you that I have an offspring to produce?' said he.

'That's right,' said I, 'but look, what are the chances of making a child in such a place? One in 200,000?'

'Well,' said he, 'nevertheless there is a chance. And I know how to augment it.'

He was already entering the house. 'Come on! I can't miss any chance whatsoever. That's my mission, *Je sème à tout vent!*'

A thick, heavy woven fabric of wool covered the horizontal surface made of timber and forming the bottom of the drawing-room. The upper side of the drawing-room was covered with fine white plaster moulded into 'guirlandes,' and attached to laths fastened to the lower side of the timber work supporting the floor above. On the sides, the drawing-room was divided from its surroundings by solid structures of bricks relatively thin in proportion to their height and length. They were covered on the drawing-room side with paper, highly decorated in brown, red and violet.

There were four openings: three of them serving as entrances with wooden structures moving on hinges for closing them, and one, not very large, filled with panes of glass fixed in a movable frame and covered by a sheet of pale yellow cloth lowered from a roller above, and by a sheet of green cloth hanging on a rod and drawn across so as to keep out sun and draught.

There were borders of gilded wood holding a painted representation of a vase of flowers; a three colour print of a naked young girl playing a musical woodwind instrument having a long curved reed mouthpiece, the tube furnished with holes, some meant to be stopped by fingers, others by keys; there was also a big border of carved wood holding a picture produced by chemical action of light on a sensitized paper, and representing specific persons, namely: a team of eleven cricket players.

There was a 5-foot high nickel column supporting a bulb-shaped glass containing a short, fine, coiled wire made of a very hard metal, only fusible at very high temperatures. 6.3×10^{18} electrons were passing through that wire each second, which — measured in units of intensity — equalled 1 *Ampère;* and as the force supplied in that Borough by the 'Electric Supply Company Ltd.' was 100 *Volts,* it gave the power of $1 \times 100 = 100$ *Watts;* and the planetary electrons of the atoms of the very hard metal of which the coiled wire was made tried to repel the flow of 6.3×10^{18} electrons supplied each second by the 'Electric Supply Company Ltd.' at the price of 0.4×10^{-23} pence per electron, and were opposing it with the resistance of 100 *Ohms* — thus raising the motion of molecules of the fine wire sufficiently to make it glow with the light output which (thanks to the fact that the wire after being coiled was coiled again upon itself under British Patents: 226,455 and 441,207 by the female workers of Osram Manufacturers of G.E. Co. Ltd.), was not smaller than 1590 lumens; — but since a certain device, composed of yellow stiffened silk, was attached to the nickel column supporting the bulb-shaped glass, and intercepted most of the electromagnetic waves that were meant to stimulate the retina and arouse visual sensations, the drawing-room was filled with partial darkness.

A part of the drawing-room was constructed in a special manner: there was a cavity in the brick structure, in the bottom of which a frame with iron bars was fixed. There was a decorative moulding placed across the top and on either side of the opening of the cavity, and a stone shelf projecting above.

On the frame with iron bars there were some pieces of organic rock, mostly of plant, and to a lesser degree of animal origin, and above them three roughly hewn pieces of wood. The pieces of rock and wood were rapidly combining with the oxygen present in the atmosphere, which process was accompanied by a glowing mass of gases; the resulting heat and light were radiating from it into the drawing-room. But, after having travelled through a few feet of space, most of the radiation was intercepted by a combination of sofa and chair, upholstered, and having a layer of thick soft material placed over springs, on which three females were seated.

They were not old. Their youth was just slipping away, but their organs producing small, $1/125$-inch eggs, still possessed their full powers, and the eggs, if allowed to be fertilised by a male, still would develop into new individuals.

They stood up to greet us when we entered, and we realised at first glance that they belonged to a super-family which possessed three characteristics differentiating it from the rest of the Anthropoidea: erect gait with its spinal modifications; articulate speech; and the highly specialised faculty of reasoning. They immediately started to use that faculty, opening a discussion about being affected by the general atmospheric conditions prevailing at a specific time and place, namely, the temperature, the amount of moisture in the air, the direction of wind, clouds, etc., and about the effects these phenomena have on health and complexion.

There were still some minor features differentiating them from the other Anthropoidea: their bodies were naked, if one discounts those parts which showed a blonde or brunette thread-like outgrowth of epidermis, being a modification of the skin's 'touchbodies,' and still retaining to a certain extent the function of touch, and if one discounts also some fine, soft, cotton fabric, pervious to radiation; their faces, covered with some scented, reddish oily compound, were non-projecting and with a facial angle of 80 deg.; chins well marked; fore-limbs relatively short; thumb (with its pin-point-pared and red-painted nail) functional, but great toes (in light and loose red pom-pommed slippers) nonopposable; they had large fleshy muscular protuberances at the back of their hips, small canines and rudimentary wisdom-teeth. They smoked American cigarettes, one could bet one's bottom dollar that their appendices were vermiform, and that they had laryngeal pouches, remnants of 'howling apparatus'; they had ear-muscles and tails, — these tails consisted of three vertebrae which would have been movable by means of extensors, flexors, and agitators, had not these muscles atrophied. When they were 5 to 8 weeks old in the wombs of their respective mothers, their tails contained 8 to 11 vertebrae, and it is a mystery why they did not keep and develop these organs of propulsion and steering.

We sat down beside them on that upholstered combination of sofa and chair, and then an old woman in a white apron brought us glasses of a beverage which had been produced by (1) converting the grain of barley by a process of germination into malt, then steeping it in hot water and converting its starch into sugar and dextrin; (2) by drawing the liquid off and boiling it with the bright, yellowish cones of the female plant *Humulus lupulus;* (3) by adding some cells of certain fungi and letting them convert the sugar into water with one H atom replaced by hydrocarbon radical; (4) by draining it from all suspended matter and storing for some six weeks before sending it to the consumer.

We drank it with pleasure, and the three women drank it also. We all still had our eleven thighs at right angles to our trunks, while our bodies themselves were upright, with their weight resting upon, and supported by, that combination of sofa and chair. But we were packed closely together and a form of energy possessed by our bodies in virtue of the motion of their molecules was conducted from one to the other and raised everybody's temperature, already high because of the energy radiating from the pieces of rock and wood and the luminous mass of gases. To make a comparison: A 6 ft., 14-stone navvy doing hard work requires some four large calories per minute, a calorie being the amount of heat required to raise the temperature of one kilogram of water by 1° C.; and each gramme of alcohol we drank in our beverage, already oxidising in our living tissues, yielded the energy equivalent to raising the temperature of a kilogram of water by 7 deg. C., and this energy *had* to be changed into work performed by our organs.

So we started to sweat in order to get rid of that heat in the form of 'latent' heat required to evaporate water; but this evaporation, being scented, stimulated our olfactory senses; and our saliva, produced in response to it, stimulated our gustatory senses; and the air-waves produced by the vocal organs of the three women stimulated our auditory senses; and the rose light, reflected by the projections of their breasts, stimulated our visual senses; and each change in the position of our own muscles and tendons stimulated our kinaesthetic senses; and each change in the position of our heads stimulated our senses of equilibrium.

'You are a glamorous girl, really you are,' said Bayamus.

The woman he spoke to rose, took him by the strap of brown leather which encircled the narrowest part of his trunk, between ribs and hip-bones, said 'Come on, darling!' and when he got up and stood on his roller-skate, left and right feet in the air, she burst out laughing and drew him to the door.

We had more room now. And only six feet to the three of us.

I didn't intend to go with either of the two remaining women to the other room, where a piece of furniture with all its parts (the case of cotton material, stuffed with feathers, and the wooden frame, with rows of wire springs, which supported it), was permanently prepared for love-making. It wasn't that I didn't want to. I liked them both very much. I have always liked brothels and so-called professional women. True professionals have in general certain magnificent features: they are moderate in character and temperament; they are of sound cool judgment; not given to extremes in opinions and prejudices; avoiding vehemence of feeling and expression, or violence in action. They possess a keen, natural perception of what is right and fitting, a quick apprehension of the right thing to say or do; instinctive skill, adroitness and discretion in dealing with persons or difficult situations. They don't ask personal questions and they intrude on nobody with accounts of their own private life, which remains free from professional business, and which they keep well closed to the public in general. Their mind is impartial, just, their intelligence thoroughly formed, developed by training and experience; not superficial, or childish; their thoughts and actions resulting from these mental faculties are prudent, wise, based upon careful deliberation; their movements are well thought out; complete in every detail. Their organisms are ripe, fully developed, having reached maximum growth, but they have and express a moderate opinion of their own abilities and qualities, they are not boastful, arrogant or self-assertive, they are essentially modest. They are upright, straightforward; not inclined to defraud, to deceive, to claim what does not belong to them, or more than they are entitled to receive; they are trustworthy, fair-minded, scrupulous in judgment and action, they are sincere, willing to face facts, veracious, not given to distorting the truth, and their work is conscientiously performed. Yet Bayamus was there, and I don't like to be associated with anybody. I don't like pleasure-trips to the seaside, or excursions to museums, in joint stock companies. In general I am fond of company and not averse to society, but smelling the sea or looking at pictures is something too personal to be experienced in public. When I'm with witnesses, the sea ceases to smell, pictures become colourless, and love-making becomes obscene. This is because the very presence of company suggests that the whole thing is a result of premeditation, that it was deliberately planned and contrived in advance, that it was meditated on, schemed and designed beforehand. That is what it suggests, even if it isn't so. And vice versa: without company the thing may seem to be spontaneous, even if it were deliberately planned and contrived in advance. And so I started meditating, scheming and designing beforehand, deliberately planning and contriving in advance, — to pay them a visit alone on the following day.

'You don't mind if I come tomorrow?' I asked.

'If you like.... But what about now, darling?'

'Well,' said I, 'my friend will come back in a moment and we are rather in a hurry.'

One of them rose and silently went out.

'Just as you like,' said the other. She wrapped her dressing gown tightly round her waist, took some sky-blue woollen yarn, and started knitting. Wholly occupied in interweaving and fastening the yarn together, by series of loops and knots, she began to hum a melody, with her lips closed, her vocal chords vibrating, her breath passing through her nose.

'Hein...' said I, 'are you French?'
'Of course I am,' said she. 'Do you know that song?'
'Yes,' said I.

And so she started to sing aloud the song of the Quartier Latin students.

I was sure she wasn't aware how indecent that song was. The words had lost their meaning, they were nothing more for her now than some *tra la la*, than a sort of canvas to embroider the musical sounds upon; we all lose the meaning of words we use; we become quite satisfied with verbal formulae; afraid of reality, we don't use anything but stereotyped expressions; we like to eat catchwords and we like to sleep with clichés. We look at a half-crown given to the old woman in the white apron sitting at the door, and we know the half-crown is round, with: 'GEORGIVS V DEI GRA: BRITT: OMN: REX' and with 'FID. DEF. IND. IMP. HALF CROWN. 1936' on it, but we forget it has its third, rectangular projection. We say: 'Nice drawing-room in that "house",' and we don't see the landlord, the judge, the 'Electric Supply Company Ltd.'. 'The Gas & Fuel Company Ltd.', the butcher, the baker, the grocer, the newspaper agent, the G.P.O., the cigarette manufacturers, the movie makers, the 'Marks & Spencers', the 'Woolworths', the 'John Lewises', the physicians, the pharmaceutists, the lawyers, the preachers, — all standing round the walls of the 'house', and all sharing the two £1 notes, which Bayamus had just now given to his girl.

The woman knitting beside me still sang the Quartier Latin song, and it was evident that she sang it without thinking about the meaning of the words. Yet the words existed; whether we liked it or not, they still existed, just as really as the owner of the house let to tenants exists; and as really as the official appointed to preside over the court of justice, and to hear and decide cases exists; and as really as the association of persons formed for the purpose of supplying electricity exists; and as really as the association of persons formed for the purpose of supplying gas exists; and as really as the individual who slaughters animals and deals in meat exists; and as really as the one whose employment is to bake bread exists; and as really as the dealer in dried and preserved foods, spices, condiments, sugar, tea, etc., and in various household requisites, such as soap, candles, etc., exists; and as really as the one who is entrusted with the business of owning a publication printed and issued daily or weekly containing news of the day, comment thereon, etc., and advertisements, public notices, etc., exists; and as really as the department of State which deals with the conveyance by post of letters and parcels, and also with telegraphs and telephones exists; and as really as persons occupied in manufacturing small rolls of finely-cut tobacco, enclosed in thin sheets of paper exist; and as really as the makers of shoes and boots exist; and as really as the makers of cinema shows exist; and as really as the large general shops containing a number of departments for sale of goods of various kinds exist; and as really as the person trained in, and practising the medical profession exists, who diagnoses disease, and treats it by means of drugs; and as really as the person skilled in, and engaged in, pharmacy exists; and as really as a member of the legal profession exists; and as really as the one who preaches a sermon exists; and as really as two notes each of the value of a pound sterling exist; and as really as Bayamus, and his girl exist. They, the words of the Quartier Latin song, were a part of the reality of our world, and it's a poor thing to ignore any bit of reality, or to run away from it. The woman knitting beside me still sang the Quartier Latin song. And suddenly my fists clenched, my toes bent strongly, and I felt that all my body, from head to foot, violently desired to discover the real truth contained in the piece of reality which was that song. I understood that the very action of discovering that real naked truth, may enrich the mind, store it with knowledge, develop its capacities, add beauty to the thoughts; and I knew now that the best way of discovering it, was to throw away the mystificatory aureolas of conventional, traditional, patriotic, artistic, moral, customary, 'couleur locale' associations, to do it by replacing the words of the song with definitions expressed in emotionally neutral dictionary words, rigorously accurate, conforming closely to required standards of precision. To break the poor phonetic rhymes: *'étudiants —— épatant',*

'avocat —— chocolat',

'carabins —— bois de sapin', and to find a new logical rhyme and rhythm for the new truth which, I had no doubt, would arise from it.

THEMERSON

'*Vive les étudiants, ma mère, vive les étudiants,*
  Ils ont des...' — the knitting woman started to sing from the beginning
— '*ah, c'est épatant!*'

                                                      and I
                                        started to translate:

MY TRANSLATION OF THE QUARTIER LATIN FRENCH SONG SUNG BY
THE WOMAN KNITTING THE SKY-BLUE WOOLLEN YARN

Let it continue during an extended period
    that ultimate source
    that primary element
    that principle
        which pervades organic matter
      & which enables persons engaged in the acquisition of knowledge
            to transform food into energy
            to grow
            to adapt themselves to their environment
        & to propagate their kind,

Oh my old woman
        who hath the tender
                kindly qualities of a female parent,

Let it continue during an extended period
    that state of existence in the world
    that state of existence as persons engaged in a course of study at learned institu-
                                                                              tions,

They possess their male
                intromittent organs of generation
                    which are something
                          stunning
                          ripping
                          topping
                          flattening
                          striking all of a heap
                          astounding

> dumbfounding
> stem-breaking!

Et l'on s'en fout
La digue digue daine
Et l'on s'en fout
La digue digue don!

> *'Vive les avocats, ma mère, vive les avocats,*
> *Ils ont des...'* she sang, and I went on:

Let it continue during an extended period
    that sum-total of functions which
        resist death
        & which constitute the persons engaged in the acquisition of know-
                ledge of that branch of the
                legal profession whose
                province it is to plead in
                court the cause of
                another,

Oh my human being of female sex
  oh my human being
      who art advancing in years
      & who hath the tender
          kindly qualities of a mother,

Let it continue during an extended period
    that vortex of chemical
        & molecular changes
            which take place in many trillions of cells constituting
                    the bodies of the persons
                    engaged in a course of
                    studying the knowledge of
                    that branch of the legal
                    profession whose province
                    it is to plead the cause of
                    another,

They possess their male
    intromittent organs of generation
        made from beans of cacao plant
          ground down
          sweetened
          & otherwise flavoured!

      Et l'on s'en fout
      La digue digue daine
      Et l'on s'en fout
      La digue digue don!

Let it continue during an extended period
  that physico-chemical
    mechanism of those
      who
       apply themselves to learning the
           science
         & art of the prevention
           treatment
         & cure of disease

Oh my human being
  who art still characterised by the capacity of bringing forth youth
Oh my human being
  who ceasest to be capable of being fertilised
        & bearing fruit
 but who hath still the tender
     kindly qualities of the female organism
        organism from which
       others derive,

Let them continue during an extended period
  these sum-totals of reflex actions to environment
  these transformers of energy
    who seek to acquire the knowledge
       & art of healing,

They possess their male
>> intromittent organs of generation
>> made from the solid
>> hard substance of a
>> fir-tree trunk!

Et l'on s'en fout
La digue digue daine
Et l'on s'en fout
La digue digue don!

Let it continue during an extended period
> that enduring insurgent activity
>> growing multiplying developing
>> enregistering varying and evolving
> that enduring
> insurgent
> activity of persons
>> studying the art
>>> & practice of collecting
>>>> preparing
>>>> mixing
>>>> & dispensing vegetable
>>>>> &
>>>>> mineral
>>>>> substances
>>>> used for medicinal purposes,

Oh my old human being
> who hath the tender
>> kindly qualities of a female parent,

Let it continue during an extended period
> that dynamic equilibrium in a polyphasic system
>> of persons studying the science of the nature
>>> preparation
>>> & use of medicinal drugs,

They possess their male
> intromittent organs of generation
> that...

The door opened and Bayamus came in.

'Bye, bye,' said the knitting woman without interrupting her work.

Back once more in the street I started to repeat aloud, from memory, my translation of the *Quartier Latin* song.

'That's splendid!' exclaimed Bayamus. 'You should recite it at the Semantic Poetry reunion.'

'You are crazy, Bayamus,' said I.

'Why?' said he. 'You should!'

Chapter 10

Rhododendron

*

We had to take a longer way because the bridge was tired. It was an ironbridge. But its particles, acted upon by the continuous stress from the heavy vehicles, lorries, and tanks which passed over it day and night, underwent changes of their relative positions which rendered the bridge more and more liable to rupture with the advance of time. It was necessary to give it some rest, allow the displaced particles to readjust themselves and recover.

So we took a longer way, shaped like a $\supset$, and when we got to the upper end of the $\subset$, I was suddenly struck by the sight of a sheet of paper displayed in the window of a tobacconist. It was a poster advertising the Semantic Poetry Theatre. Looking at it, my eye caught something which at once impressed deeply all my visceral organs, but I didn't come to verbalising what it was. The impression was in my viscera but it didn't affect the muscles of my speech-apparatus.

'The funniest joke I know,' said Bayamus, 'is that Jesus Christ was composed of approximately as many protons as Herr Goebbels.'

I didn't see anything funny in it and I kept silent. In front of us was a path of bare earth, with shrubs planted on either side. They were evergreen, with spikes instead of leaves, bearing yellow flowers. A male bird, with the two very long exterior retrices of its tail curved in the shape of a lyre, walked there with a stiff, pompous, affected, self-conscious gait. Somewhere behind us, upon a permanent track of steel rails, ran a shrill, clear, piping sound, produced by a jet of steam in the whistle of a locomotive engine, but it was too far to hear it.

On the right, there was a street. People were coming in and out of shops, they were crossing the road and buying newspapers at the corner. A-man-leaning-against-a-lamp-post shouted to another:

'But doctor, I have a real guilt complex. When I'm leaving the theatre I do not meditate upon the play I have just seen but I notice immediately a beggar standing in the street. When I'm eating my lunch, I can't taste it, because I can't help thinking that even the cheapest lunch of a navvy was earned for him by poor Indians and Negroes.'

'Do you say: "rhododendron" each morning, as I told you to?' asked the other man loudly.

'Yes, doctor, I do. It doesn't help!' shouted the first.

'Well, then try to realise that all these things happen because in your infancy you sucked too much at your mother's breast!' said-the-man-whom-the-other-man-called-doctor, and he got into his car.

There were plenty of cars, black and blue, red and yellow, green and grey, running along the street. At the corner, an old woman was trying to sell a few bunches of liliaceous herbs with little green flowers in whorls of large oval leaves.

A bystander who had evidently heard the last words spoken by the man called 'Doctor,' approached the man who was still leaning against the lamp-post:

'Breast-feeding is best, Sir, but Utent Barley and milk is an excellent substitute, digestive and nourishing, inexpensive and easy to prepare. If you really want to forget beggars, Indians and Negroes....'

'Well, Sir,' answered the man leaning against the lamp-post; and he pointed a business-like finger at one of the cars running along the road — 'Here's a 10-h.p. quality saloon bristling with improvements! For performance — a quieter, more flexible power unit; redesigned cylinder head giving extra power; improved gearbox and back axle; variable ratio cam gear steering. For comfort — deeper seating with centre arm rest at rear; heavily sound-proofed body panels; flush-fitting sliding roof. You are dealing with Utent Barley, and I'm dealing with these things. Buy one of them for £310 plus approx. £87 Purchase Tax and I'll send you a 1d. stamp for a copy of this invaluable booklet on substitute Breast-feeding.'

'Look here, Sir,' said a young, athletic-looking man, 'what really makes you think about beggars, Indians, Negroes, etc., is constipation. Constipation plays havoc with your temper because it congests your liver. It upsets your digestion because it unsettles your stomach. It prevents your being sociable, cheerful and practical, because poisons contaminate the whole of your body. Yet there is a simple remedy for this condition — and millions know it to be a timely course of Czam's Pills. Keep some Czam's Pills by you — they are gentle, natural, effective and reliable!'

'Excuse me, gentlemen,' a young smart blonde woman said, smiling, 'I'm glad to meet you face to face. I have been a sufferer from chronic indigestion a good many years. My husband brought home a tin of Ytt's Antacid Powder and persuaded me to give it a trial. I obtained quick relief. To be able to eat any food you fancy, knowing you will no longer suffer pain due to beggars, Indians and Negroes, is indeed a miracle made possible by this wonderful Powder!'

'As for me,' cried a grey-haired lady just passing along in slow-motion on her push-bike, 'I am still taking Sun tablets and am feeling A.1. They are wonderful and I cannot speak too highly of them!'

'Now, now,' said a gentleman in a soft, green hat, 'I've come here from Tilbury. Listen. I have used Ood Poultry Spice for over 10 years and would not keep poultry without it. I never have any sick birds and can always get them over their moult in 6 weeks. I have actually had them lay all through the moult and I get over 200 eggs a year from all my birds.'

'I quite agree with my Honourable Friend from Tilbury,' said a man in gold-framed spectacles, 'but to get the most wear out of your eggs, don't wait until they get thoroughly dirty before cleaning them. A little Owp on a clean rag completely erases your guilt complex. Inspect your hens regularly and treat the dirty places with Owp, especially necks and elbows and cuffs. Owp doesn't affect the colour; leaves no odour. Safe to use anywhere because it can't catch fire!'

'It can't catch fire! It can't catch fire!' loudly exclaimed a woman wearing a long white feather on the top of her hat. 'And do you think Atom can catch fire?! Oh, Sir, listen to me, I beg you, and you will exclaim with joy: *Ah-h, Blessed Relief for my conscious!* Sore, tender, aching souls feel like new after a soothing Atom footbath. Atom releases oxygen — cleanses pores of stale acid. Weariness vanishes, throbbing pain is washed away. The 3/1½d. pink packet solves your problem, Sir!'

'I have nothing against 3/1½d. pink packets,' said another woman, but a young man with a baby in his arms interrupted her:

'I don't intend to say that I have anything against them, but...'

'Don't interrupt me, please,' said the woman. And she started again: 'I have nothing against pink packets, but remember, Sir, your problem is hidden all over your skin, not only in the skin of your feet....'

'And what about the crevices between the teeth...' the man with the baby in his arms started again.

'Please don't interrupt me,' said the woman.' All your skin, sir, is a highly sensitive organ. Its 2,000,000 pores must be kept active with regular baths. Its fine nerve network should be stimulated with cold showers or vigorous friction rubs. Once your skin begins to work as Nature intended, you will find you have acquired an extra sense. Only when you have developed your skin-sense can you enjoy to the full the luxurious comfort a warm bath can give; the fresh touch of new underwear; the soft caress of sea breezes on bare limbs, and above all, the carefree rapture of Oyt Talc after the bath — the most exciting experience your skin-sense can enjoy. In stimulating your skin-sense Oyt Talc stirs up a calm, silky confidence, the feeling of certainty and the conviction that the beggar-Indian-Negro problem is just as you want it, and that feeling lasts all day!'

'And what about night?' the young-man-with-a-baby-in-his-arms started once more. And turning to the man who was still leaning against the lamp-post, he added: 'I hope I can help you, Sir! What is the best way to clean Dental Plates and False Teeth? Obviously with a brush. Only brushing can clear the tiny particles out of the crevices between the teeth. Why not try to clear your problem with a brush and Oyl Denture Powder 6d. and 10½d. double size?'

'That's all nonsense!' exclaimed an irritated voice behind him. 'Solution of his problem is: ACROSS — 1. Dressed crab; 7. Denominator; 8. Assess; 10. Front; 12. Dab; 14. Use; 15. Hue; 16. Marsh Mallow; 18 and 19. Month of May. DOWN — 1, 8 and 16. Dad and Mum; 2. /D/Ennis; 3. S-am; 4. Do-n/ot/; 5. Ratio; 6, 11 and 17. Bar the way; 9. South; 10. Freda; 13. Baron; 15. H-i-lum.'

'Quite so,' said another man speaking with his pipe between his teeth. 'Quite so, that's the solution, but it will not help him. Solutions don't help people. What he needs is 10 new KOREANS in his garden. These new Chrysanthemums are the latest Horticultural wonder. Easy to grow, very hardy and producing an abundance of flowers in lovely new pastel shades difficult to describe. This collection includes Apollo, Mars, Jante Wells. Ten well-rooted outdoor plants, packed in moss, ⅔d. carriage paid.'

'What's all this talk?' I asked Bayamus when we struggled our way out of the crowd. But Bayamus, instead of answering me, pointed to a great building on the other side of the square, and I knew that it was the Theatre of Semantic Poetry.

I wanted to repeat my question, when I heard somebody's steps approaching quickly. From the direction of the lamp-post a man was running after us. He was old, tall, grey-haired, and he wore a big, blood-red flower in his buttonhole. He cast a swift hasty look in all directions, and then said in a whisper:

'Listen, gentlemen. I promised a one-guinea prize to the sender of the first correct solution on a postcard examined on Wednesday morning:

Black: 9 pieces
White: 7 pieces
1 p 1 k 2 p 1 / 1 K p b p 1 P 1 /
3 K t 4 / 3 Q 4 /
/ 8 / 7 P / 8 / b R 1 B p 2 p /
White to move and mate in two.
Plenty of variety!'

Chapter 11

Theatre of Semantic Poetry

*

I intended to enter the Theatre quietly, without attracting anybody's attention, and to sit somewhere at the end of the auditorium. But when we found ourselves in the wide open door, I saw the eyes of some hundred people directed towards us. Instinctively I took a step backwards, and at once I had the unpleasant feeling that by thus exposing Bayamus' third foot I was behaving disloyally towards him.

At the same moment two men in evening dress approached us with gestures of welcome. Now I was certain that they were Bayamus' acquaintances and that he was a well-known person in that circle; so I took one more step backwards.

But Bayamus didn't answer the two men's friendly gestures; he entered the theatre, while the two men approached me.

'Hallo!' said one of them. 'Nice evening.'

'Quite…' said I.

'Happily, the west wind ceases to blow,' said the other.

'Yes,' said I.

'If you don't mind,' said the First, 'we'll go that way.' And he showed me a corridor on the left.

I went with them, rather astonished that they made such a fuss of me. I thought they wanted to show me the cloakroom, or that, maybe, they wanted me to sign the club-book, if it was not an open public meeting. 'Do they make as much ceremony over each new visitor?' I asked myself. I was just wondering about it, displeased, since I thought the recital had already started, when they stopped at a door on the right.

'Well...' said one of them.

'Well...?' I asked. And immediately I felt that he had interpreted my question somewhat incorrectly.

'Good !' said he. And he opened the door.

They entered and I went with them. There was a table standing halfway between the door and the opposite wall, and three chairs on one side of the table. They showed me the chair in the middle, and when I sat down I saw that instead of being in the audience I was facing it from the platform. Some hundreds of pairs of eyes were looking straight at us.

'Ladies and Gentlemen,' said the gentleman on my left, 'I have pleasure in announcing that The Semantic Poetry Reunion is now open.' And he went on to speak about the art and poetry of the Middle Ages, and that of the Future. Several times he referred to the poetry which was going to be delivered here in a moment, and on these occasions he made a little bow in the direction of his right. Therefore I looked, not without curiosity, at the gentleman on my right, and I wondered what kind of poetry he would recite to us.

Then the gentleman on my left sat down, and the gentleman on my right rose.

'Ladies and Gentlemen,' he began, and went on to speak about the art and poetry of the Romantic Era and of the Present. He also referred several times to the poetry which was going to be delivered here, and on these occasions he made a little bow in the direction of his left. I looked at the gentleman on my left and at the gentleman on my right and was unsure. I was wondering which of them was the poet when a terrible suspicion came over my mind. At the same moment there reappeared with a terrific clarity on the retinas (?) of my eyes the Semantic Poetry poster I'd seen hanging in the tobacconist's window, and I suddenly realised what the thing was which had impressed itself so deeply on my visceral organs but which I had not verbalised. Yes, I was quite sure now. In big heavy red letters there was my own name on the poster. Why hadn't I realised this before? My first reaction was:

'well, now I'll get up and go out. Somebody has played a poor practical joke on me. I've nothing to do with all this!' But after a while, a terrible feeling that it wasn't that, that it was something else, something different and much more horrible, came upon me. For some years I had been well aware that there was something wrong with my memory. I was quite conscious that there was a hole, in place of the memories of a few months of 1940, and I was unable to recollect anything of that time. I remembered I was in the army, I remembered one particular beautiful, sunny day, and then there was just an empty space, a nothing, and then I was no longer in the army. 'Well,' I said to myself, 'and what if I promised to hold this recital and forgot all about it?' I closed my eyes and wished that the gentleman on my right would never stop speaking. I didn't listen to him. I wanted my own brain to tell me something and quickly.

'What the devil can S.P. be?' I asked myself, while strange words started to sound in my ears:

'Kardang garro
Mammul garro
Mela nadjo
Nunga broo'

'Ah, yes,' I recollected, 'it was, — how many? — 25 years ago, when I found in my father's library a book, namely: Sir E.B. Tylor's ANTHROPOLOGY; and in it came across the poem:

'Kardang garro
Mammul garro
Mela nadjo
Nunga broo'

I didn't mind that it was composed by Australians. It was translated and I understood it much better than the poetry I had known until then.

> 'Young-brother again
> Son again
> Hereafter I-shall
> See never'

I considered it the best, the most universal poem of the world. There was nothing in it which could be specially connected with Hugo's or Mickiewicz's particular countries, with Homer's or Dante's particular time, with Byron's or Goethe's particular language, and there were no words in it the meaning of which would change according to the reader's country, time or language.

> 'Kardang garro
> Mammul garro
> Mela nadjo
> Nunga broo'

stands the trial of time, of space, and of translation. It transcends history, geography, and language.

'Each of the S.P. words should have one and only one meaning,' I said to myself, really astonished that I had any idea of what S.P. should be. 'They should be well defined. They should be washed clean of all those diverse aureolas which depend on the condition of the market. The word: **war,** for instance, carries with it different associations for different people. Thus, it is good for a political speech, but in a poem I would prefer to find instead a more exact definition, for instance, that in my Dictionary: *The open conflict between nations, or active international hostility carried on by force of arms.*

'And instead of the word: **snow,** which stimulates different harmonics in different people's minds, I prefer: *multishaped crystals, belonging to hexagonal system, formed by slow freezing of water-vapour.*'

The gentleman on my right was finishing his speech. He said one more sentence, there was something in it about a new world, and he sat down. The whole audience was waiting now and I had no doubt it *was* my turn.

I rose. In spite of everything it was rather funny to see all these people waiting for your poems, while you had no poems to recite.

'My Lord Archbishop,' I said, 'Your Excellencies, Your Graces,' I made a long pause to gain time, 'My Lords, Ladies and Gentlemen, Men and Women, Children…' I drew a deep breath and continued: 'Embryos, if any; Spermatozoa reclining at the edge of your chairs; all living Cells; Bacteria; Viruses; Molecules of Air, and Dust, and Water, — I feel much honoured in being asked to address you all and to recite poetry, — but I have no poetry to recite.

'I have no poetry to recite,' I repeated. And suddenly I felt that it was not true. My memory started to work, and I knew that something was being formed in it. Now it was necessary to gain time. 'I have no poems to recite,' I repeated, 'but I may give you the instrumentation, the orchestration of…'

And in that moment everything became clear to me.

'Well,' I said, 'you may read a musical score horizontally, following the melodic line, and you may read it vertically, following the chord structure. The same with poetry. Take for instance, Winifred Galbraith's English rendering of a Chinese poem written about the time when China sent gunpowder to Europe, and Europe a colony of Jews to China:

*
The wine among the flowers,
  O lonely me !
Ah, moon, aloof and shining,
  I drink to thee.

* *
Beside me, see my shadow,
  Rejoice we three!
Moon, why remote and distant?
  Dance with my shade and me.

* * *
This joy shall last for ever,
Moon, hear my lay,
My shade and I can caper
Like clouds away.

* * * *
And drunk we are united
(But lone by day)
Let's fix eternal trysting
In the Milky Way.

'You may read horizontally the melody of this poem, but you may also take each of its words and score it vertically for your whole intellectual orchestra, you may give each of them the flesh of exact definition; instead of allowing them to evoke the clichés stored in your mind, you may try to find the true reality to which every word points, and that is what I call Semantic Poetry.'

And then I translated the Chinese poem into Semantic Poetry, S.P., and recited it. Well, it just happened to be a Chinese poem but this is not the point. Semantic Poetry's business was to translate poems not from one tongue into another but from a language composed of words so poetic that they had lost their impact, — into something that would give them a new meaning and flavour. I had been fed-up with political oratory and with ezrapoundafskinian jazz plus joyce plus dada-merz plus some homespun rachmaninoff glossitis. Avant-garde, I thought, got to go back to Diderot, yes, Denis, of all people, to the time when men and women tried to think, yes, think, and it should start from there again. 'Well, your damn' thinking didn't prevent the war, did it?' the clever ones said. 'Well, did/(& will?) your damn' singing?'

I stood there, in front of them, and insisted on the importance of words in the *chanson,* and on the importance of the meaning in a word; on the importance of the physical fact that a rose, called by any other name, smells as sweet. I gave them lots of diction, good avant-garde Diderot dictionary defined diction. At last I felt that I had found contact with my audience, they seemed to understand what I meant, the temperature was rising higher and higher. Instead of titillating their spinal columns and trying to excite the pleasure centre of their brains by freeing the words of their semantic weight and let them loose on the ear-drums, I was enlarging that weight, spreading it on to a wider cognitive and affective spectrum. But before I relate what happened afterwards, I think that I should give here the above-mentioned Semantic Poetry Translation as fully as I can remember them now.

(This, of course, creates a typographical problem: the method itself was simple: to replace some of the key-words of a poem by their definitions. But how to do it typographically? How to replace one atomic element by the long ribbon of its spectrum? In short: How to print five, ten, fifteen words in place of one, and so that they would hold together as one entity? Well, yes, but Typographical Topography of a printed page is two-dimensional, is it not? You scan it not only from left to right but also from top to bottom. Therefore, if I have a number of words that form one entity, a bouquet of names by which a rose may be called, why shouldn't I write them as I would write the notes of a musical chord: one under another, instead of one after another? Internal Vertical Justification is the answer to our problem: How to set Semantic Poetry Translations. I.V.J. for S.P.T. Yes, I know, printers will not like it. But 'learning hath gained most by those books by which the printers have lost').

MY S.P. TRANSLATION OF THE OPENING WORDS OF THE CHINESE
POEM: 'DRINKING UNDER THE MOON,' BY LI PO.

*

        The fermented
           grape-
           juice
  among the reproductive
           parts
           of
           seed-plants

        O! I'm conscious
           of
           my state
             of
              being isolated
                from
                others!

Ah! Body attendant   revolving   keeping   & shining
      on   about   238,840 miles   by
      the   (mean)   reflecting the light
      Earth   aloof   radiated
                                                                        by
                                                                        the
                                                                        sun

      into
      my
      mouth
      I take
      &   while expressing the hope for thy success.
      swallow
      the
      liquid

THEMERSON

✶ ✶

Obtain the
    visual
        impression of a
            dark
            patch formed beside me
                by
                my body
                    which
                    obstructs some rays of thy light!

Let   influence   by   feedback   the   object of which
us   ourselves   from   is
three   each   to stimulate
                                    other   the
                                                                pleasure centre
                                                               in
                                                                our brain!

Body attendant   Why are you separated from me by 221,614 miles minimum —
    on
    the   Why is the distance to you increasing up to 252,972 miles?
    Earth!

Make thy glides
        leaps
                revolutions
                      gestures
                              & other expresses of a universal fixation for rhythmical
                                                                             movement
                        the
            keep in step with partial
                          darkness caused by the intervention
                                      of
                                      my   thy light
                                    body between
                                                              &
                                                               the surface
                                                               of the
                                                               Earth
                & with me.

* * *

```
The existence   shall
    of          continue
    this        for
    emotion     a                              every
                period      which is greater than assignable
                of                                       quantity
                time

Body attendant  Let the   vibrations of my short lyrical song
    on                    stimulate thine external ear-drum
    the                   & be conveyed to thine internal ear-drum
    Earth!                & thence to thine internal ear fluids
                Let them
                          cause impulses to pass up thine auditory nerve
                                        to
                                        the
                                        hearing
                                        centre
                                        in
                                        thy
                                        brain

            the
    I & patch          produced by the intervention
        of darkness                   of
                                      my             the surface of the Earth
                                      body between
                                                   &
                                                   thy light

        we can move
            rapidly
            like the masses    suspended    in the gases
                    of         at                of
                    minute     high              the
                    droplets   altitudes         air
                    of
                    water
            away.
```

THEMERSON

* * * *

And having the
        fermented
           grape-juice in our stomach
     absorbing it into our cerebro-spinal fluid
     paralysing various parts of our nervous system with it
     speaking thickly
     unable to maintain equilibrium
     our vision blurred and double
we get merged with one another
        cognitively
        &
        affectively

(though separated and companionless again when the sun
                                     is
                                        above
                                 the horizon)

Let us determine the place
            of
            our
            meeting which
                    shall
                          continue for a period of time
                                     greater
                                     than
                                     every
                                     assignable
                                     quantity

    somewhere
      between
145,000 million
       or is it
300,000 million
            stars constituting that particular 'island universe'
                    of
                    which
                     our
                      solar
                       system
                      is
                  a   part.

BAYAMUS

MY S.P. TRANSLATION OF THE OPENING WORDS
OF A RUSSIAN BALLAD:

'HAIDA TROIKA,
THE SNOW'S DOWNY,
THE BELLS ARE RINGING... &C.'

'Ladies and Gentlemen,' I said before reciting the poem, 'When I was six years old, in 1916, in Russia, I was once taken in a "troïka" for a drive. In the S.P. Translation you will hear now, I find a better account of that wonder which enchanted my eyes, the eyes of a child, than in the original ballad.'

Heigh
    my large   flowing mane
   three powerful   coarse   and
      solid-hoofed   long   tail
      domesticated mammals with

      all   all   all
      your   your   your
      3 x 4   3 x 4   3 x 4
      feet   feet   feet
      in   in   having
      the   the   no
      air   invisible foundation in any substance
      together elastic   capable
                gaseous substance   of
                     which   resisting
                     surrounds   penetration
                     the Earth   by other
                                         substances

             at one stage of each stride;

THEMERSON

    &

at another stage of each stride:

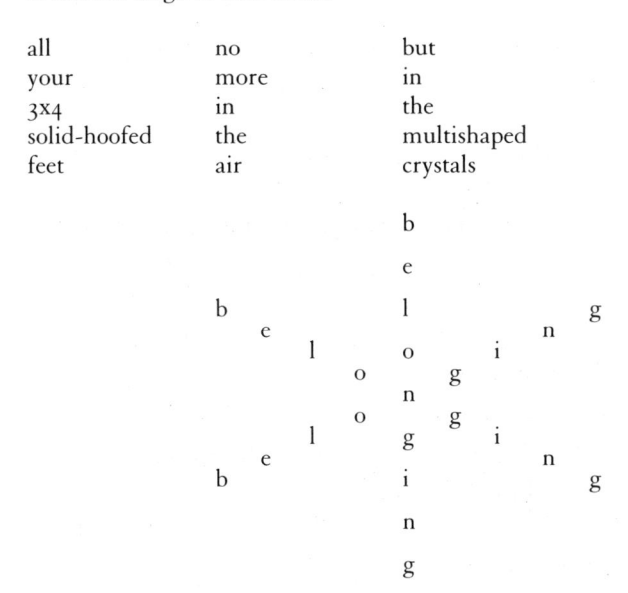

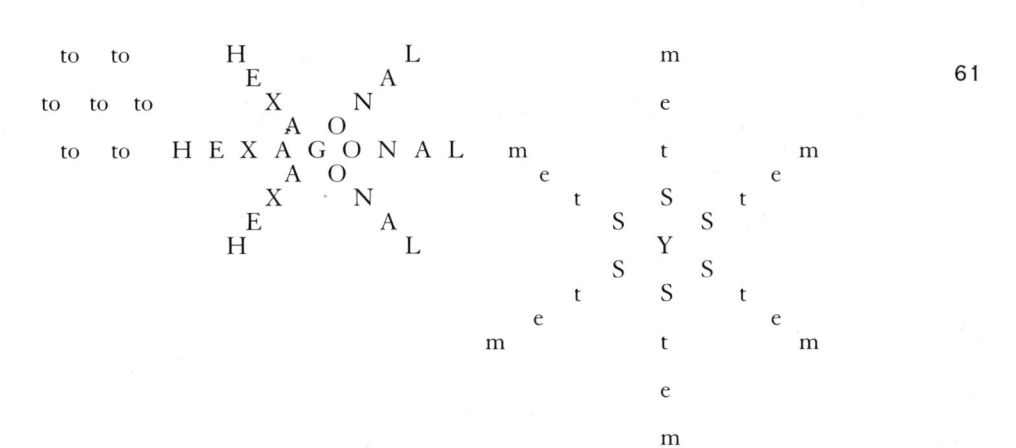

```
all              no           but
your             more         in
3x4              in           the
solid-hoofed     the          multishaped
feet             air          crystals

                              b
                              e
             b                l              g
                 e            o         n
                   l          n     i
                     o          g
                              o
                                g
                     l        g      i
                 e            i          n
             b                n              g
                              g
```

```
to   to      H         L          m
          E       A
to  to  to     X    N             e
          A  O
to   to  H E X A G O N A L    m             t          m
          A  O                      e
             X  .  N                     t       S       t
          E       A                      S       Y       S
          H       L                      S       S
                                    t    S       S      t
                                    e                   e
                              m                         m
                                         e
                                         m
```

formed by slow freezing of water vapour.

Their (the crystals') texture is like the fine
                        soft
                            plumage under a bird's feathers

Their (the crystals') appearance
                    is like light
                  fluffy
                    substance resembling
                          fine
                          soft
                          plumage under a white
                                    bird's feathers

Hung at the necks of the three powerful
                      solid-hoofed
                      domesticated mammals
the small
   hollow
     cup-shaped vessels closed at the upper end
                 of   open at the larger lower end
                 metal struck
                        by
                        strikers suspended inside them
                                  from the top

                emit periodic compressions and decompressions of air
                  periodic compressions and decompressions
                  which exist independently of whether
                  there is any ear to hear it
                            as a clear
                                vibrating
                                resonant sound...

THEMERSON

THIS IS THE S.P. TRANSLATION OF THE PRAISE OF CREATED
THINGS WHICH SAINT FRANCIS MADE WHEN THE LORD
CERTIFIED HIM OF HIS KINGDOM.

Most   complex
         most specialised and differentiated
         best adapted for dominating environment more variously
                                           and extensively
         having power and authority over all things
         able to do all things
         excellent in matters of conduct concerned with the difference
                                         between right
                                                 &
                                                 wrong

         virtuous
         observant of obligations
         dutiful
         conscientious
         well-behaved
         indulgent Lord

Thine be the praise
       the glory
           the honour
       & all benediction

To Thee exclusively
       only
           & to no other are they due

and no member of the highest order of mammals
       is fitted by character or quality
       to mention Thee

Be Thou glorified
           & magnified by worship
                      or by recital
                              esp. in song of Thy greatness
                                      & goodness

My Lord
> does it mean: Lord belonging to me
> > or: Lord to whom I belong

Be Thou glorified
> & magnified with every one of things
> > > not self-existent
> > > but produced from nothing
> > > > by Thee

above all
> *that* male and having the same parents as we
> > incandescent
> > approximately spherical
> > heavenly body
> > round which the planets of our planetary system
> > > > rotate in elliptical orbits
> *which* gives the day and lightens us therewith

And it is beautiful and radiant with the great splendour
> > of 114,700 tons of light pressure ex-
> > erted on the exposed earth-surface

to Thee
> extending upwards far above any level or base
> > it bears similitude

Be Thou praised
> my Owner
> > of Sister Moon
> > of that female and having the same parents as we
> > > satellite of the Earth

> > > & of the self-luminous celestial bodies
> > > > intensely hot
> > > > glowing masses
> > > > situated at enormous distances from the solar system
> > > > the nearest being over 4 light-years away
in the expanse in which they move hast Thou formed them

THEMERSON

        clear
        & precious
        & comely

Be Thou glorified
    & magnified
  my Proprietor
          of our Brother Large-Scale Movement of Air caused by convec-
              tion effect in the gaseous envelope surrounding
              the Earth

        & of the composition of nitrogen
                oxygen
                argon
                carbon dioxide
                neon
                helium
                krypton
                xenon
   with the addition of
      small amounts of water vapour
                          hydrocarbons
                          hydrogen peroxide
                          sulphur compounds
                        & dust particles

       & of the masses of vapour formed in the upper atmosphere
       & of fair and of all: bad
                           good
                           fine
                           wet
                           hot
                           windy atmospheric conditions

by the which Thou givest to Thy creatures
            the sum-total
       of environment forces
                acting on them
                      providing their necessary food
                and furthering their existence

Be Thou praised
> my Ruler

>> of our Sister Cessation of the function of the body as an
>> organised whole

>> of our Sister Cessation of the functions of the body's many
>> trillions of cells

> from whom no man living may escape

The divine
> supernatural   anger
>> vengeance
>> misfortune
>> misery
>> ruin
>> destruction will be upon those

whose bodies
> in sins incurring perdition unless repented of
>> and
>> forgiven
ceased to function as organised wholes

> Praise ye and bless my Lord
>> and give Him expression of gratitude
>>> grateful acknowledgment
>>> of
>>> obligation
>> and act as servant to Him
>> work for Him
>> help Him
>> assist Him

> forward His interests
> supply Him with goods
perform the duties or functions which He needs
> satisfy His wants

> with great meekness

& lowliness of mind.

AND THIS IS THE TRANSLATION OF A POLISH POPULAR SONG THE WORDS OF WHICH PUT INTO ENGLISH AS LITERALLY AS POSSIBLE, ARE:

HOW NICE IT IS WHEN DURING A LITTLE WAR	— BIS —
THE UHLAN FALLS FROM HIS HORSE	— BIS —
HIS COMRADES DON'T REGRET HIM	— BIS —
THEY EVEN TRAMPLE HIM	— BIS —

(Before reciting my translation I gave the audience the melody of the song, which is:

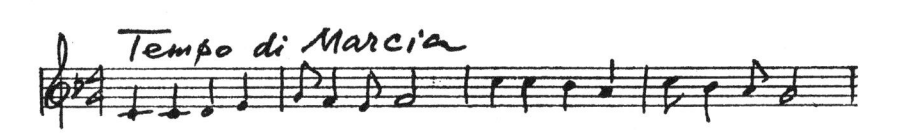

Tempo di Marcia

'Ladies and Gentlemen,' said I then, 'that melody gives a very high patriotic emotion to anyone who listens to it or sings it; it gives a joyful feeling, briskness, sprightliness, and I would like to call it a physiological song, unless scored for the more intellectual orchestra of S.P., as follows:')

How nice it is in that jolly good open
                        conflict
                        between nations
How pretty it is in that jolly smart active
                        international hostility
                        carried on by force of arms

When a light-cavalry soldier
      armed with a weapon of offence
            & defence
        consisting of a pointed iron head
              fixed to a shaft   9
                      or 10 feet in length
      used for thrusting
        & parrying

THEMERSON

  passes through space from the level of the spine of his horse
       to the level of the earth

      From the level of the spine of his horse
        to the level of the earth

His partners

  participators in that open
       conflict
       between nations

companions

  associates sharing the same conditions of this active
           international hostility
           carried on by force of arms
    undergoing the same experiences as he does

  do not feel any grief
      sorrow
      sympathy for him

  do not regard him with desire to help
         relieve
         spare

They even tread upon him
    so as to crush him
      with the modified forms
        of the toe-nails
         of their horses

They even tread upon him
    so as to crush him
      with the flat-strips of iron
        shaped to fit their horses' hoofs
        open at the back
        placed when hot upon the under surface of the hoof
        &
        fastened on with nails.

(To end I recited the S.P. Translation of a Nursery Rhyme, sung by English mothers to their children. 'For us, adults,' I said, 'the words have lost their meaning, they are merely conventional signs of a somehow nonpersonal reality. What if the child's mind apprehends them as in this S.P. Translation?')

TAFFY WAS A WELSHMAN.

Taffy was a male native of Wales

Taffy was a person who practised seizing the property of another unlawfully
        & appropriated it to his own use and purpose

Taffy came to the structure of various materials
       having walls
            roof
            door
        & windows to give light and air
he came to that structure which was a dwelling for me

And there he appropriated to his own use
        one of the limbs of the dead body of an ox
        prepared and sold by a butcher

I went to the structure of various materials
       having walls
            roof
            door
        & windows to give light and air
I went to that structure which was a dwelling for Taffy

Taffy was not there

Taffy came to the structure of various materials
        having walls
            roof
            door
              & windows to give light and air
Taffy came to that structure which was a dwelling for me

And there he appropriated to his own use
        the part of the ox skeleton
        containing in its cavity
        the fat substance
        the vascular tissue
        which had formed the red bloodcorpuscles of the ox

I went to the structure of various materials
        having walls
            roof
            door
              & windows to give light and air
I went to that structure which was a dwelling for Taffy

Taffy was lying upon a piece of furniture
            consisting of a mattress
                & the wooden frame which supported it

I took the part of the ox skeleton
    the part containing in its cavity
        the fat substance
        the vascular tissue
        which had formed the red bloodcorpuscles of the ox

And by a sudden sharp blow
I broke open that part of Taffy's body
        situated on top of the spinal column
        which contained the great mass of nerve-cells
        the functioning of which
                is
                    mind.

Chapter 11

(Continued)

✶

I've mentioned already that my performance won an applause expressed by clapping of hands, shouting, etc. Several times my recitation had been interrupted by exclamations like 'Listen! Hear! Hear!' True, sometimes they were ironical, and at the end some people, imitating sounds made by a cow, cried: 'Boo!' in order to express their disapproval of my person or my S.P. translation, but that could not spoil the heavenly feeling of relief which came upon me the moment I realised that this unexpected strange adventure was over.

The two gentlemen in evening-dress shook hands with me and disappeared. I looked for Bayamus but couldn't see him among the departing public. One of the electric bulbs suspended above my table went out. An usherette came to me and handed me a small card.

> *Why didn't you recite the S.P. Translation*
> *of the Q.L. Students' song as I asked you? —*
> *Bayamus —*

I looked about me again but didn't see him.

'It's funny,' I said to myself, 'for someone to put questions and disappear before receiving an answer.'

A young woman in red, accompanied by a still younger man, approached me.

'We are going to have a bottle party. There will be some painters and poets. Would you like to come with us? We are going by car straight on from here...' she said.

But I was still looking for Bayamus.

'I'm sorry,' said I, 'I've an appointment already.'

'Pity,' said she, 'your friend Bayamus will be with us.'

I wanted to say that in that case I would go with them, but at that very moment I felt that I couldn't move. My legs were as if frozen; my feet as if stuck to the floor.

'Well...' I began, and suddenly I felt a wave of heat.

The young woman in red drew in air sharply and nervously through her fine white nostrils.

'Something stinks in here!' she said.

Then, and with real horror, I realised that my vesical sphincter was out of order, and that the sensation of the wave of heat was caused by the fluid secreted by my kidneys, transferred by the ureter into my bladder and thence discharged from my body through the urethra. I knew it contained a large proportion of water together with some of the waste products of my metabolism. And I understood that it was the minute particles of this very fluid, each of them perhaps not greater than $1/10000000$ of a gramme, and the gaseous molecules of it, which had entered the nose of the young woman in red, acted on the peripheral end of its olfactory nerve, set up nerve-impulses and produced in the olfactory centre of her brain that impression of smell, the unpleasantness of which was due, I thought, mostly to the fact that the evaporating molecules were the molecules of the colourless, pungent, soluble, alkaline gas called ammonia.

'Well...' I said, exerting myself to speak calmly, 'I'm sorry I can't go with you now. If you would be so kind as to leave me your address I'll come, and with pleasure, in an hour.'

'Certainly,' said she. And her companion tore a card from his notebook and, writing a few words on it, left it on the table.

'Without fail!' said she.

'Yes,' said I.

'Bye, bye,' said she.

'Bye, bye,' said the young man.

'Bye bye,' said I.

After they had left I waited a moment, and, tentatively, with a quick slight drawing-in of air through the nose, tested the scent around me. There *was* a smell of ammonia. My heart was beating quickly, and I felt a cold perspiration on my forehead. 'Well,' said I to myself, 'first thing: no panic! Calm! You will think it over again afterwards. Now try to change your mood.' I pretended that nothing had happened, and started to think of something else. 'I'm definitely fed-up' — that was what I thought — 'I'm definitely fed-up with us all, my good people. Fed-up with Thee, Jesus Christ, and with you, Niels Bohr, and with me myself, as well. I'm fed-up with Christ's teaching which, during the past 2,000 years, turned out to be the worst method of unteaching men to slaughter each other, and perhaps the best method of teaching them hypocrisy; I can't help being fed-up with Niels Bohr and his atomic wonders, even if someone shows me how much better it is to finish the war by dropping two atomic bombs; and I'm fed-up with me, and with you, and with all of us, because of several handfuls of hundreds of different reasons. I am perfectly aware that all this is my personal affair, that it concerns nobody, and I do not obtrude it upon anybody else. I am living like others, eating and drinking like others, working like others, making love like others, going to the cinema like others. But something as small as the hammer or the anvil or stirrup bones, the three small bones of my middle ear, is broken in me. Definitely and irreparably. There are some dozens, or dozens of hundreds, or hundreds of thousands of people living, working, eating, drinking, discussing problems and going to the cinema, who have also something in them definitely and irreparably broken. Nobody knows that, and nobody ever will know that, because they hide the very fact that there is a small nothing broken in them; because they pretend to be the same as they were before the war; and because they want to take that secret with them into the grave. I'm one of them, and I'm fed-up with them as well.'

The second electric bulb went out, but it wasn't any darker than it had been before. I looked at the table before me and saw a small card lying there. It carried the name of a *Mrs.* and her address, both strange to me. I couldn't recollect how it had appeared here. But I recognised perfectly well two large transparent vessels standing beside it on the table. The first one contained a pair of infant human beings joined together by a fleshy ligature, the second one — just a normal female foetus in the womb, in an advanced stage of development. The circular space I stood on was surrounded by four circular platforms rising tier upon tier, each one of them being protected by a handrail supported by black and white painted bars. But there were no listeners there now.

The part of the hemispherical ceiling directly above the table consisted of 120 translucent sheets of a hard and brittle substance made by fusing silicate with some other materials. Midway between the hemisphere and the table the bony framework of a human body from which all the soft tissues had decayed or had been removed, was hanging on a thick, strong cord of intertwined fibres of flax. This cord passed over a small grooved wheel contained in a block fixed in the centre of the translucent hemisphere. The other end wound round a small wooden cylinder with a short handle, fastened to the pilaster near the door.

'It's funny of Bayamus,' I said to myself, 'to leave the Theatre of Anatomy and to wander around for several hours in order to come back to the Theatre of Anatomy and enter it through the other door. Or,' I continued after a while, 'is it the door we come through that is the most important? or what we experienced on our way before coming?' It was rather a trite remark and, being disgusted with it, I felt angry with Bayamus who had left me by myself.

A man in white trousers and a blue jacket, with a yellow cravat at his neck, appeared in the doorway. He seized the short handle and turned it. The cylinder paid out the thick, strong cord which passed over the small grooved wheel, and the bony framework of a human body from which all soft tissues had decayed or had been removed passed silently through space, down to the level of my table.

It was fearfully and wonderfully made.

I grasped the card lying between the vessels, turned quickly and went out.

Chapter 11

(Continued)

*

Once again in the street, I looked around me and from several thousands of stimuli which rushed upon me I immediately chose the *gestalt* of a painted and illuminated board bearing the sign TOURING CLUB and the name GREAT WINDOWS HOTEL.

'We have no rooms,' said the porter.
'I wanted one for a very short time only,' said I.
He looked at me suspiciously.
'All our rooms are occupied,' said he.
'When I say: a very short time, I mean: one or two hours.'
'We are not that kind of place,' he said coldly.
'What do you mean?' I asked.
He took a newspaper from the counter, folded it, and put it on his desk.
'Visitors are not allowed to enter the rooms of our guests,' said he.
'Well,' said I, 'you misunderstand me. I have no intention of receiving any visitors.'
'And you want a room for one hour?'
'Yes,' said I.
He scrutinised me sharply. I was sure he suspected I was looking for a place to commit suicide or something.
'You have no luggage with you?' he asked.
'Look here,' said I, deciding that in the circumstances one must commit

what is literally a lie in order to convey what is essentially true, 'my luggage is at the station. My train is leaving in three hours or so. Have I no right to hire a room for two hours? I'll pay you for the whole night. In advance. But don't keep me standing here, because I want to take a bath at once, and sleep for one hour.'

He rose. 'I'm sorry, Sir,' he said, and it was the first time he had called me 'sir'. 'Number 7, Sir!' and he rang the bell for a servant.

We went to Number 7 which was on the first floor. I immediately undressed, emptied my pockets, gave my trousers (and jacket) to be ironed, and took a bath. Then I regained my room and lay down on the huge wooden carved bed, a fine fake of the Great Bed of Ware (Hertfordshire, England).

Chapter 11

(Concluded)

✶

But then the door opened
and the servant came in
bringing my clothes.
I put them on
and extended my muscles fully
by stretching my limbs;
at the same time,
my mouth opened widely,
owing to an involuntary
muscular
contraction.
I looked round me
and felt I had nothing more to do
in that alien room,
Room Number 7
of the GREAT WINDOWS HOTEL.
After paying the bill I realised
that if I bought cigarettes
I would have no money
for the 'bus.
I did not enter the tobacconist's shop, — and,
nevertheless, went on foot.

Chapter 12

Bottle Party

★

The room was packed with people. From the first moment I felt there was something strange about them all. Not in their behaviour though (they were sitting quietly around, on chairs, on cushions, and on the floor) — but in themselves. However, when I entered, the gentleman standing in the centre showed me immediately to a chair, and then, for a time at least, all my attention was directed exclusively to him.

Over a white close-fitting garment reaching to his waist he wore a black coat with tails, with a division between them, and a button at the top of each. The lower part of his body was hidden in a black garment extending from the narrowest part of his trunk to the ankles and having a separate tubular opening for each leg. So 82 per cent of some 15,000 square inches of the surface of his body was shut off from sight by textile-fabrics, and if one also subtracted the 6 per cent hidden in his leather shoes, — only 12 per cent was left to be seen. That 12 per cent consisted almost entirely of a very pale skin, partly covered with hair lubricated with some scented ointment. There were openings in the skin in several places. In two of them were seen parts of his eyeballs: part of the sclerotic coats, pearly white on the outer surface; cornea, transparent and showing an iris in which the pigment cells were in such quantity and so distributed that they gave the impression of a clear sky-blue colour. Two other openings conducted to his organs of hearing. Two more served as passages for air to and from the lungs and to convey odours to his olfactory nerves. And one, when he opened his lips, showed the fleshy muscular organ, serving purposes of taste, mastication, swallowing, and of speech.

He wore several rings of gold and silver, one of them set with a gem. They adhered tightly to his skin, where it covered his fingers.

Well, I'm quite aware that the above description of a few details of the 12 per cent of his surface available to sight may just as well fit several other individuals of the same species. What constituted his more personal characteristics were some things which did not exist within his reach but ought to have been there. My first feeling was, there ought to be a silk top-hat in his left hand, and a pair of white gloves and a long pliant whip used to incite horses in a circus, in his right. But one shouldn't classify individuals according to their appearances. I know a family butcher, London, w.9, who could play perfectly well the role of a refined aristocrat in continental films, and I agree that the bodies of many peers are perfectly suitable for the role of butcher. The gentleman standing in the centre of the room had the appearance of a ring-master, but what he said had nothing to do with that profession.

'I repeat,' he said, continuing his speech interrupted by my entrance, 'Semantic Poetry is also *against* something. It is against provincialism. Against a limited intellectual outlook. Isn't that so?' — he asked suddenly, addressing me directly.

'Yes, I suppose it is,' said I.

Then, as though my 'yes' had been given by an ancient Greek priest, inspired by a god, he turned his head triumphantly around, and emphasising his words with a gesture, said:

'You see?'

Nobody answered and he was quite satisfied with that.

'I know 46 languages,' he continued, 'not all of them perfectly well, but I can read in 46 languages easily. And I assure you I prefer to read Russian literature in English translation, English literature in French, French in Spanish, Spanish in German, German in Italian, Italian in Norwegian, Norwegian in Portuguese, Portuguese in Polish, Polish in Yiddish, Yiddish in Hebrew, Hebrew in Rumanian, Rumanian in Swedish, Swedish in

Turkish. When I read a translation I feel the author cannot cheat me so easily. He cannot delude me with the sonorities of his words and with all the associations each of his words carries in the original. In the translation I can see the 'couleur locale' from the outside, not as one who is himself participating in it, not as one born in the same parish as the author, but as a man of the world. Am I not right?' he asked.

'Quite,' said I.

'You see?' he said to his audience, and continued: 'We are divided horizontally and vertically and across in provinces and provinces and provinces. The same word has different echoes in each of them, and alas it is just these echoes, not the words themselves, that are considered by writers and readers as the most subtle poetical material. Isn't that so?' he paused, waiting for an answer from me.

'Quite,' said I, reluctantly, for I began to be irritated at having to endorse everything he said.

'You see?!'

And then he continued:

'An international language does not solve our problem. It merely suppresses the phonetical and grammatical differences which separate us. But there exist differences of a higher degree, separating even people speaking the same language. Like paths and alleys overgrown with hardy, rank-growing weeds, the words we use are overgrown with our individual, private, provincial associations, which tend to choke the meaning. They do very well for political purposes. They may be good for prose. *But,* Ladies and Gentlemen, not for poetry!' He suspended his voice to stress with an impressive pause the importance of his statement. 'Poetry, Ladies and Gentlemen, ought to be built with bricks which change as little as possible during the ages and across the frontiers. It ought to extend not only in time but also in space, to be not only eternal, but also international, inter-provincial, inter-individual; human; divine!'

'I see...!' somebody cried suddenly from the corner.

And at that moment my attention was transferred from the speaker to his listeners. I have already said that from the first moment I entered the room they seemed to me to be somehow strange. However, it was only now that I realised why I had that impression. They were monsters. Their bodies were most fantastically deformed, and I was sure these deformities were not acquired, or due to accident, disease, the maintenance of abnormal conditions in the course of a trade or occupation, were not deliberately contrived compressions at the dictate of custom, religion, etc. — but were congenital.

There was an old man 2 feet 5 inches high, a woman with her two eyes fused in a single median socket, a Chinese giant more than 9 feet high, a middle-aged woman with a long white beard, whiskers and moustaches, a man whose head grew beneath his shoulders, a young girl with a strangely asymmetrical face, twins with their breast bones united by a band of flesh; it was only now that I noticed that the young man I had seen in the Theatre, with the lady in red, had seven fingers on each hand, and I couldn't imagine what kind of deformities they hid under their clothes, which were tailored in a way not seen in the fashion-plates of any time or place. 'Well,' I said to myself, 'maybe my first impression was right. Maybe he is a ring-master.' But now he was speaking rather in the manner of a teacher.

'I think I know what you are thinking. You're thinking that what I've just said is a repetition of what you said at the Theatre. No, my dear sir, it isn't. I'm not repeating your thoughts, I'm developing them.'

I couldn't take my eyes off the rings which glittered on his fingers. One of them fascinated me. It was so much like the one, set with the beryl, I used to have, and lost, years ago, I didn't even notice when.

'Don't think I'm not your friend,' he continued. 'I am. And I like your dictionary game. I agree that there is more in it than in all those romantic, surrealist, dadaist, automatic, or combinatorial ways of making familiar words look as if they were not familiar. All the same, you'll not deny that it is deductive. It is based on verbal mathematics, and not on the properties of the universe. No, my dear sir. We have to take our poetry more seriously. We've got to base it not on: "$'p' = 'p^{1'} + 'p^{2'} + 'p^{3'}$... as you find them in your dictionary," but on: "$'p'$ is true if p – as you find it in life." Once you forget to be empirical, your appealing to the meaning of a word, too, may deceive you and present you with an unnecessary scholastic puzzle. For instance: you may hear that a man, after he had got 164 dollars out of a Jew, delivered him to the Gestapo, and you exclaim with astonishment: *"How can a Christian do it?!"* You are surprised because you have in your mind only the deductive definition of the word: *"Christian,"* your full exclamation being: *"How can a person who professes the religion and doctrines taught by Jesus Christ and His Church, and who adheres to the code of conduct enjoyed by them — do it?"* You can't solve that problem and you are puzzled by it. But try and get a slightly more inductive definition in your exclamation; would it not run somewhat as follows:

How can one

one who was baptised after he was born;

one who was told to be good because, if he wasn't, a Jew would come and take him away in his sack;

one whose lymphatic glands were attacked by tuberculosis, who had lice in his shirt, and stank of cabbage which was the principal dish of his dinner;

"Stop it," the old dwarf said.

But the ring-master took no notice of him and continued:

one who was allowed as a boy to treat with scorn another boy, called Abram, whose lymphatic glands were attacked by tuberculosis, who had lice in his gabardine and stank of onion which was the principal dish of his dinner;

"Shut up!" the old dwarf repeated.

But the ring-master went on:

one who was told he couldn't have two-pence to buy ice-cream because there was rent to be paid to that rich Jew, father of...

"The Jew!" the young man whom I first met in the Theatre with the lady in red, and who had seven fingers on each hand, jumped up from his chair. "My house is a decayed house, / And the jew squats on the windowsill, the owner, / Spawned in some estaminet of Antwerp, / Blistered in Brussels, patched and peeled in London…"

But the ring-master didn't stop:

>   one who was told: aren't you ashamed? this dirty Jew Isaac is better than you in geography!;
>   one who was told: don't be as stupid as this Jew Yoyne is;
>   or: as arrogant as the Jew Chaim;
>   or: as cowardly as the Jew Mendel;

"I wish you would shut up," said the dwarf.

>   one who was taught that the sweet aryan Jesus was sold by a Jew called Judas;

"And what, maybe He wasn't?!" the twins said.

>   one who was told: the sweet aryan Jesus wanted to save the world and make everyone happy, but He was murdered cruelly by the Jews;

"Well, wasn't He?" asked the twins.

>   one who was told: the Jews are sleeping on gold stolen from Christendom;

The young man with seven fingers on each hand had a rich, golden voice. "The rats are underneath the piles," he recited. "The jew is underneath the lot. / Money in furs. The boatman smiles…."

But the ring-master ignored him:

>   one who was told: he couldn't go to the University because his place had been taken by Jews;

The young man's voice was warm and gracious. It delighted the ear. "What is important," he said, "is the unity of religious background; and reasons of race and religion combine to make any large number of free-thinking Jews undesirable. — And a spirit of excessive tolerance is to be deprecated."

The ring-master, however, didn't pay any attention to him and continued:

> one who was told: he had to free Christianity from those to whom even God's Love had closed the entrance to Heaven —— — do i⸺

Well, you see, when you put the right inductive definition in your puzzle, the puzzle dissolves. Because Semantic Poetry does not arrange verses into bunches of flowers. It bares a poem and shows the extra-linguistic data hidden behind it. There is no room for hypnosis in its rhymes and rhythms. Semantic verse is lucid and sober. If it happens to be bitter or funny, as it does at times, it is not because one has seasoned it with wormwood, or charged it with laughing bubbles of Nitrous oxide, but because it is *it* itself that squeezes that bitterness and funniness out of the reality of the world of which they have always been, and will for ever remain, the original and final ingredients.'

I was rather tired by his exposition and wanted to ask him whether he had seen Bayamus, but he was talking without interruption, and still with the gestures of a ring-master.

'Poetry must be *"simple, sensuous,* and *passionate"* said Milton. And what is more *simple* than replacing definiens by definiendum? What does appeal more to our *sensuousness* than the latter, the definiendum, seen as if for the first time, seen through, X-rayed to show a bit of naïve empirical reality? What is more intense and fervid than the *passion* to see truth taking off her coat of traditional beliefs, tales, sayings, customs and behaviourisms! Am I not right?' — he turned to me again for endorsement.

'Quite,' I began, but he was already making his triumphal ring-master gesture.

However, this time he stopped suddenly and asked:

'Who are you?'

I was rather surprised by this unexpected question.

'I was invited to this party by a lady in the Theatre of Semantic Poetry. I was told my friend Bayamus would be here too. I shall be grateful if you will tell me where he has...'

But at that moment he burst out laughing.

'Damn you!' he shouted. 'We know all that very well. My wife invited you at *my* special request. And when I'm asking: Who are you? I mean: what is your definition of yourself?'

The old dwarf filled up a glass with whisky and offered it to me.

'Nina!' He turned to the woman with the beard, whiskers and moustaches, 'would you like to have one more too?'

'You can't ask me, would I like to have one more too, because that is his *first* glass,' said she in a deep, low, resonant voice.

'But it is not *your* first glass,' said the dwarf.

'I don't say it is, Klaud,' she said, 'and I didn't correct your saying: *one more,* what I did was to correct your saying: *too.*'

'But he's drinking *too,*' the old dwarf whined.

'I don't say he isn't,' said she, 'but if the judge asks a witness and the witness says he heard you saying *"would you like to have one more too,"* he, the judge, may deduce that he, the gentleman, has already had a drink, which isn't true. You see?'

'But who is talking about judges, Nina? What have judges to do with it?' the dwarf asked, evidently frightened.

She put her glass behind her on the floor.

'Nobody ever knows...' she answered, twirling her moustaches with both hands.

'Quiet, please, Ladies and Gentlemen! We are discussing a serious question!' said the 'ring-master.'

And at the same moment, something told me he wasn't telling all these stories without some special purpose. Something told me all his speech was merely an introduction made to prepare the way for what would start now.

'And according to you, Ladies and Gentlemen,' he said, 'who is he? what do you think?' — pointing his finger at me — 'Who is he, that strange 5 feet 7 inches tall gentleman with only five fingers on each hand, with two eyes, each in its own socket, with his head growing on his neck, and with other particularities hidden under his clothes?! Who is he, where is he, when is he?'

'Well,' the woman with the asymmetrical face said, 'he's there, on the chair.'

'Is he? Oh, how clever you are!' exclaimed the 'ring-master'. 'He is there on his chair,' he repeated scornfully. 'But is he also in that part of space where his hair is? And what if I cut his hair? Will he still be there or not? And what if I cut his leg off? Is he in his leg too or not, I ask you?! Or, maybe he is in my leg, not in *his*? Ha, ha, ha!'

'Don't talk nonsense,' the man whose head grew beneath his shoulders said reproachfully.

'Be quiet, my dear Karl. I am not talking nonsense, I assure you. You can't define him exactly in space. Well, you can say: here he is, there he is not, but you can't fix the particular point where he ceased to be, because you have no precise definition of who he is.'

'He is a good fellow,' said the woman with both her eyes fused in a single median socket.

'I'm not saying he isn't, Clara. No! He *is* a good fellow. A jolly good fellow!' He struck his knee with the palm of his hand and with a curious smile said to me: 'I'm sorry, I didn't want to hurt you!'

'In any case it wasn't *my* knee being hurt,' said I.

The Chinese giant suddenly stood up. His head was bowed a little, otherwise it would have touched the ceiling.

'I would like to dance,' said he.

'Very well, Chiang. You may dance,' said the 'ring-master.'

'But I would like to dance with your wife,' said the giant.

'I'm very pleased to hear that, Chiang. She is there, in her room,' he pointed to the door on his left, behind him, 'but she'll soon come and join us.'

'Well,' said the giant, 'then don't talk nonsense till she comes, please.'

'What nonsense, Chiang?'

'Any nonsense! About the gentleman: who he is, where he isn't, and so on.'

'Look, Chiang, what if I cut your ear and transplant it behind one of mine? Wouldn't it be the case that you would exist partly where I am, and not only where you are?'

'That's some more of your nonsense,' said the Chinese giant. 'I am where my brain is, where my memories are registered!'

'Splendid, Chiang, splendid! But what if a part of your memory is cut out from you and transplanted, for instance, into me? What in that case is the meaning of the word *you* or of the word *I*?'

'Well,' said the giant, 'it would be a new thing; and it is just silly to speak with old words about new things.'

'But that new thing exists,' cried my 'ring-master,' and pointing once more to me — 'He is that new thing!'

'I object!' said I, standing up.

But he was still pointing at me.

'Tell me!' said he provokingly, 'where is your memory for several months beginning with June, 1940?'

'I object!' I repeated quite automatically, surprised that he seemed to know more about me than I had thought earlier on.

'It's not necessary to object,' he said. 'We are all serious people here, and none of us can be offended by listening to the truth. Please sit down and I'll tell you.... It was a very hot, sunny day of June, 1940...' — he started and I sat down again, frightened, and at the same time very unhappy, as if that which was the cause of my fear had already been accomplished.

But at that very moment the door opened and the lady in red came into the room. She was accompanied by Bayamus rolling on his roller-skate, and at first, when the door was moving on its hinges, I even had the impression that I saw his hand squeezing her elbow and then withdrawing rapidly.

She evidently heard the last sentence.

'Oh, please!' she exclaimed, approaching us quickly, 'don't be so cruel, darling! I know what you are going to tell him, it's all perfectly true, and your intentions are of the best, but I'm afraid, darling, you don't know how to do it with all the delicacy needed in this case. It needs a feminine touch. Let me tell him myself, darling...' and without waiting for his answer she came very close to me and touching my forehead with the sharp polished nail of her forefinger, said:

'Do you know that your head was cut off?'

I couldn't refrain from smiling.

'I'm surprised to hear that,' said I, 'I think my head is still on my body.'

'Oh, yes,' said she, and she was very charming indeed when she repeated: 'Oh, yes! But it isn't your body!'

'Isn't it?' I asked, trying to be affable with her.

'No,' said she, 'Prof. Kravtchenko cut your head off your body five years ago.'

'That's very hard to believe,' said I.

'Well, I saw it. I saw it myself at a private screening,' she said. 'He connected your head with an artificial heart and with artificial lungs, and it was living. I saw it very clearly. Your head was standing, I think that's the right word, standing on a large dish, and it reacted to all sorts of stimuli. It made wry faces, its mouth watered, it slept during the night and opened its eyes in the morning, and when Prof. Kravtchenko's female-assistant showed it a mirror, which was very nasty of her, its eyes wept. You don't remember that?'

'I'm sorry,' said I, 'I don't remember that.'

'That's strange,' said she. '*He* remembers all that very well,' and pointing at her husband, she asked: 'Don't you, darling?'

'Certainly I do!' said he.

'You see?!' she turned to me. 'You see,' she repeated, 'Prof. Kravtchenko did the same thing with him. And then Prof. Kravtchenko connected your head with his body, and his head with your body! Isn't it marvellous! He joined all the veins and arteries and nerves and the trachea and the spine, it must have been a true work of precision, a jeweller's masterpiece!'

'Do you mean to say, Madam,' said I, 'that my body isn't mine but his, and that his body isn't his but mine?'

'Yes,' she said with a graceful smile.

'Yes,' he echoed, 'if you consider, as I do, that the head is that which determines which of us is you and which I. I warn you, however, that it isn't a perfect determinant, because part of your biography and part of your memory are registered not in your brain, but in your spinal chord; I mean: in *my* spinal chord, and reciprocally part of my biography is registered in yours.'

'Oh, please! Don't complicate it all with your definitions, darling!' exclaimed the lady in red.

'I am not complicating anything, my dear, but I like the whole truth to be said and my intention is to discuss the whole thing now at once and to decide....'

'Darling!' exclaimed she. 'You promised me....'

'I didn't promise you anything, my dear. Quite the contrary, I told you that I would...'

'Well, then,' she interrupted him, 'but at least not in my presence.'

At that moment the Chinese giant suddenly stood up and said:

'Excuse me, Madam. Your husband promised me a dance with you. You are not going away now? Are you?'

'I'll come back in a minute, Mr. Chiang,' she answered, turned away, and went out of the room, closing the door behind her.

An idea I considered funny at the time came into my mind.

'I have a dark-coloured spot on my skin,' I said, 'I was born with it. If you don't mind I will show you that I still have it on my shoulder.'

'Have you looked at it since 1940?' asked the gentleman I still called the 'ring-master.'

'I don't remember any particular moment when I have looked at it since then,' said I, 'but I'm sure it is still there.'

'Yes! You are sure, though you haven't looked at it!' exclaimed he. 'But I look at it each morning in the two mirrors I have specially arranged in my bathroom. Yes, sir! Your spot is here, on my shoulder!' — and he started undressing.

He took off his dress-coat but had scarcely had time to withdraw the studs from the button-holes of his old-fashioned shirt-front when an ear-piercing scream came from the corner of the room, where the twins with their breast-bones united by a band of flesh were sitting.

'Ah! Ah!' — they screamed hysterically, 'you monsters! A-ah! you devils! Both of you! Ah! Ah! Devilish! Artificial monsters! Ah-h, Jesus, save us!'

'Silence!' ordered the 'ring-master,' and then he added with indignation: 'The bowel!'

'What does he mean? Who is the bowel?' asked the dwarf.

'All of you!' said the 'ring-master'. 'The bowel has not had time to adapt itself to modern soft, starchy food, to the modern sedentary nature of occupation, to all the modern conditions produced by modern life. Its action is incomplete and often stops altogether. And you, too, you can't adapt yourself to modern conditions produced by modern science. You scream when you hear of transplanting somebody's head, as if there weren't more extraordinary experiments! You see a new thing, and you scream, frightened, but I say you are frightened only because you have no name for it yet. Don't be stupid! The time will come and you'll invent a name for it, and then you'll be calm and convinced you know all about it.'

'Give me a glass of whisky,' said one of the united twins.

'Two glasses,' said the other.

Bayamus was still near the door he had entered through, and I stood up with the intention of approaching him. But the 'ring-master' stopped me.

'Excuse me,' he said, 'there is a point I have to discuss with you frankly and openly.'

'I'm listening,' I said, quietly.

'The point is,' he said, 'that I have a baby.'

'I'm glad to hear it,' I said.

'Well,' he said, 'the point is, it isn't my baby, it's yours.'

'What do you mean?!' I said. 'I scarcely know your wife, I didn't meet her till this very evening.'

'That's the reason!' he said, 'It's I who made your baby with her.'

'I beg your pardon, Sir?' said I.

'Oh!' he exclaimed helplessly. 'It's only the head which is mine, the rest of my body is yours. Don't you understand that?'

'Well....' I started.

But then he hung his head and whispered:

'And I... I want to have my own, my own baby by her.'

'You mean,' I said, and stopped, afraid of finishing the sentence.

'Damn it!' he said irritably. 'I'm talking to you, openly and frankly, as man to man, as every man ought to once in his life, and you're answering me with these: "I beg your pardon...." "Well...", "You mean..." How annoying! Yes, what I mean is you ought, *you* must make *my* baby with her, I beg you!'

I wondered for a moment about what he said.

'And do you think,' I asked, 'that your wife will agree?'

'What?!' he said, 'certainly she will agree! She has to! We were married in church, Sir! She made an oath in the most solemn manner, with an appeal to God, she made a binding promise to make children with me, my *own* children, that means the children grown from the ovum fertilised by the sex cells which are in the body which now belongs to your head, not to mine. That's clear, Sir!'

It was obvious that he considered the matter already settled. I implored Bayamus with my eyes, but he turned quickly to the window and pretended to look out.

'Would you like to see your baby?' said my 'ring-master,' 'I have no objection to your taking it with you, if you like. That's your paternal right.' He went to the door and opened it. 'Darling, the gentleman would like to see Barbara!'

He showed me into the other room, but he himself remained in the first one and closed the door behind me.

There I really saw a baby, in a sort of bed with high sides and mounted on rockers. The 'ring-master's' wife was sitting on the chair behind it. She glanced straight into my eyes and then her face turned red. She stooped quickly over the cradle.

'May I introduce Barbara to you,' she said, taking off the little pink coverlet.

The first thing which struck me was that the girl was very tightly bound up from her waist down to her feet, just like an Egyptian mummy.

'What's that?!' I couldn't refrain from asking, indignantly. She went to the door and turned the key.

'He has never seen her without bandages,' said she. 'And he never will.'

Then she came back to the cradle and started to unfold the strips of soft, pliable material.

The little girl awoke but didn't cry. After a moment she smiled, glad and happy, and the bandages once off, I saw her three plump pink legs shaking joyfully in the air.

'You understand that my husband mustn't know,' said the lady in red.

I kept silent.

'He would be terribly jealous,' she added.

'Well,' I said, smiling, 'I thought you expected me to be jealous, as I was promised that I would see *my* baby.'

'Oh,' she said perplexed, 'I didn't see it from that point of view.' And covering little Barbara she added quickly — 'But you'll keep it secret, I hope. You are not going to tell him?'

'I'm certainly not going to tell him,' I said.

She wondered about something for a long while.

'And when will you come to visit us again, sir?' she said at last.

'It depends on you, Madam,' I said, and felt that my face went as red as hers.

'Well,' she said, and very quietly this time, 'my husband insists that you should start to visit us after the next shedding of a part of the lining membrane of my uterus, together with the unfertilised ovum. I expect it to be at the end of next week, sir.'

'I am looking forward to it, Madam,' I said, retreating to the door.

But she looked at me astonished:

'Wait a minute!' she exclaimed, 'you are forgetting Barbara!' She took the girl out of the cradle. 'What an absent-minded man,' she said, wrapping the baby in the swaddling bands and the coverlet.

When I took Barbara from her arms, she turned the key and opened the door before me.

The twins united by a fleshy ligature were still sitting in the corner. The woman with her two eyes fused in a single socket was sleeping on the chair. The old dwarf was climbing on the knees of the young girl with the strangely asymmetrical face, while the Chinese giant and the woman with a long white beard, whiskers and moustaches were dancing in the centre of the room.

'I'm glad you're taking your baby,' said the 'ring-master.'

'I see!' exclaimed the man whose head grew beneath his shoulders.

With Barbara in my arms I went out.

To my surprise Bayamus was waiting for me in the street.

'You have come at last,' he said. 'I haven't had an opportunity to congratulate you on your recital! It was grand! Really! But why didn't you recite the *Quartier Latin* poem? Were you ashamed? No!'

'Thank you, Bayamus,' said I. 'I have to congratulate you, too. You are a true mutant, that's what you are!'

And I showed him Barbara, who was sleeping again.

'Yes...' he said, 'I knew...' and he took the baby from my arms. He looked at her very tenderly and I saw that his nose became wet. He tried to take a handkerchief out of his pocket but he couldn't manage it, and he gave me the baby to hold. But when it was in my arms again, he suddenly struck the earth with both his side feet and as quickly as a motor-bike ran away on his roller-skate.

THE END

Cambridge, London, 1944

The Life of

Cardinal Pölätüo

with Notes on his Writings

his Times and his

Contemporaries

Part One

1

On the twelfth of September 1862, an elderly maiden lady asked the brothers Goncourt:

'Et puis, pourquoi sommes-nous faits en viande?'

Cardinal Pölätüo overheard these words, and turned his back in distaste. He had spent the previous night at the villa of the Countess Kostrowicki; who, as the first beams of the rising sun broke through the stained glass of the casement, had said to him: 'My dear, I am sure that you have started a new life in me; a boy, to be precise. I can already feel it in my bosom, and I intend to carry it for not less than seven years. I believe that, in general, one carries one's young for too short a time; one expels it into the world too soon; which is, undoubtedly, the reason why men of genius are so scarce. Besides, shall I not thus be confident that I shall not conceive again during those seven years, and shall not my confidence put my mind at rest and ease at all those moments when it is most desirable? Could you not, my dear, you who are a son of the great bosom of the Church, say a little Mass to strengthen my resolve?'

At the time, Cardinal Pölätüo hadn't taken these matinal confidences very seriously. It had on the contrary put him in very good spirits to hear that he had become the Author of a spiritual son, whom the Countess would mature in her bosom over a period of time marked by the recurrence of so many astronomical coincidences. And it was only the question put to

Messieurs de Goncourt by the elderly maiden lady, that stirred his imagination.

'Can it be that the Countess' intent is to make our son *en viande?*' he asked himself.

2

At the end of September 1880, Cardinal Pölätüo received a letter that gave out a faint fragrance of perfume. Before slitting open the envelope, he placed it in front of him on his writing desk, and said to himself: 'After we have read this letter,' (the Cardinal always addressed himself in the first person plural; he reserved the singular for the Lord and his footman) 'we shall imagine that we had a presentiment and that we foresaw the content of this letter. Let us try now to precise in words what we shall afterwards like to consider foresight. And in order to avoid becoming a victim of banal self-delusion, let us confide these words to a scrap of paper.'

And, in the margin of a secular magazine, he wrote as follows:

'— *it is from a woman who is asking for money: we shall have prayers said for her;*

'— *it is from a woman who is asking for a prayer: we shall have money sent to her;*

'— *it is from a Jewess who wishes to see the Pope: we shall write a letter to her;*

'— *it is something rather serious: we shall do nothing for the moment;*

'— *it is something even more serious: we shall act in a way which, when we have read this letter, we shall consider to be proper.*'

Whereupon he reached for a pair of long Venetian paper scissors, slit open the envelope, and drew out a dove-grey card covered with the quiet, sloping handwriting of the Countess. It announced the birth of a beautiful, plump baby boy, — named Wilhelm/Guillaume.

> '.... I should not like you, Eminence, to take it amiss, that I carried him for a whole eleven years longer than was settled between us. Eighteen years en somme. However, I trust that Y.E. will agree with me that to produce a poet one needs at least nine times more time than to produce an elephant. Et Guillaume n'est pas un éléphant, je vous assure: il est un Apollinaire.
> Kissing the Sacred Purple, I am, my Lord,
> Yr. aff. cousin,
> Angélique.'

After having reread the letter, Cardinal Pölätüo glanced at the margin of the secular magazine on his desk and began to ponder which attitude to adopt. Ought one to pray for her? Ought one to send her money? Ought one to write to her? Ought one to do nothing? Or, on the contrary, ought one to take the way which one considers proper?

'Perhaps in this particular case the most appropriate action is to refrain from taking action,' he said to himself at first. But after reading the letter for a third time, he came to the conclusion that to leave things where they were might become even more dangerous to the Holy Cause than it was to himself.

3

If you were to have asked Cardinal Pölätüo the name of his birthplace, he would have been obliged to search for it in his official documents, as it had never been noted in his memory. Indeed, he had never revisited that foreign country through which the post of galloping horses was carrying his mother to Rome where she had intended to be delivered of her child.

But if you were to ask him when the event took place, he would answer you with great precision.

Cardinal Pölätüo was born on New Year's Day, 1822. And he was baptised the next morning, in a wayside church.

Now, I can't agree with those historians who don't treat this year of 1822 with the greatest respect. Indeed, I consider it to be the year that distinguishes itself the most in the whole first half of the nineteenth century: the year which opened a new epoch in the history both of Rome and of the development of European and Christian thought. Their eyes fixed on 1804, on 1812 or 14 or 15, on 1830, 1848 and other wonderful dates, some historians seem not to notice the significance of a certain bashful decree that was promulgated in just this year of 1822; a decree which, by permitting the publication and sale in Rome of books treating of the movement of the heavenly bodies, nullified the most solemn enactment of the Congregation of Prelates and Cardinals, dated 22nd June 1633, videre licet:

'Terram non esse centrum Mundi, nec immobilem, sed moveri motu etiam diurno, est item propositio absurda, et falsa in Philosophia, et Theologice considerata ad minus erronea in fide.'

From the time when a certain man of the Church managed to outwit the Inquisition by dying a natural death sufficiently quickly after publishing his *De Revolutionibus Orbium Coelestium Libri VI,* dedicated to His Holiness Paul III, two hundred years had to elapse before cardinals and prelates were able to understand that men may find it very easy to digest the ideas of Copernicus, Galileo and Kepler *at the same time as* those of Joshua; and that to become acquainted with certain astronomical facts, and to toy with natural laws, need not necessarily constitute a danger to the Church.

Young Pölätüo's life began in this precise year of 1822, and so it seemed to him quite natural that he saw the spines of the Copernican cosmographies set out publicly on the open shelves of the pious bookshops, while the thought that science would develop not to the detriment of Lord Jesus but to His Glory, was perfectly obvious and self-evident to him. No, if he felt a danger, as he did, he felt it neither among the physicists nor among the astronomers, busy with dead matter, nor even among the naturalists, nosing into the matrix from which living creatures are made, but among the poets; — the poets who dare to attempt alchemy — not with that Materia Prima which, in conjunction with *Forma Corporeitatis* constitutes the Body of Man, but with the *Substantial Form* which transcends the Law of Change and constitutes the Soul of Man; — the poets who interfere with Its *vis cogitativa;* the poets who cause accidents to happen to Its precious Immaterial Substance; who meddle in their own irresponsible way with this only Origin of All Vital and Mental Performances, the Origin created each time individually by God for each body, and ordained by Him to be entrusted to the priest's care, and not to their suspect influence. The most evil thing in the world today is Poetry. And as, for the Cardinal, Voltaire was a poet, it would be difficult to say that he felt danger where there was none.

Taking all this into consideration, we can better understand the anxiety of Cardinal Pölätüo who was now reading Countess Kostrowicki's letter for the fourth time.

'O Lord,' he said, 'if we have begotten Thine Adversary, we will erase him from the surface of the Earth in whatever way we shall consider proper. This we promise Thee.'

4

'Well?' said King Umberto.

'Well, Sire, whether or not that thought which Cardinal Manning called madness still lingers in the Most Holy Head, in your head, at all events, there can be no doubt that your Temporal Power is given you by God.'

'Well…?' repeated the King.

'Well,' Pölätüo continued, 'if we were to tell you, Sire, that there lives a person among us who may become a real danger to the Church, would it not be your duty to take action?'

'Who is it?' demanded Umberto.

'Sire… It is a male child. It had its first birthday a few days ago.'

The King moved his chair nearer to Pölätüo.

'Is he a member of the House of Savoy?'

The Cardinal made him wait for an answer:

'No, Sire. His mother is only a Polish Countess.'

'And the father?' asked Umberto, looking into the Cardinal's eyes.

'A son of the Church,' Pölätüo replied after a pause.

The King leant back comfortably in his chair, crossed his legs and scratched his knee-cap.

'I don't see upon what pretext the son of such a couple might advance a claim to the throne.'

'There is no question of that, Sire.'

'Well,' said Umberto, 'I don't see how a one year old child who has no birthright to the throne can be dangerous.'

'Sire,' said Pölätüo solemnly, 'We must disclose one fact of the greatest importance.'

'Yes?' said the King.

'He is a poet,' said the Cardinal.

'Well?' said the King.

These tediously repetitious well? well? well? were vexing the Cardinal's ear.

'Well,' he said, 'your attitude will, we hope, change, Sire, when you learn that he is not made of marble, or myth, or paper. His mother carried him for a period which would have sufficed to produce nine elephants one after another; you will understand, Sire, that as a result she has made him entirely en viande.'

The Cardinal thrust his hand into the red of his robe:

'And a poet made en viande,' he concluded, 'constitutes the greatest danger to the Church, to Civilisation, and to the House of Savoy!'

He then drew out a small, scented, dove-grey envelope:

'Here is the letter we received from his mother.' And holding the dove-grey card in one hand, and his gold framed spectacles in the other, he began to read:

'.... today Guillaume has his first birthday. He is already a big, pretty boy and he's beginning to talk. What am I saying? Il peut déjà versifier avec grâce. When he hears the fairy tale that his English nurse tells him, doesn't he shout, for half an hour afterwards, the two beautiful rhymes: sword — Lord, sword — Lord?'

'I should have thought,' said the King, 'that, using these two words, one could write a poem which would be most papalist and most royalist.'

The Cardinal crossed his arms on his breast and said:

'Sire, it is desirable, it is necessary, it is imperative that you be told the true meaning of these two words. Ten years ago, immediately after the dogma of papal infallibility was pronounced, two men published two books. One man was Darwin, and his book was *The Descent of Man;* the other — Swinburne, and his: *Hymn of Man (during the Session in Rome of the Oecumenical Council).* We have nothing against Darwin. Nothing at all. We believe that we could reconcile him, and all these physicists, geologists and astronomers, with the Bible, — just as Thomas Aquinas reconciled the Bible with Aristotle. And we trust that one of the future Holy Fathers will be able to make out of Pölätüomism an authority to guide catholic minds, just as Leo XIII is today doing with Thomism. No, Darwin is no danger to our philosophy. But the other man, — Swinburne; listen, Sire…'

The King interrupted the Cardinal, and began, himself, in a rather uncertain tone of voice:

'*"Let there be light, O Italy!"…*'

'Yes, yes,' the Cardinal interrupted him, impatiently: ' *"O Italy!"*, but what sort of Italy? Not, by any chance, a *Republic?* With *"freedom and the sovereign sun"* replacing il Sovrano Ranieri Carlo Emanuele Giovanni Maria Ferdinando Eugenio Umberto? Look, Sire, when Rome was ours, he, Swinburne, dedicated his book to Mazzini. Now, when Rome is yours, are you quite sure, Sire, that at this very moment he isn't writing a poem dedicated to this Passanante who three years ago, with a knife in his hand, made an attempt on your life at Naples? Are you sure, Sire, that he isn't at this very moment sharpening his rhyming pen against you, "Umberto the good"?, he who flings himself at "the supreme evil, God!". No, Sire, if Swinburne is by any chance on the pay roll of *your* Congregation of Propaganda, cross him off! Listen, Sire…

'*"By the name that in hell-fire was written, and burned at the point of thy* sword, *Thou art smitten, thou God, thou art smitten: thy death is upon thee, O Lord. And the love-song of earth as thou diest resounds through the wind of her wings: Glory to Man in the highest! for Man is the master of things!"*'

Fathomless silence suddenly ensued in the bit of the space-time continuum located between 6.14 and 6.15 p.m., and between the King and the Cardinal. When the clock at last struck the quarter, Cardinal Pölätüo said:

'To Swinburne's compatriots and correligionists, whose chief interest and concern lies in commerce, a poem means nothing politically. Never was a single act of their parliament influenced by an argument set in rhyme! That is why they allow their poets this devilish freedom to utter whatever blasphemy the printing ink will stamp. Their queen?, no, she doesn't see any connection between Poetry and Politics either! They are *immune,* Sire, — and we are using this word here not in its ecclesiastical but in its new, apothecary, sense — the English are politically immune from the poison of Rhyme. This is not so elsewhere, however. Poor France learned it the hard way; the Tsar of Russia sends his poets to Siberia; Plato exiles them from his Republic; Bismarck would like to muzzle them all and send them to Hell; and if Dr. Angelicus were living today, would he not confirm that we must refuse freedom of conscience, and execute those true heretics — the poets — first, because faith is an act of will and murderers of the Soul are worse than murderers of the body?!'

The sound of a trumpet and the clatter of horses' hooves filtered in through the curtained windows. A detachment of household cavalry was mounting guard.

The Cardinal continued:

'Have you paid sufficient attention, Sire, to these two rhymes in Swinburne's poem: *sword/Lord?* Do they not look to your eye like two stones of burning sulphur thrown at the crown and at the tiara? Do they not resound in your ear like a double shot of dynamite discharged by that subterranean conspiracy which for the last ten years has been trying to break the rock both under your throne and under that of St. Peter? Do they, or do they not, Sire? And now, Sire, that you hear of a poet who is not yet even two years old and already borrows these two cryptic words to versify like this old atheist and revolutionary —, aren't you horror-struck at the thought of what this boy will write when he is as old as the man, — what he will write in 1914?'

'What are you trying to say?' asked the King.

'We have sworn to the Lord God Almighty to erase this poet from the surface of the Earth,' answered the Cardinal.

'Swinburne?' asked the King.

'No; the son of Countess Kostrowicki,' Pölätüo answered.

Umberto looked at the Cardinal for a moment and shrugged his shoulders. But Pölätüo went on:

'We were not successful in discovering where he is now; but we are sure it's somewhere in your kingdom. And… Behold, Sire! If God did not stop the hand of Herod, King of Judea, do you think He will stop yours?'

'Well,' said Umberto. 'Well…' he repeated. 'Italy is much larger than Judea. The statistics for 1871 give 26,801,154 subjects. Today, in 1881, this number has increased to 28,459,628. That means almost a whole million, a million Innocents! Whilst Bethlehem was a tiny hole where you couldn't possibly count more than 6 Innocents, or, let us say: 10!'

'Longin the Sage, cited by Barhebraeus after Jacob of Edessa, says the number of Innocents massacred was between 1800 and 2000.'

'Well, then, let's say there were about a dozen little souls,' said Umberto.

'The Greeks assure us that there were 14,000!'

'I doubt it,' said the King.

'The Syrians mention 64,000!'

'Apologists,' answered King Umberto, 'give twenty as the maximum.'

'Yet certain mediaeval authors, based on the Apocalypse, say 144,000!'

'It's still not a million,' retorted King Umberto.

Cardinal Pölätüo smiled bitterly.

'Yes,' he said. 'When it was a question of exterminating Our Saviour, nobody worried about how many Innocents would have to be massacred; but when it's a question of liquidating this Adversary of God, we do sums, calculate, reckon…'

'Oh well,' said Umberto. 'All the same I'm sure it's more difficult than it may seem... To massacre a million one-year-olds!'

'Not even half a million,' interjected Pölätüo. 'We are not counting the girls.'

'Half a million little boys!' sighed Umberto. 'Now if they were only twenty years old, if they could only be serving in the army...'

Cardinal Pölätüo quickly offered his hand:

'Then you promise me, Sire, that in 19 years time, in 1900...'

'Oh, if that will reassure you, Eminentissimo Signore...'

5

Assured that the casus of the poet would be liquidated in 1900, Cardinal Pölätüo saw stretching in front of him the wonderful prospect of nineteen years free from the anxiety which had troubled his mind and harassed his conscience. All was calm again. There, in the centre of the parquet floor, reposing heavily on its five spiral legs à la Bernini, stood, waiting for him, his huge mahogany desk.

He rang the bell, and ordered his manservant to fetch Berkeley. Then he sat down in his armchair, in front of the desk, and placed on it some sheets of white paper and some quills he selected from a silver tray.

The door of the study opened, and the manservant brought in Berkeley, a small Black-and-Tan Manchester Terrier, on a green satin cushion bordered with a yellow fringe. A few months before, when Pölätüo had received Berkeley as a present from Cardinal Manning, he had immediately been struck by the terrier's resemblance to a miniature roe: the same slender legs, the same expression in the round black eyes, the same grace of movement, — and since it seemed to him that it was the Form of Roe-ness appearing through the Form of Dog-ness which in fact actualised the matter of which the dog consisted, he had wanted to call it 'Aristotle,' but had refrained because of his esteem for St. Thomas Aquinas — and in recognition of the friendship he felt for the English donor, he gave the dog the name of the Irish Bishop Berkeley.

In the right-hand bottom drawer of the Cardinal's desk, shut up in an old casket inlaid with mother-of-pearl, there was a bit of boot-lace. Berkeley knew this drawer very well. He would run up to it, sniff at the metal fixtures, and with his black roe's eyes look up at the Cardinal in expectation. Then Pölätüo would turn the key in the lock, open the drawer, and take out the bit of boot-lace from the inlaid box. Berkeley would sniff avidly at it, then turn his back. The manservant would lift up the little dog, or on occasion the Cardinal himself would bend down and fix the boot-lace to its tiny, trembling tail. Upon which Berkeley would bark, twist round into a circle, and begin a magnificent game of chasing the boot-lace. Cardinal Pölätüo called this game 'Berkeley,' or else a more complicated name: the David Hume Solipsist Demonstration.

Usually Pölätüo waited until Berkeley, tired out from his endless chase, lay down on the green cushion. But this time he gestured impatiently to the manservant to remove Berkeley from the study. He hitched his armchair up to his desk, dipped his quill into the ink, and wrote at the top of a white sheet of paper:

1: So far as Berkeley's mind is concerned, there only exists the Idea of a black streak running away from his eyes, or the Idea of a smell running away from his nose: Matter has no existence for him unless it is the sum of a logical process, a constituent part of the Mind of God.

2: Hume forces Berkeley to catch the boot-lace. Then to eat it, and his tail, and then all the rest from the tail to the head within which the Mind is contained, so that eventually nothing is left except the Idea.

Cardinal Pölätüo dipped his quill again and wrote:
  How did Hume succeed in cheating Berkeley with this trick?
  And why don't we with our Black-and-Tan Manchester terrier???

In making these question marks, Pölätüo splayed out his nib. He threw it away, selected another, and wrote:
  Because in the First Case Words were chasing Words,
  But in the Second Case Matter is chasing Matter.

He felt a little uncomfortable in his armchair. He pulled it still nearer to the desk, sat deeper down in it, and picked up his quill again:

Would not this imply that words which follow one another according to the rules of a logical universe may nevertheless lead us to a fallacy in the physical universe?

Quickly, he inscribed under this sentence a fat, cursive:
NO!

Then, with deliberation and no haste, he wrote:
It only implies that the reasoning was fallacious.

And in the margin he added:
The physical universe cannot be fallacious, for the truth of actuality is indubitable.
Dvlp in dtl t.prblm: Emprcsm as t. fnl Tst in Lgs.

After which he continued:
Where was the fallacy in the reasoning?

He considered this for a moment, stroking his lips with the quill-feather. Suddenly a revelation, flooding in, came silently on him. He bent over the desk, flicked some ink off the quill, placed a virgin sheet of paper in front of him, and inscribed calligraphically:

Here beginneth

the beginning

of the

Prolegomena

to the

Philosophy

of

Pölätüomism

6

From that day on, Cardinal Pölätüo left all his everyday affairs to his secretary, and devoted all his (Pölätüo's) time to his (Pölätüo's) work. Not to lose any more of the precious minutes which they both used to spend in mending the points of his quill nibs, he acquired some Birmingham-made nibs of steel alloyed with silver, keeping only one swan quill for the decoration of his desk, and a few crow quills for fine lines. 'If we only write one page a day,' he said to himself, 'in the nineteen years which we have before us, the total number of pages will be:

$$\begin{array}{r} 365 \\ \underline{19} \\ 3285 \\ \underline{365} \\ 6935 \\ \underline{+5} \\ 6940 \end{array}$$

Even if only 10% of them are of lasting value, we shall still leave, for the edification of the world, a work of 694 pages.'

He glanced at the pages he had written the previous day, and noticed that they were not numbered. On the top of the first page he wrote:

pagina 1

and on the second page, which bore the words: 'Here beginneth' &c., he wrote:

pagina 2

Then he took a fresh sheet of paper, wiped his pen in a little egg-cup-shaped metal penwiper filled with horse-hair and began:

pagina 3

Pölätüomism distinguishes two categories of knowledge:

1
DIRECT KNOWLEDGE

&

2
INDIRECT KNOWLEDGE

We,

Pölätüo,

have Direct Knowledge

of the existence of God.

They who employ indirect methods deny that God is known by the Gentiles through created things. Let us assume that they are right. Let us assume that Indirect Knowledge gives us no evidence of the existence of God.

He revealed Himself to us and we have seen Him; not through the Embassy of our eyes but directly in the parieto-occipital region of our brain. We spoke to Him, and He answered us, and we heard Him in the Inner End of our Ear. We felt Him with all our direct senses. We are a Witness to His Existence.

But we by no means demand this of it. Indirect Knowledge, based on the Intermediary of the Outer End of the Eye and the Ear and the Nose, claims rather to explain, if not now then in the future, us, OURSELVES;

therefore also us who have had Direct Knowledge of the existence of God.

N.B.*1 to pagina 1.*:
AND THIS EXPERIENCE OF OURS BREAKS THE VICIOUS CIRCLE OF HUME WHO CLEARLY DID NOT HAVE DIRECT KNOWLEDGE OF THE EXISTENCE OF GOD.

In order to do this, Indirect Knowledge will move all the cog-wheels of physics, chemistry, biology, sociology, educational theory — And in contradistinction to some authorities we find no blasphemy in it; on the contrary we commend it,

since:

is not all the content of the right column an effort to answer the question which is implied by the left column, namely: AFTER WHAT FASHION does God reveal Himself to us?

Direct knowledge teaches us that we are God's creatures, distinct from the animals and from the angels.

Indirect knowledge, however, teaches through the theory of evolution by natural selection that we, with the other monkeys, are descended from a common ancestor; — and we should not be at all scandalised if Darwin's successors were to find that finally, or rather originally, we were descended from crustaceans, from primordial ooze, and from inorganic clay — THE CLAY FROM WHICH ADAM WAS KNEADED —
— And in contradistinction to some authorities we find no blasphemy in this; on the contrary we commend it,

since:

is not all the content of the right column the answer to the question which is implied by the left column, namely: AFTER WHAT FASHION did God knead us from clay?

N.B.: *If you have a definition of 'Man' then, whatever the definition is, you must agree that, however big and tumultuous was the evolutionary throng of creatures from which mankind is descended, there must have been the first single couple among them that fits your definition. What is wrong in calling the couple by the name of Adam and Eve?*

Direct knowledge teaches us that human language is God's Gift.	*Indirect knowledge teaches us, through the mouth of Herr Herder and the lips of Mr. Darwin, that language was invented by man and developed gradually.*
	— And in contradistinction to some authorities we find no blasphemy in this; on the contrary we commend it,

since:
is not all the content of the right column the attempted answer to the question which is implied by the left column,

namely:
AFTER WHAT FASHION did God teach Adam to make up the names of all the fowls of the air and the beasts of the field?

Cardinal Pölätüo put down his pen for a moment. Then he glanced at the clock and felt on his palate the sudden taste of crab mayonnaise, onion soup, and goose stuffed à la Romaine. Yet there was no mayonnaise, nor soup, nor goose, in the space bounded by the four walls of his study. He glanced once more at the clock, picked up his quill again, and wrote:

DIRECT KNOWLEDGE	INDIRECT KNOWLEDGE
We felt the taste of mayonnaise. We felt the taste of goose.	*We observed that there was no mayonnaise, onion soup or goose in our sensory field. And we find no blasphemy in this: on the contrary, we commend it,*
We had direct knowledge of onion soup, one hour before dinner-time.	

since:
Is it not precisely indirect knowledge which, in this instance, by showing that there is no onion soup even though we feel it, reminds us that the Vanitas of Experience is not the same thing as the Presence of Reality?

N.B.: *In the case of our direct knowledge of the existence of God (see above), indirect knowledge by no means stated that there is no God; merely that it gives us no evidence of His existence. In the present case, however, in the case of our direct knowledge of the onion soup, indirect knowledge positively stated that there was no onion soup in the universe of our dwelling.*

His nose wriggled with some agitation. He took the very first page of his MS, *pagina 1*, the one that began with the words: 'So far as Berkeley's mind is concerned, there only exists the Idea of…' and in the bottom margin he wrote as follows:

N.B.: *When God brought a bird to Hume and said: 'Give this a name!', Hume pointed his finger at his own skull, and said: 'Goose.' When God brought the bird to Berkeley and said: 'Give this a name!', Berkeley pointed his finger at God, and said: 'Goose.' But when God brought the bird to Adam and said: 'Give this a name!', Adam pointed his finger at the bird which God had brought him, and said: 'Goose!'*

Whereupon, he continued:

DIRECT KNOWLEDGE	INDIRECT KNOWLEDGE
During our last visit to King Umberto, the King crossed his legs and scratched his knee-cap. Yesterday our secretary saw the King's Private Secretary, who said that the King's consciousness had no knowledge that his knee-cap had itched.	*Observation of the matter of which the King consists allows us to infer the fact that the knee-cap itched. Such a process of reasoning does not seem at all blasphemous to us: on the contrary we commend it,*

since:

has not indirect knowledge the right to warn us that God's Law exists, and watches over us, always and everywhere, even when we are not conscious of it?

Pölätüo stopped for a moment, without lifting his pen from the paper. Then he quickly transferred it to a fresh sheet and wrote:

However:
The King's knee-cap was scratched by a hand which was connected with a Mind not conscious of the itching (namely the King's mind); not by a hand which is connected with a Mind conscious of the itching (namely our, Pölätüo's, mind).
Reflexio:
The world would seem much simpler if things occurred in the following sequence:

1:   *We notice that the King's knee-cap itches;*
2:   *We say: 'Sire, your knee-cap itches';*
3:   *The King answers: 'Tante grazie, Eminentissimo Signore';*
4:   *He scratches his knee-cap.*

The Cardinal sat, pen in hand, and didn't notice when the pen, unthinkingly, drew the following figure:

This drawing had always exercised a certain fascination on him. When Pölätüo was one year old, a French savant, M. André Marie Ampère, discovered that if you grasp an electric conductor with your Right Hand so that the current flows in the direction pointed by your Thumb, then the magnetic induction encircles the conductor in the direction of your Fingers. This *Right Hand Rule,* as it was called, used to puzzle young Pölätüo: Why should it be the Right Hand and not the Left Hand?, he used to ponder. There was no reason for it being one and not the other. And if there is no reason for it being so, then the Right Hand Rule is not a Physical Law but an Arbitrary Decree. Because whenever something occurs without reason, it occurs because it has been chosen. And if it has been chosen it must have been willed. And doesn't the existence of Will imply the existence of Person? And who is the Person who willed that the Universe be governed by the Right and not the Left Hand Rule, — if not the Creator? Is it not so, therefore, that Indirect Knowledge supplies us with better and more tangible points of departure than those used by Thomas Aquinas in his courage to prove the existence of God?

Pen in his right hand, he stood up, crossed the floor, and left the room. When he came back after a very short while, the pen was in his left hand. He sat again at his desk, transferred the pen to his right hand, and wrote as follows:

To perform the action of scratching one's knee-cap does not demand the co-operation of both forms of knowledge: direct and indirect.
However:
To perform the action of writing down
THE PHILOSOPHY OF PÖLÄTÜOMISM,
which is based on direct knowledge,
demands the previous cognizance of all that can be taught by
Indirect Knowledge!

7

Cardinal Pölätüo was determined to investigate all that indirect knowledge could teach.

In the autumn of 1881 he set out on an embassy to Paris, in order to thank the French Government for the congratulations they had sent to Leo XIII on the occasion of the publication of his Encyclical *On Civil Sovereignty*, issued after the assassination of Tsar Alexander II. During his stay, he visited Louis Pasteur, and on p. 127 of *Pölätüomism* he wrote:
Louis Pasteur, an ardent scientist and a serious Catholic, has faith in two things:
1:   God;
2:   the principle of immunisation by inoculation. We don't see why the second faith should be thought blasphemous to the first.
On the contrary, we commend it, since:
if disease is God's Punishment, then recovery is God's Grace. Hence is not Louis Pasteur a carrier of God's Grace?

From Paris he went to Bonn, where he visited F. A. Kekulé. Bonn he left for Amsterdam, where he visited G. A. Van't Hoff. On p. 190 he wrote:
Kekulé showed me his symbol:

$$\begin{array}{c} H \\ | \\ C \\ \diagup \;\; \diagdown\!\!\!\!\! \\ H-C \quad\;\; C-H \\ \| \quad\quad\;\; | \\ H-C \quad\;\; C-H \\ \diagdown \;\; \diagup\!\!\!\!\! \\ C \\ | \\ H \end{array}$$

But he did not pray to it.

He said that around this ring one may place other groups of atoms, and that this synthesis, which permits the production of dyes, drugs, gun-cotton and poison gas, opens up a new epoch in the history of mankind, And we find no blasphemy in this, since:
if it is God's Will to send calamities and blessings among us, then is it not right and proper to welcome this Kekulé who perfects the Instruments of all these calamities and blessings?

On p. 215 he wrote:
Van't Hoff was v. pleasant. He informed us that a molecule is not built symmetrically, and that crystals may be left-hand and right-hand. Our Belief was in no way weakened by our discovery how God built His molecules and crystals.

In 1882 he left for London, and saw Karl Marx. It was in his brief account of the meeting that he used for the first time the singular 'I' instead of the plural 'we.' Since that time 'I' and 'we' tend to replace each other both in his speech and in his writing. *'Quand j'écris et parle de moi au singulier, cela suppose une confabulation avec le lecteur; il peut examiner, discuter, douter et même rire. Mais quand je m'arme du redoutable nous, je professe; il faut se soumettre.'*
— this quotation comes from Brillat-Savarin, and not from Marx. It is copied on the verso of p. 419 of *Pölätüomism*. On the recto of the same leaf, he wrote: *Il signore gentile... I would like to write 'vecchio' but for the fact that he's only four years older than I. It is his having seven children, — or is it his thinking of human affairs that makes him grow old so rapidly? I admire him because there is no trace of poetry in him. He has so far carefully avoided the use of those notions which have been produced and injected into our spiritual life by irresponsible poetic activities. He keeps strictly to orthodox ontological notions. For him, wine and bread will not be symbols for blood and body, they will be blood and body without reservations, real in their own right. He is a pure product of that Western World for which organised Christianity laid the foundation, and he will never be accepted on any other Continent, whether pagan or gentile, unless he makes room for the name of Jesus in his teachings. To do this, however, may be our (and our missionaries') business and not his. To be precise, he told me: 'the course of history is primarily determined by economic factors.' And in, con-*

tradistinction to some authorities, I find no blasphemy in this. Is not Almighty God permitted to determine the course of history by economic factors, if that is His Will?
He also told me: 'the mode of production in material life determines the general character of the social, political, and spiritual processes of life.'
Entirely agree:
this conclusion is a timely sign given to the Church by God, that she must not let temporal power slip from her hands, but must — through kings and queens, presidents and governments, — influence the mode of production in material life and thus determine the general character of the spiritual processes of life. Therefore I find no blasphemy in this new discipline; on the contrary, I commend it.

In 1883 Cardinal Pölätüo didn't leave Rome, but had sent to him Kleb's newly discovered Diphtheria bacillus, the Tuberculosis bacillus just discovered by Koch, and Vogel's list of the spectra of 4,051 stars.

On p. 850 he wrote:
I have looked at the spectra of 4,051 stars, I have seen through the microscope numberless groups of endless streams of Tuberculosis bacilli stained with Methylene Blue — and, suspended between this huge infinity and this minute infinity, I understand by direct knowledge that in contradistinction to the views of some authorities, indirect knowledge builds its microscopes and telescopes to the further Glory of God.

In 1884 Cardinal Pölätüo left for New York, in order to make a call to Boston over the world's first trunk-line. It was from New York that he sent a post-card to the International Conference, then in session at Washington. He proposed that the meridian should be fixed, not through Greenwich, which is just two or three miles southeast of the dome of St. Paul's in London, but through the cross on the dome of St. Peter's in Rome. On his return to Europe, he met Schiff and heard him lecture on the thyroid gland.

In 1885 he visited Krupps', where Alfred's son, Friedrich Alfred K., showed him the prototype of their 100-ton gun; and the Hôpital de la Salpêtrière in

Paris where he heard Charcot lecture, and saw brains and spinal cords preserved in labelled and numbered glass-jars.

In 1886 Goldstein showed him a hole in a cathode, through which positive rays passed; in the autumn he received a present of Robert's photograph of the nebula in Andromeda, framed together with a reproduction of Tintoretto's *Origin of the Milky Way;* and in December he received a postcard from Ralph Capeland, telling him of his discovery of helium in the Great Nebula of Orion.
Indirect knowledge confirms conclusively that the Greatness and Wisdom of the Creator is limitless.

— he wrote on p. 1079.

In 1887 Cardinal Pölätüo crossed the Atlantic for the second time. From the ship he straightaway took the train to Cleveland, Ohio, in order to verify with his own eyes the Michelson-Morley experiment. Cardinal Pölätüo had foreseen that he would discover a minor error in the manner by which the apparatus was fixed to the stone floating on the surface of the mercury. He did not, however, find any error. And yet, in spite of this, whether the apparatus was placed in the direction of the earth's movement, or against it, or across it, there was no change in its readings; the ray of light travelled at the same speed; as though the earth did not move in the Aether. On his return trip across the Atlantic, Cardinal Pölätüo had his Manuscript brought out of the coffer, shuffled the leaves together, took a blank sheet of paper, inscribed at the top:

pagina 2244

drew a line down the page from top to bottom, and wrote:

SUMMA CONTRA GENTILES THOMASI AQUINAS

...let us take as principle that which is already made manifest (xiii), namely that God is altogether unchangeable.

From the foregoing it is also clear that God is eternal.
For whatever begins or ceases to be, suffers this through movement or change.
Now it has been shown that God is altogether unchangeable.

Therefore He is eternal, having neither beginning nor end.

Again. Only things which are moved are measured by time: because time is the measure of movement, as stated (Arist: 4 Phys. xi. 5).

Now God is absolutely without movement, as we have already proved (xiii).
Therefore we cannot mark before and after in Him.
Therefore in Him there is not being after non-being, nor can He have non-being after being, nor is it possi-

NOTES ON THE MICHELSON-MORLEY EXPERIMENT

...let us take as principle that which is already made manifest (1887), namely that the velocity of light is altogether unchangeable.

From the foregoing it is also clear that the velocity of light is absolute.
For whatever accelerates or decelerates, suffers this through movement or change.
Now it has been shown that whatever the direction of the rays of light, its velocity in the Wind of Aether is altogether unchangeable.

Therefore its motion is absolute, having neither acceleration nor deceleration.

Again. Only changes in velocity are measured by inertial reference system: because an equation of movement has the same form for two objects moving uniformly with one another, as stated (Newton: De Motu ii).

Now Aether is absolutely without movement, as Michelson and Morley have already proved (1887).
Therefore we cannot mark upstream and downstream in It.
Therefore in It there is not inertia to a change in Its state of rest, nor can It have inertia to a change in Its state of

ble to find any succession in His being, because these things cannot be understood apart from time.

Therefore He is without beginning or end, and has all his being simultaneously...

motion, nor is it possible to find any direction in Its space, because these things cannot be understood apart from relation to our or some other body.

Therefore there is no Aether...

Cardinal Pölätüo looked out through his cabin porthole at the sea, covered with foaming white waves; then he wrote:

...and in this consists the notion of eternity.

...and in this consists the notion of non-existence.

In 1888 when the whole Christian world, with Pope Leo XIII at its head, was transported with joy at the abolition of slavery in Brazil, Cardinal Pölätüo left for Karlsruhe, to meet Hertz. 'I don't know whether or not the Aether exists,' said Hertz, when they looked in at the little Bierstube near the Polytechnic, 'but I know that there do exist electromagnetic waves, which differ from visible waves only in that they are not visible. I have refracted them, I have reflected them, I have polarised them, I have passed them through a prism, I have measured their velocity; and it is identical with the velocity of light.' 'Herr Professor...' began Pölätüo, but he realised that Hertz was not a Gentile, and he didn't finish the sentence. As has already been said, he, Pölätüo, was born on New Year's Day, which is the festival of the Circumcision of Christ, and it always made him feel awkward to stand face to face with men whose foreskin had been cut off.

Afterwards, on p. 2609, he wrote:

1° Indirect Knowledge also has her prophets. The name of one is J. Clerk Maxwell: 20 years ago he predicted the coming of Heinrich Rudolph Hertz.

2° If the discovery of these e-m waves destroys the mechanistic view of the structure of the world, will it not be the task of Pölätüomism to elaborate a new

philosophy, taking the chapter in S. Thomas Aquinas entitled 'That in God there is no matter' in the sense 'That in God there is neither matter nor wave'? —
3° or, on the contrary, should not the task be to elaborate it in the sense 'That God is wave', the Aetherlessness of which was demonstrated by us (p. 2244f), the Absoluteness of which was proved by Michelson and Morley, and the Existence of which was evidenced by Hertz —?
He paused for a moment, and then added:
4° ...If all absolutes are banished, if every motion is relative, (if the same Newtonian equation applies to A moving towards B, as to B moving towards A; if it makes no difference whether Henry IV goes to Canossa, or Hildebrand, i.e. Gregory VII, to the German Emperor), then indeed, indeed, the existence of God cannot be demonstrated. If, however, if it can be shown that absolute values exist, it can also be proved that God exists. Now, do not scientists show us that some things are absolute? Have they not convinced us that the velocity of light is terminal, ultimate and unconditioned? Again: Is it not absolute, the space in which a Foucault pendulum swings, taking no notice of the earth that rotates underneath? And again: Is it not so that the water in the bucket will ascend to its sides when it is forced to revolve in front of your eyes, but will not do so when you try to run around it? Is not, therefore, 'Ignorance,' precisely, — ignorance of the laws of physics, ignorance of the existence of absolute values, — the name of that force which does not stop Mr. Bradlaugh from getting the English House of Commons to pass his Bill permitting atheists to substitute an affirmation for an oath in courts and in Parliament?

In 1889 Pölätüo left for Paris to glance at the Congress of the 2nd International. Later in the year he received a model of Edison's kinetoscope and Dreyer's recently published New General Catalogue of 7,084 nebulae.
On p. 2974 he wrote:
We find no blasphemy in the fact of the existence of this Congress. If the Lord God chastises us with war, we have no doubt that the leaders of the International will, just like anybody else, each in his own country, vote in favour of war credits.
And on the next page:
The kinetoscope is an instrument which, just as much as the means of production

in material life, will determine the 'general character of the social, political and spiritual processes of life' (pide: vagina 419). For this reason it should be in the hands of the Church.

In 1890, one week after Leo XIII published the Encyclical *Sapientiae Christianae*, namely 17 January, Cardinal Pölätüo left for Cambridge, where he met Sir James G. Frazer. On his way back he stopped in Paris for a rendezvous with Pierre Janet.

On p. 3339 he wrote:
Pierre Janet informed me that if one guides the mind of a patient so that he recalls the situation during which he received the shock, and if one afterwards explains to him that the shock was of no importance, and presented no danger to him, then it sometimes happens that the patient's mind and body recover. Should this system of healing spread, I should envisage it as a threat to the institution of the confessional. And since, in his Encyclical Sapientiae Christianae, *the Holy Father stated: '. . . it is abundantly clear that rulers of States are free to administer their own affairs, and this not alone with the Church's passive toleration, but plainly with her active co-operation,' then should not the Church show more active co-operation in helping the rulers of States in their freedom to control medical practice? (I have installed electric light in my palace.)*

In 1891, on p. 3704, he wrote:
I have received two volumes of The Golden Bough *by Sir James. Religion as a branch of anthropology, archeology, psychology and sociology And in contradistinction to some authorities, I find no premeditated blasphemy in this; on the contrary I commend some of these writings, since they show me AFTER WHAT FASHION God constructed the Way through which men may come to knowledge of Him.*

In 1892 Cardinal Pölätüo had Weissmann's *Aufsätze über Vererbung*, which had just been published in Germany, translated to him.
Indirect knowledge is eating itself up. Here Weissmann half engulfs Darwin: stating that what a man does with his mortal body, SOMA, has no effect on his

potentially immortal body, OVUM+SPERMA. For thousands of years the Jews have been circumcising themselves, but they still have sons with foreskins born to them. Ever since the creation of the world, husbands have been perforating their brides, but they still have daughters with hymens born to them. How then can Darwin's race of adapted organisms come into the world, if fathers and mothers are not potent to transfer their acquired characteristics to their children in their SPERMA & OVUM?

In 1893 Cardinal Pölätüo jotted down for future reference Wien's newly discovered Universal Constant, giving the ratio of wavelength to the Absolute temperature of the emitting body, viz:

$$0.294 \text{ cm}°$$

and with this note he left for Lima in connection with the papal arbitration in the Peru-Ecuador boundary dispute.

In 1894, with 1°: Charcot's papers on hypnosis,
        2°: Kruger's *Catalog der Farbigen Sterne,*
        3°: Langley's *Internal Work of the Wind,*
in his attaché-case, he left for Guiana in connection with the papal arbitration in the Anglo-Venezuelan boundary dispute.

In 1895 he went to Haiti in connection with the papal arbitration between Haiti and San Domingo. From there he proceeded to the town of Trinil in Java, to see for himself the place where Dubois had discovered two molar teeth, a fragment of the skull, and the femur of a creature which was named by Dubois *Pithecanthropus Erectus*. This relic Dubois had of course taken with him. After breaking off a piece of volcanic matter probably belonging to the Pleistocene era, and taking it as a souvenir, Pölätüo set out on a journey to Munich, where W. K. von Röntgen, without opening the Cardinal's purse, made him a photograph of five silver Lira, 20 Centimes, 3 Marks, and a small trunk-key. On his return to Rome, Cardinal Pölätüo hung up this photograph beside that of the nebula in Andromeda and the Tintoretto reproduction already mentioned.

In 1895 he left for Abyssinia, in order to make an appeal to the Emperor Menelik on behalf of the Italian prisoners-of-war, and then for America, on the Potomac, where he observed Langley's aerial tests with his flying machine. Returning through Amsterdam, he visited Zeeman, who demonstrated how the sodium lines in the spectrum dilate when the flame is placed in a strong electro-magnetic field. Then he passed through Paris, where he saw Becquerel at the *Academie des Sciences* for a few moments at his announcement of the strange conduct of Uranium compounds, which were capable of blackening a photographic plate packed in black paper, and discharging the leaves of an electroscope from a distance.

In 1897 Gustave Canet showed him his 75mm field gun *à tire rapide;* J.J. Thompson sent him an off-print of his paper on cathode rays, and Atwater proved that the Cardinal discharged as much energy in heat as he ate.

In 1898, when Mme Curie was out, he visited her laboratory in the rue Lhomond; after which he met the Graf von Zeppelin, who showed him the blueprints of his cigar-shaped balloon, which was moved through the air by propellers.

In 1899 Häckel sent him a presentation copy of his *Die Welträtsel,* and Campbell reported that the Polar Star is a triple. In June he took part in the Volta Centenary Conference at Milan, and, from 18 to 23 September, in the National Electrical Congress, which was opened by Umberto I and the Queen.

On 29 July 1900 Cardinal Pölätüo finished the 6935th sheet of paper. '10% of these pages,' he said to himself, 'contain the basis of *Pölätüomism.* But which of them constitute this 10%?'

On the Cardinal's desk, beside his manuscript, lay a paper on Loeb's experiments on chemical fertilisation, and a book entitled *Traumdeutung* by a certain Freud. He pushed this printed matter to one side.

'Indirect knowledge will never stop,' he said to himself. '*"La verità è figlia del Tempo,"* yet, if one is to create a philosophical system, one must choose not only the place of departure but also the time to say "Basta!"'

'Basta!' said Pölätüo, and took in his hand the sheet numbered:

pagina 6935

On it was written:

Hypothesis:

In the final moments of death-agony the soul lives ever faster and faster.

Exemplum:

If this agony lasts 2 (two) seconds,

then: during the first 1	second the soul lives 1	second
during ½ of the remaining 1	second the soul lives 10	seconds
during ½ of the remaining ½	second the soul lives 10^2	seconds
during ½ of the remaining ¼	second the soul lives 10^3	seconds
during ½ of the remaining ⅛	second the soul lives 10^4	seconds
during ½ of the remaining 1/16	second the soul lives 10^5	seconds
during ½ of the remaining 1/32	second the soul lives 10^6	seconds
during ½ of the remaining 1/64	second the soul lives 10^7	seconds
during ½ of the remaining 1/128	second the soul lives 10^8	seconds
during ½ of the remaining 1/∞	second the soul lives ∞	seconds

TOTAL = 2 seconds   TOTAL = Eternity

Thus:

in accordance with indirect knowledge, the soul dies after two seconds and simultaneously:

in accordance with direct knowledge, the soul lives eternally.

Indeed, the 2 seconds in question may belong to some long forgotten past in the time historical, but they shall remain for ever and ever, amen, in the time divine. And there is no contradiction between these two statements, — as we have just demonstrated by mathematical means. In fact, why not use mathematics to show physicists and historians that the notion of Time is not as simple as it seems to appear to the bodies of their clocks? The new Century, the XXth from the birth of Christ, will see a multitude of ideas developed in, and permeated by, the most highly specialised mathematics.

Pölätüo inspected this page very carefully, dipped his pen again and wrote: *A philosophical system requires no proof that It Is So: its one and only requirement is logical consistency. Though logical consistency may be considered useless if the system can be disproved. Which is not the case so far as the above hypothesis is concerned.*

He crossed his legs (in 1900 Pölätüo, alone among the cardinals, still wore knee-breeches and red stockings), and scratched his knee-cap. Suddenly this reminded him of King Umberto and the year 1881. 'Nineteen years have passed,' he said to himself; 'in '81 I was 59 years old, now I am 78.' His ear caught the low creak of the opening door. He turned round. In the doorway stood his young secretarial assistant.

'Don't say anything for a moment! Wait!' the Cardinal commanded.

He got up from his armchair, went over to the book-shelves, and searched for a long time. Finally he found a yellowed copy of a certain secular magazine dated 1880. This he laid on his desk. In the margin was written in fading ink:

'— *it is from a woman who is asking for money: we shall have prayers said for her;*

'— *it is from a woman who is asking for a prayer: we shall have money sent to her;*

'— *it is from a Jewess who wishes to see the Pope: we shall write a letter to her;*

'— *it is something rather serious: we shall do nothing for the moment;*

'— *it is something even more serious: we shall act in a way which, when we have read this letter, we shall consider to be proper.'*

Pölätüo sat down again, looked through these notes, and then turned to his secretary:

'Yes?'

'I have just received a telephone call from Monza: The anarchist Gaetano Bresci has assassinated the King!'

Cardinal Pölätüo strained forward in his armchair.

'Then our telephone is already working?' he exclaimed.

Keeping up with the times, the Cardinal, who had travelled specially to New York in 1884 in order to speak to Boston by wire, had installed the telephone in his own palace. The yellow box had hung there since the previous May, but till this moment nobody had ever got through on it.

8

'Why did God not stay the hand of the anarchist Gaetano Bresci?'

The Black-and-Tan Manchester Terrier, Berkeley, had died long before (in 1885 — or was it perhaps in '86?), but in the lower right-hand drawer of the desk there was still a bit of boot-lace shut up in the little mother-of-pearl casket. Cardinal Pölätüo automatically opened the drawer, pressed a little button on the casket, smelled the boot-lace for a moment, then slammed the casket and shut the drawer again.

'Why?' he repeated.

He went over and stood in front of a large Venetian mirror which turned red in reflecting his robed figure, and asked himself:

'Was it not in order to stay the hand of King Umberto, who promised me, nineteen years ago, that in 1900 he would solve the problem of Countess Kostrowicki's son?'

'Assurdo!' he cried out, turning his back to the mirror; 'I swore to God that the poet Guillaume would be erased from the surface of the earth, and I have direct knowledge that God accepted the sacrifice.'

He moved over to the desk, placed his palm on the high battery of 6935 pages of manuscript, and continued:

'It would not surprise me, if God would not accept my sacrifice of Ampère, of Darwin, of Maxwell, of Thompson, of Michelson & Morley, of Marx & Engels, of Röntgen & Lorentz, of Zeeman, of Maria Sklodowska-

Curie. We have often shown, in our *Pölätüomism,* that a proper grasp of their indirect knowledge supports, does not undermine God's Church. No!, I mean: Yes, Scientists do not deny the existence of the Soul; they confirm it, like the bookbinders who confirm the existence of the Bible: After their own fashion. But why should God not want to accept my sacrifice of Countess Kostrowicki's son?'

He marvelled at this for some time; then went on:

'Yes, it wouldn't surprise me if God were not to accept my sacrifice of Marx & Engels. It is written, Thou shalt not steal. And it is written, Thou shalt not covet thy neighbour's house, thou shalt not covet thy neighbour's wife, nor his manservant, nor his maidservant, nor his ox, nor his ass, nor any thing that is thy neighbour's. The Church defends private property. But the definition of Capital which emerges from the Scriptures is not the same definition as that which is given by Marx, of Capital growing from the concentration of surplus value. Therefore it is not that which the Church defends that Marx attacks.'

For a moment Cardinal Pölätüo wondered whether he ought not to take a fresh sheet of paper, numbered p. 6936, on which to fix these thoughts. He stretched out his hand for his pen, — but he withdrew it.

'"Socialism," "communism,"' he soliloquised, ' — we are not quite sure which is which. One, we are told, promises "from each according to ability, to each according to work performed," and the other: "from each according to ability, to each according to need." How does the former propose to measure the spiritual work performed by us, we wonder! No, we definitely prefer the latter, the one that promises to pay us according to our needs, which happen to be not inconsiderable. Indeed, we find it an improvement on the communism of the Essenes, who were forbidden to own two cloaks or two pairs of sandals.'

He gazed at the pair of Venetian paper scissors on his desk, as if they were a crystal.

'Undoubtedly, some people attach too much importance to the whole trend. Lord Rosebery fears it spells "the end of all things." A miss Rosa Luxemburg hopes it is "the promise of the millennium." O, no! The former need not be afraid. And the latter should not have any illusions. The Institution of Communism, or Socialism, whichever it is, will not endure. It can't possibly become the Redeemer of Mankind, because it doesn't think in terms of Mankind. It thinks in terms of Nations, and we shall see the Day when sooner a prince will help his serf, and sooner a Rothschild will help a poor Hasidean, than a rich worker of one country will help a poor worker of another. This prophecy is so crystal clear to whoever can read the Soul of the common people, and see that an indelible little Charles Maurras resides in each: "La nation est le plus vaste des cercles de communauté sociale. Brisez-le et vous dénudez l'Homme. L'Homme y perdra toute sa défense, tous ses appuis, tous ses concours. La nation occupe le sommet de la hiérarchie des idées politiques." Yes, these heavy scissors of industry that cut the cloth for the new Essenes' cloaks... It is a perfectly intelligible proposition, they say, that they ought to be nationalized. Behold: they will not say that they ought to be internationalized. They will keep thinking in terms of Nations, id est: in terms referring to what differentiates peoples from peoples; and thus the Church of Christ will remain the only Institution that thinks in terms of all Mankind, id est: in terms referring to what peoples have in common. Our Sole Lord and Saviour, even as He is depicted by the masters, is not clad in costumes cut to the fashion of any folk. In which Catholicism lies Our Holy Mother Church's strength. Because what is built on what differentiates peoples from peoples will not, and what caters for what is common to all Mankind will, endure the evolutionary processes. Therefore we do not see any danger to the Soul in this new Doctrine.

'And it wouldn't surprise me if God were to refuse my sacrifice of Karl Marx.

'But wherefore, O Lord, wilt Thou not accept my sacrifice of the poet Guillaume?

'Is it that Thou seest not that he is Thine Adversary?

'Is it that thou seest not that a Pair of Scissors cannot cut a Soul in two, but a Pair of Rhymed Words can — ?'

At the edge of the desk, left there by his secretary, a flimsy fascicule was lying, written by a young poet, Filippo Tommaso Marinetti. With the long nail of his little finger he pushed it so that it fell straight into the waste-paper basket.

'… Rhymed, or Unrhymed!' he added, and crossed the room with slow step. As he passed the mahogany pedestal on which stood a Majolica vase, verdant with small asparagus leaves, a new thought suddenly came to him:

'1° The Countess Kostrowicki's son was born in 1880 in Monaco,' he spoke slowly and loudly, as if he were counting each syllable. 'But long before that, namely in 1861, Victor Emmanuel II had sold Monaco to France.

'2° The Countess Kostrowicki's letter of 1881 was indeed sent from Italy. BUT THIS IS NO PROOF that the Countess Kostrowicki's son is NOW in Italy!'

'3° And if he is not now in Italy, then the Massacre of the Innocents would be aimless bloodshed.'

Cardinal Pölätüo went to the window, drew back the curtain, and lifted his eyes to the heavens to thank God for His Wisdom in not staying the hand of the americanized anarchist Gaetano Bresci, who had jumped on to the King's carriage and inserted four revolver bullets in the King's chest; and to thank God for His Wisdom in thus staying the hand of the King, who was about to have made a Massacre of 20-year old Innocents, among whom Guillaume might not have been included.

Whereupon Cardinal Pölätüo sat down at the telephone and spent six hours putting calls through to all capitals of the world.

All that night, 29/30 July 1900, and all next day, all the Christian world on all the Earth's sphere, in all dioceses and parishes, searched for the Countess Kostrowicki's son.

9

'The Church is for l'Action Française and not l'Action Française for the Church,' said Charles Maurras.

'That doesn't make any difference,' replied Pölätüo.

'Doesn't it?'

'No. If l'Action Française were an Instrument of the Church, you would do what I am now requesting, because I would have ordered it of you; if the Church is an Instrument of l'Action Française, you will do what I would otherwise have ordered, because I have requested it of you.'

'Your Eminence has told me that you approach me as a private individual, and not as a representative of the Vatican.'

'Quite,' answered Pölätüo. 'Which is why I likewise approach *you* as a private individual, and not as a representative of l'Action Française.'

'Garçon!' Charles Maurras called. But when the waiter appeared he dismissed him with a wave of the hand, and resumed:

'To go back to Anatole France. I can assure Your Eminence that he is not the kind of man he would seem to be from his books. Last week I was walking along with him towards "les Immortels," and on the Pont des Arts he stopped for a moment and said: "As a matter of fact the inner man in me is a royalist too!"'

'If that is so,' replied the Cardinal, 'then Monsieur France is wise enough not to set his inner man against history. Monsieur France is wise and modest enough to treat his own opinions and emotional impulses with the sense of humour which informs his observation of the opinions and emotional impulses of his contemporaries. You, on the other hand, Monsieur Maurras, are conceited; it was your personal inclinations that made you invent your principles; you ended by believing in those principles; and now you wish to impose them on your contemporaries by a coup de force.'

Charles Maurras rapped on the marble table-top with his signet ring:

'And you?' After a pause he added 'Your Eminence?... Does not what you impose on your contemporaries arise from your own personal inclinations?'

'No!' replied Pölätüo. He drew a circle on the table-top with his finger. 'No,' he repeated: 'my private inclinations are quite different...' He drew more circles on the table-top. 'What I really wanted was to become a watchmaker. Did you ever see the clock which Henri de Vick constructed for Charles V in 1379? I wanted to construct a clock like that. Possibly I would construct it today from the electromagnetic waves which Hertz has just discovered. But that technical point can't interest you. I have a sort of nostalgia to have been a watchmaker. But I was capable of examining this personal inclination of mine and instead I became a tiny Pinion, a Pawl in the Clock Universal.'

'Perhaps in the case of Your Eminence,' said Maurras, 'the inclination to become a Pinion or a Pawl was stronger than the desire to become an Horlogier. But to go back to the death of the President, Félix Faure: it reminded me of the death of the Archbishop of Paris, Harley de Champvallon, but with this single difference that the role of the Princess de Lesdiguières was played by a Delilah bribed by the Jews...'

'Why go back to all these questions?' interrupted Pölätüo: 'all except the one I want to discuss with you.'

'Eh bien!' exclaimed Charles Maurras impatiently. 'Eh bien; what do you want of me, Monsieur? I am an intellectual, quand même... Do you want me to strangle him with my own hands Monseigneur?' He stretched out the palms of his hands, and with his white fingers spread out, he waved them to and fro in front of the Cardinal's face. 'Do you want me to throw him from a bridge into the Seine? Do you want me to smite him under the ribs with a poisoned dagger? Or in the shoulder with a lead bullet? Do you want me to order my youths to string him up from a lamp-post? Or do you want me to steal some cholera bacilli from the Laboratoire du feu Monsieur Pasteur and pour them into his glass? Do you...'

'Silence!' the Cardinal ordered. He kept his clenched fist on the table-top, and from his eyes poured flashes of anger, thunderbolts of indignation and whirlwinds of disgust. Only after several long seconds did he put his hands on his knees, the left on the left, the right on the right, and say quietly: 'Are you insinuating that we would entice you to commit murder? Do you think that we would take upon ourselves the blood shed or coagulated in the crime? Do you imagine that we would dare to stand before our Maker, stained with the sin of our fellow creature?'

'In that case,' said Charles Maurras, 'I've not understood a word. You told me, Your Eminence, that for some reason or another, which I have no desire to examine, you want to erase him from the surface of the earth. And now you tell me that you don't wish anyone to commit the crime of assassination on your behalf. That's a contradiction which I don't understand.'

On the bench near the edge of the pavement a white-haired old man sang, to the tune of *La Casquette du Père Bugeaud*, a song dating from the previous August:

>Il paraît que la s'maine dernière,
>Un dreyfusard très connu,
>Comm' le général Brugère,
>A reçu du plomb dans... l'dos.
>>As-tu vu
>Le trou d'balle, le trou d'balle,
>>As-tu vu
>Le trou d'balle à Labori?

Cardinal Pölätüo pushed aside his glass of grenadine and said:

'St. Augustine stated: "Knowing that because they did this in military service they were not murderers but *ministers of the law*, not avengers of their own wrongs but defenders of the public safety, he said to them..."

'"When a man in obedience to his lawful superiors slays another man, no law of the State regards him as a homicide..."'

'And St. Athanasius stated: "To kill the enemy in battle is both lawful and worthy of praise..."'

'If you intend this to mean,' said Charles Maurras 'that you want Kostrowicki sent to the front, I take the liberty of remarking that we have no war on at the moment.'

'There is always a war on somewhere in the world,' answered Pölätüo.

'But not every war is right and just,' said Maurras. 'And if you like quotations, I can quote too:

'St. Clement said: "If the Christian faith has come upon thee in the profession of arms, obey the captain who giveth *just* commands..."

'And St. Thomas Aquinas stated: "In order that a war may be *just*, three things are necessary. In the first place, the authority of the Prince, by whose order it is undertaken. .. In the second place, there must be a just cause; that is to say, those attacked must have, by a fault, deserved to be attacked... In the third place, it is necessary that the intention of those who fight should be right..."

'Now, how can we make Kostrowicki think that it *is* right?'

The drunken old man on the bench sang:

> *Toute la gendarmerie*
> *Cherche l'assassin inconnu,*
> *Qu'a eu cett' barbarie,*
> *De blesser un homme au... dos.*
>   *As-tu vu*
> *Le trou d'balle, le trou d'balle,*
>   *As-tu vu*
> *Le trou d'balle à Labori?*

'St. Augustine stated,' answered Pölätüo 'that *unless* certain of the injustice of a war, the citizen is bound to support his Government, since civil authority comes from God, and since the citizen is likely to be less in a position to know all the material facts than are his statesmen.'

'Of the latter I'm sure,' answered Maurras. 'Except when those statesmen are all republicans,' he added. 'But to go back to Kostrowicki: he is a French citizen, and France is not at war at the moment. How can Kostrowicki know where he should go? Which war, of all those which are on at this moment in the world, is not unjust?'

'In every war,' answered Pölätüo, 'if an aggressor causes injustice, the cause of the invaded is just, as is that of him who defends the invaded.

'St. Athanasius stated: "He who, when able, does not ward off injury from his comrade, is as guilty as he who does the injury…"'

Charles Maurras twisted his ring from his finger and spun it round on the table-top.

'And if,' he said, 'we were now to send Kostrowicki to China, and he says to himself in his conscience that the invaded party is neither the Christian missionaries, nor Baron von Ketteler, but the Boxers, and if he therefore calls the latter his comrades, what then? Will it not do injury to Your Eminence if he dies in battle under the command of a pagan Chinaman?'

'St. Augustine stated,' said Pölätüo, ' "A man can fight justly for maintaining public peace at the command even of a sacrilegious man, when what is commanded of him is either not contrary to God's precept, or not certainly against it."'

The drunken old man on the bench sang:

> *À sa terrible blessure*
> *L'avocat a survécu*
> *Quoique ce soit une chose bien dure*
> *Que d'avoir un' ball' dans… l'dos.*
>   *As-tu vu*
> *Le trou d'balle, le trou d'balle,*
>   *As-tu vu*
> *Le trou d'balle à Labori?*

'Well,' exclaimed Maurras, 'let's assume that he paints his face yellow, that he adopts Chinese nationality, and that the authority of the Prefect of

Shantung is derived from God. Even that doesn't imply that Kostrowicki will want to fight: Francis de Vittoria stated in *De Jure Belli*: "If a subject is convinced of the injustice of a war, he ought not to serve in it, even on the command of his Prince... Soldiers also are not excused when they fight in bad faith... Hence follows the corollary that subjects whose conscience is against the justice of a war may not engage in it whether they be right or wrong. This is clear, for 'whatever is not faith, is sin...'"

'That is exactly why I appeal to you,' said Pölätüo.

The drunken old man on the bench sang:

> *On court chercher pour l'extraire*
> *L'éminent docteur Reclus;*
> *Secondé par un confrère,*
> *Il lui fait des fouill' dans... l'dos.*
>   *As-tu vu*
> *Le trou d'balle, le trou d'balle,*
>   *As-tu vu*
> *Le trou d'balle à Labori?*

'Why?' asked Maurras. 'What for?'
'That you may convince him that at least one of the sides must be just; that you may inoculate him with faith.'
'I?' asked Maurras in surprise.

The drunken old man on the bench sang:

> *M'sieur Doyen à la rescousse*
> *Accourt; mais... turlututu,*
> *Le blessé qu'avait la frousse*
> *N'veut pas lui montrer son... dos.*
>   *As-tu vu*
> *Le trou d'balle, le trou d'balle,*
>   *As-tu vu*
> *Le trou d'balle à Labori?*

'Yes, you' said Pölätüo; 'you are the only man who can do it. You know how to address the youth of today; you know how to appeal to them. Kostrowicki is only 20.'

> *Bref, après tant de souffrance,*
> *L'avocat est revenu*
> *Prendre sa place à l'audience*
> *En gardant sa ball' dans... l'dos.*
> *As-tu vu*
> *Le trou d'balle, le trou d'balle,*
> *As-tu vu*
> *Le trou d'balle à Labori?*

'All right,' said Charles Maurras, 'I'll try to send Kostrowicki to China. That's settled. But to go back to Esterhazy and Schwarzkoppen, I've heard that...'

> *Il a fait une bell' harangue,*
> *Son bagout a reparu,*
> *Y a rien qui délie la langue*
> *Comm' d'avoir une ball' dans... l'dos*
> *As-tu vu*
> *Le trou d'balle, le trou d'balle,*
> *As-tu vu*
> *Le trou d'balle à Labori?*

1 0

Yes, there is always a war on somewhere in the world. On 31 December 1900 Cardinal Pölätüo received a letter from Charles Maurras. On the third page he read:

'... *as to Kostrowicki, I saw him in person today. He introduced himself: "Je suis Guillaume Apollinaire dit d'un nom slave pour vrai nom." As far as going to China was concerned, he wouldn't hear of it. "Que Vlo-ve?" he answered. In any case, he would probably have got there too late, for it appears that the Patriotic Harmonious Fists will surrender, accept an ultimatum, and pay an indemnity of 334,000,000 Gold Dollars. I shall now attempt to persuade him to go to Chile or the Argentine. Argentina is expanding her fleet, and Chile is introducing conscription for her army and navy, so one may anticipate that he will get his chance over there. However, if Kostrowicki's case is not an urgent matter to Your Eminence, c'est à dire: if Your Eminence would wait until say 1917, his fate and your problem would be solved here in France. This is a safe bet, in my opinion, due to the Second German Naval Law, just enacted on 12 June, concerning their seventeen-year plan for rebuilding their fleet. But to go back to the case of Waldeck-Rousseau's cabinet, "la loi du 30 Mars 1900" and the wave of strikes — (à propos: what is Your Eminence's opinion on the question of persuading Kostrowicki to take a job in a factory? For instance, if he'd been working at Martinique, he would have had his chance of perishing at the hands of L'infanterie de marine on 10 February; if he'd been working at Chalon-sur-*

Saône, he would have had his chance of perishing at the hands of the gendarmerie on 3 June, &c.) — I'm assured that Aristide Briand's view...'

In 1901 Cardinal Pölätüo received a letter from Charles Maurras, in which he read:
'... as to Kostrowitzki (because this is how he spells his name, at least in "Grande France," where he has just published some poems) — I had a talk with him in the last day or two, and urged him to go off to the Boer War. I told him of the fate of the coloured workers in Australia, and I directed his attention to the plans of the English in the Kingdom of Ashanti. To which he answered that he was on his way to Honnef and Neu-Glück bei Cherpleis, in Rhineland (of all places!), as a tutor to la vicomtesse de Milhau's daughter. What is Your Eminence's opinion on sending him off to the Far East when he comes back from Neu-Glück? The construction of the Trans-Siberian railway will undoubtedly lead to conflicts over there, and he will get his chance.
To go back to the person of Jaurès, I would direct Your Eminence's attention to...'

In 1902 Cardinal Pölätüo received a letter from Charles Maurras, in which he read:
'... as to our Kostrowitzki, I'm afraid that for sending him to South Africa it is now too late. I urged him to go to Nigeria or to the Far East, where that conquest of modern civilisation, the railway, should soon pay for its whistle.
To no effect.
To go back to the election of 27.IV and 11.V...'

In 1903 Cardinal Pölätüo received a letter from Charles Maurras, in which he read:
'.......... he didn't go off to the Far East, but my expectations have been verified by the events. Today, as doubtless Your Eminence already knows, the Russians reached Yalu. This year, for a change l would be inclined to send him to British Somaliland, but I'd first like to know Your Eminence's opinion on Venezuela or, eventually, Macedonia. To go back to the fact that Émile Combes

is opposing the abolition of the Government Credits for the Church: it will surely be known to Your Eminence that Combes once intended to become a priest, and prepared a thesis on St. Thomas Aquinas. Non sequitur? I leave it to you. However, Your Eminence should not jump to the conclusion that the affair of the liqueur produced by the Fathers of Chartres...'

In 1904 Cardinal Pölätüo received a letter from Charles Maurras, in which he read:
'.......... he doesn't understand at all what is going on at Port Arthur. The Pacific is no longer the issue: Bolivia and Chile are signing a treaty. I tried to suggest to him some other places where he would also get his chance. Rimbaud would have been seduced immediately by the very sound of a name like LHASSA-EKUMEKOS-HERRERO!!! Kostrowitzki replied: "Je marche vers Auteuil, je veux aller chez moi à pied, dormir parmi mes fétiches d'Océanie et de Guinée. Je peux dormir chez moi." To go back to Léon Daudet's London visit to H.R.H. le Prince d'Orléans: it took place at the Carlton, not at the Savoy; on the other hand, if the question is that of President Loubet's Rome visit to the King of Italy, I'm inclined to think that the section of Cardinal Merry del Val's letter of 26.IV., which begins: "Par suite, si quelque Chef de Nation catholique infligeait une grave offense au Souverain Pontife en venant prêter hommage à Rome à celui qui contre tout droit détient sa souveraineté civile..." &c., may expedite disestablishment here, and this...'

In 1905 Cardinal Pölätüo received a letter from Charles Maurras, in which he read:
'... as to Monsieur K., the Japanese finished their job in August without his participation. In September I suggested to him that he should leave for Mytilene; I also described as well as I could the attractions and charms of Serbia and Austria, who are now starting their Pig Customs Duty War. He answered: "maybe some other time," as he was in a hurry to get to a certain English bar in the rue d'Amsterdam, where he had an appointment with a Spaniard P. R. Picasso and a Jew Mr. Max Jacob.
To go back to the verdict of the Court of Cassation on 12.VII., I beg Your

Eminence to take into consideration the fact that Dreyfus acquitted ought to be even more informed qu'il n'est pas Français. "Dehors les barbares!" c'est le nouveau cri national, and if Your Eminence wants to get to the bottom of the problem, I...'

In 1906 Cardinal Pölätüo received a letter from Charles Maurras, in which he read:
'.......... I think he would have left for Natal, to fight the English under the King of the Zulus, or to fight the Zulus under the King of Great Britain, could he have taken with him the métèque Picasso and the Jew Jacob. What would be Your Eminence's opinion on that eventuality?
To go back to my book (just published) "Le dilemme de Marc Sangnier," the judgement that it constitutes no common platform on which atheism and the Catholic Church could...'

In 1907 Cardinal Pölätüo received a letter from Charles Maurras, in which he read:
'.......... neither Persia, nor Nicaragua, nor Honduras, nor the English bombs at Casablanca were able to distract his attention, even for one moment, from a new philosophy of cubes, which has just been invented by the Picasso whom I mentioned last year, and a certain Mr. Braque, who, to our distress, happens to be a Frenchman.
To go back to the waiters' strike, Your Eminence should know that it was not just the question of refusing them the right to wear moustaches and beards; the deeper aspect...'

In 1908 Cardinal Pölätüo received a letter from Charles Maurras, in which he read:
'.......... the chance he would have had in Bosnia and Herzegovina he missed. The same applied to Crete, Bulgaria and Venezuela. But Your Eminence must not be discouraged. On the contrary, I recommend to Your attention one of the November issues of the "Daily Telegraph" giving the interview with the Emperor, who did not hide the fact that while he, Wilhelm, was favourably inclined

towards England, the German people are hostilely disposed. I assure Your Eminence, as I did in 1900, that if Mahomet will not come to the Mountain, the Mountain will come to Kostrowitzki. To go back to the affair of the 100,000 francs which Mme de Loynes left to Léon Daudet's wife: together with the 200,000 francs which had been collected in other ways, they were immediately used to make l'Action Française into a daily paper. As to the organisation of the Camelots du Roi, does Your Eminence think that such matters as Thalamis' lectures at the Sorbonne on Jeanne d'Arc, and the transfer of Zola's body to the Panthéon, could be, from the point of view of politics...'

In 1909 Cardinal Pölätüo received a letter from Charles Maurras, in which he read:
'.......... *neither the Congo nor even Mauritania stimulates his imagination in the direction of Your Eminence's wishes. But patience, Your Eminence! The peaceful Protocols, signed last November by the Germans and MM. Pichon and Clemenceau by no means imply that the Mountain, of which I gave you news last year, has broken its journey. On the contrary; see the sentence of the Hague on 22.V., in the case of the German deserters from our Foreign Legion...'*

In 1910 Cardinal Pölätüo received a letter from Charles Maurras in which he read:
'.......... *I don't recommend Wadai or French Equatorial Africa. The Mountain approaches under its own steam.*
To go back to the scandal over A. Briand, in connection with the General Strike of railwaymen...'

In 1911 Cardinal Pölätüo received a letter from Charles Maurras, in which he read:
'.......... *there are chances in Tripolitania with the Italians against the Turks, or with the Turks against the Italians. Personally, I would like to keep him here; the Mountain approaches with huge strides. It is already, if one may say so, aboard the gunboat "Panther" stationed at Agadir. In that connection I recommend Your Eminence to look through the issue of "l'Action Française" dated 2.VII. I refer to*

the paragraph in Bainville's article: "Those who consider such a state of affairs as acceptable or even bearable lack foresight. To those of us who can see a little way into the future, war seems inevitable, if the Republican Government remains in power."
To go back to my book "Kiel and Tangier," which Your Eminence will certainly have received by now...'

In 1912 Cardinal Pölätüo received a letter from Charles Maurras, in which he read:
'.......... I expect that Your Eminence is impatient, with such chances in Tripolitania, in Montenegro, in the Balkans, with Greece, Bulgaria, Serbia rising against the Turks; with the Triple Alliance (including the Catholic Hapsburgs) backing the Mohammedans against the Christian peoples of the Balkans. But I think Your Eminence realises that the Cambon — Kiderlen-Woechter talks, and the convention signed by Herr Schön and M. Poincaré on the subject of Morocco and the Congo will not stop what we call in our correspondence the Mountain approaching Kostrowitzki. I am taking the liberty of sending under separate cover my new book "La politique réligieuse," trusting that, in contradistinction to some authorities, Your Eminence will not...'

In 1913 Cardinal Pölätüo received a letter from Charles Maurras, in which he read:
'.......... Bulgaria, Rumania, Serbia: child's play. The Mountain approaches. "Cette fois il faut en finir et Votre Majesté ne peut se douter de l'enthousiasme irrésistible qui, ce jour-là, entraînera le peuple allemand tout entier," stated Von Moltke to the King of Belgium. In this "Peuple allemand tout entier" he most certainly included those Kameraden on the other side of the Rhine who promise our Socialists never to vote for War Credits.
To go back to the question of the Kaiser's decree, it reads: "We, Wilhelm, by the Grace of God Emperor of Germany... decree that there shall be: (i) The Battle Fleet consisting of:..." but Your Eminence certainly knows it by heart by now. The important thing is what the English think. If the English think there will be a war, there will be no war; if, on the other hand, they think there will be no war,

there will be a war. Well, the Everyman English think as follows: "Today relations between Germany and England have vastly improved: this year (1913), the two governments have evidently arrived at some understanding, the effect of which will be to check the mad race in naval armaments and to lower the speed at which the costly Dreadnoughts are produced. Kaiser Wilhelm has for some time past concentrated his efforts on the maintenance of peace, and neither he nor his subjects have any desire to plunge again into the miseries of a European struggle." Bah!
P.S.: I take the liberty of sending to Your Eminence Léon Daudet's book L'Avant Guerre *(articles and essays on the German Jewish Spy System in France since the Dreyfus affair).*
P.P.S.: I assure Your Eminence that it is M. Daudet's habit to burn letters, and to forget the names of his correspondents.'

In August 1914 Cardinal Pölätüo received a letter from Charles Maurras, in which he read:
*'...Ça y est! (*THE MOUNTAIN HAS COME TO MAHOMET!*). In connection with His Holiness Pius X's "condemnation" of "l'Action Française" in January, I think that I may now direct Your Eminence's attention to...'*

1915. The Cardinal's note: *'The leaders of the International have voted, each in his own country, in favour of war credits. Which means that Socialism or Communism, whichever it is, has become National. Which means that it is no longer a Rival of our Holy Mother Church, the Spouse of Christ, who alone remains Universal.'*

In 1916 Guillaume (Kostrowitzki) Apollinaire was wounded in the head by a shell splinter. He was twice trepanned, but died of the Spanish influenza, in hospital, on 10 November 1918, while the crowds in the streets around shouted: 'À bas Guillaume!'

After receiving the news of the death of Guillaume, the poet, and the abdication of Guillaume, the Kaiser, Cardinal Pölätüo decided to set his hand once more to his *Philosophy of Pölätüomism,* work on which had been interrupted in 1900.

He realised, however, that in the meantime indirect knowledge, that buttress of direct knowledge, had outstripped him considerably. Without wasting time, he immediately began to study Planck, Thomson, Ramsay & Soddy, Einstein, Rutherford, Punnett & Bateson, Russell & Whitehead, Moseley, Watson, Bragg, and Pavlov's theory of conditioned reflexes.

And then (on New Year's Day, 1922) he picked up St. Augustine (412 A. D.) *Ad Marcellinum* and read:

'Let those who say that the doctrine of Christ is incompatible with the well-being of the State, give us an army composed of soldiers such as the doctrine of Christ requires soldiers to be. Let them give us such subjects, such husbands and wives, such parents and children, such masters and servants, such Kings, such judges, yea, even such taxpayers and tax-gatherers, as the Christian religion has taught that men should be, and then let them dare to say that it is adverse to the State's well-being! Nay, rather let them no longer hesitate to admit that were this doctrine obeyed it would be the State's salvation...'

'Couldn't one apply Pavlov's theory of conditioned reflexes to making people obey this doctrine of Christianity?' the Cardinal thought to himself.

He put a sheet of paper into his *macchina da scrivere* and tapped out with two fingers:

```
In order to evoke reflexes we must have stimuli.
Stimuli may be positive or negative;
exemplum: food or pain.
These stimuli are in the hands of the secular,
Temporal power.
```

He thought for a few moments more, then tapped on:

> But a man is not a dog.
> To a man, material stimuli are unnecessary.
> To a man, it is enough to <u>say</u> that he will be comfortable or that he will suffer.
> And these stimuli, positive and negative, are accessible to the hands of the Church.

The typewriter bell struck the end of the line. Pölätüo turned the roller. Then suddenly his fingers began to jump about on the keys of their own accord:

> But these stimuli are already in the hands of the Church: HEAVEN and HELL!

Pölätüo tapped out the exclamation mark, and in great ecstasy he marvelled at the Wisdom of the Church, to whom all matters concerning Man had been revealed hundreds of years before the discoveries of Indirect Knowledge. Compared to this Wisdom, the 6935 pages of the *Philosophy of Pölätüomism* seemed to him an infinitely small speck of dust.

And then a new idea possessed him:

'But if...' he began to order his words in his mind, 'but if these stimuli have been in the hands of the Church for two thousand years, then WHY are husbands and wives, soldiers and subjects, parents, children, masters, servants, Kings, judges, taxpayers and tax-gatherers, not such as the Christian religion has taught that they should be?'

He coughed, and stretched out his hand to tap this sentence on the typewriter; but in the interval between the cough and touching the keys — another idea occurred to him.

PART TWO

11

In the year in which G.B. Shaw was born, Cardinal Pölätüo was already 34, and it was therefore not surprising that some three-quarters of a century later, in the year in which G.B.S. still felt vigorous enough to go visiting Moscow, the Cardinal preferred to sit in his armchair.

This armchair had been built by a young architect from the Bauhaus school of Architecture (Dessau), of the name of Jan Rybka, who had been converted to the Roman Catholic faith. Some of his friends were of the opinion that he had been converted to Roman Catholicism from Judaism. Others, however, and Jan Rybka would agree with them, felt that he had been converted to Roman Catholicism not from Judaism, of which he knew very little, but from the Weltanschauung of the Bauhaus's functionalism. And so, while some of his friends were eager to point out that his baptism had *not* freed his person from a number of his pre-baptismal characteristics — that it had left intact the lower lateral cartilage of his nose, for instance, — others found some vestiges of Bauhaus ideology in the armchair he had built for Cardinal Pölätüo.

Indeed, under the sumptuous Gobelin upholstery of the armchair, there was a skeleton of bent and welded steel tubes not unlike those invented by Laszlo Moholy-Nagy, the harbinger, the true Virgil prophesying *(Time has conceived, and the great Sequence of the Ages starts afresh. The First Chair of the New Age is already on its way down from Factory to canteen. The wooden chair shall end, and bent chromium shall inherit the whole world. Smile on the Chair's birth, Machina, your own mass-produced Apollo is enthroned at last.)* the approach of the shining stools and chairs of American milk bars.

The function of the skeleton of steel tubes was to prop, support, reassure the bony framework of the Cardinal, whose muscles, as time marched on, grew weaker, and whose osseous tissue became more and more frail. Yet it was the most universal armchair. In it was a vessel of the shape of a young duck beheaded across its long neck, designed by Jan Rybka according to data supplied by the Cardinal's physician. There was an infra-red-rays generating device. There was an electric motor which would silently change the shape of the armchair so that the Cardinal could not only sit in it when he wanted to work, but also alter it slowly to the kneeling position when he had to pray, and then spread it horizontally and rest with his back upon it when he wanted to sleep but was not inclined to move to his bed.

The at least treble-soulness of his armchair disturbed the Cardinal again and again.

>No cat is a dog;
>Mimi is a cat;
>∴ Mimi is not a dog.

Why is what is valid for animals not valid for furniture? You can say: 'No cat is a dog,' but you cannot say: 'No armchair is a praying-desk.' The Cardinal's armchair *was* a praying-desk. And a bed *too*.

'Stripped of accidentals, what is the essential function of the Chair?' he asked himself. And he felt a grudge against Jan Rybka who, as all neophytes are sooner or later bound to do, had thus confronted his (Pölätüo's) brain with such a trinity of essentials that the Cardinal felt obliged to revise the method of classification he was used to. But otherwise the armchair was most comfortable.

On the left-hand side it possessed a sliding shelf which could be turned so that all the written and unwritten pages of his *Philosophy of Pölätüomism* found themselves placed at a suitable angle beneath the Cardinal's eyes. On the right-hand side of the armchair there was another shelf on which his dictaphone was lying in wait. It was a German invention, very new then. A thin iron wire passed between two electro-magnets, connected in the usual way with the microphone, and, as the wire moved, its consecutive particles became magnetized to a greater or lesser degree according to the vibration of the voice. He didn't use the device much. His mind was not lazy, but it was slow like the formation of an embryo in the womb, or like the growth of stalactites, or the maturing of wine. It worked at the rate of one cluster of ideas every few hours, and the Cardinal felt self-conscious, remorseful and embarrassed when the thin iron wire moved virgin pure through the machine, registering nothing but its own electric noise. Besides, the Cardinal was used to working in solitude, and the sound of his own voice made him feel as if he were in a crowded protestant joss-house. No, he didn't like the machine. He preferred a passive and patient pen and a piece of paper.

Nevertheless, the iron wire of the dictaphone was a fascinating thing to possess and to look at. He held a length of wire in his fingers, scrutinized it, and contemplated. Unlike a grooved gramophone disc, the wire possessed nothing that could be seen; nothing that one could smell, taste, or put one's finger on. Who, uninitiated, would surmise that the length of wire contained a message? Yet, it was sufficient to let it pass through the machine at the right speed to be able to hear the Cardinal's voice:

'...EVEN PERTRANT RUSSELL CANNOT GETRIT OFALL THE UNIVERSALS ANTRETAINSSSI MILARITY FATHER TOUGLAS COULTYOUPLEASE TELL JONATHAN TOREMEMPER NOTTO LEAVE HIS HOOVER IN MY STUTY HE'S ALREATY TONE SO TWICE THIS WEEK ITS RUPPERPIPE LOOKS LIKEA SERPENTOF PARATISE ANTIT TISTURPS ME OR WAS IT ITENTITY?' *click!*

How do we know that there are not many more things in the universe that look as innocent as the thin iron wire and yet contain a message? It might be that all charts, diagrams, graphs — such as those curved or broken lines that show the changes in rainfall for a number of centuries, or the fluctuation of the price of pig-iron, or the rising and falling of his own temperature when he was having his tonsils removed, — it might well be that they would all reveal a message, if one only knew at what speed and through what kind of machine they should be allowed to pass. But why only charts, diagrams, graphs? Perhaps all things in the Universe are patterns that only need to be properly played back and deciphered...

He glanced at the bunch of fresh violets that Father Douglas, his secretary, had placed (as he used to every morning) on a mahogany pillar by the window. At the same time he was conscious of a drop of water that had just disengaged itself from the end of his urinary canal and was now entering the vessel designed by Jan Rybka. Like a scientist who is interested in everything, or, which amounts to the same, like a Christian who believes in the doctrine of the creation of *all* things by God, he refused to divide created things into decent and not decent — all were equally good and entitled to testify to the presence of Nature and God: a bunch of violets as well as a drop of amber-coloured fluid of peculiar odour. It might well be that the bunch of violets and the drop were also only patterns which could reveal a message, if one only knew how to play them back, at what kind of speed and through what sort of machine.

He imagined himself putting the bunch of violets into a dictaphone of some curious shape, and pressing the button. What would it announce? And in what language? Would it be in Latin? He cast down his eyes and smiled gently at the naïveté of the suggestion presented to him by his own brain. Or, perhaps, a kind of Latine Sine Flexione? — He rejected the idea as soon as it came. It was doubtful whether it would be a word-language at all. Must everything be expressible in a word-language? Of course not. But — here the Cardinal puffed softly in the direction of the left shelf, and the pages of his manuscript flapped as if animated by a breeze — but, if this were so, if there are things in heaven and earth that cannot be expressed in words, then his own work, the *Philosophy of Pölätüomism,* which was built of words, must inevitably be incomplete.

A bumble-bee came in through the half-open window, and immediately attacked the bunch of violets. Cardinal Pölätüo pressed the button of his dictaphone and began:

'Even God...'

But now the bumble-bee left the bunch of violets and began to circle round the microphone. The Cardinal was annoyed. He constrained himself to finish the sentence and then wound back a length of the iron wire and pressed another button. The voice came from the loudspeaker:

'...ITS RUPPERPIPE LOOKS LIKEA SERPENTOF PARATISE ANTIT TISTURPS ME OR WAS IT ITENTITY? *click!* EVEN GOT BZZZZ... AFTER HEHAT REVEALET HIMSELF IN THE WORT BZZZZ FOUNT IT NECESSARY TO REVEAL HIMSELF IN JESUS CHRIST BZZZZ *click!*

The Cardinal switched off the machine.

'That's how God revealed Himself. But how can *man* do so?' he asked.

The bumble-bee was now circling under the ceiling. Berkeley would have been barking at the bumble-bee. But Berkeley was no longer there. He had died many years before. The Cardinal pressed a button and the armchair began to move slowly to its kneeling position.

'In what kind of language can man reveal himself, if there are things in his *person,* if there are things in his *existence,* that cannot be put into words?' he continued.

There was a clumsy moment when, in its metamorphosis, the armchair had already ceased to be an armchair, but had not yet become a praying-desk.

'In what kind of language can he reveal that not verbalisable thinking he undergoes when he, for instance, thinks that he doesn't think of the imminence of his own death?'

Now the piece of furniture had passed completely from the class of armchairs into the class of praying-desks. He meditated for a moment. Then he turned the emerald ring on his finger and whispered:

'Is not Kneeling the language in which to reveal the unverbalisable thought that makes a man kneel before his Creator?

'Is not Throwing balls the language in which is revealed the unverbalisable thought of the *"Jongleur de la Sainte Vierge"* who, instead of saying his prayer, juggled before the image of the Virgin Mary?

'Is not Killing the only language for the unverbalisable thinkings of Adolph Hitler,

'and Houses — for Le Corbusier's,

'and Lines and Rectangles — for Mondrian's,

'and Ludus Tonalis — for Hindemith's?

— just as the life of Jesus Christ is the language for God's.

'And is not this armchair a language which helps Jan Rybka to understand that part of his existence which is: to be a craftsman, just as kneeling helps him to understand the whole of his existence, which is: being a mortal?'

He felt gratified. Every part of his argument seemed to him to dovetail as perfectly as if he had just pushed in the last piece of an enormous jigsaw puzzle.

Suddenly, however, a new doubt entered his heart:

'Yet,' he began, 'if *kneeling* be the language of myself as a mortal, *words* are still the language of myself as a philosopher. Can I not use them if I use them as I use my knees, as Jan Rybka used steel tubes and upholstery, as Mondrian used lines and rectangles, as *le Jongleur de la Sainte Vierge* used balls?'

The bumble-bee was no longer there under the ceiling, and peace reigned in the Cardinal's study. He glanced anxiously at his manuscript and asked himself:

'But, were I to use words in that way, wouldn't the *Philosophy of*

Pölätüomism become the *Poetry of Pölätüomism?*'

The word 'poetry' did not bring the name of Apollinaire with it. For years now the Cardinal's mind had seemed to be perfectly void of any such reminiscence. Instead, he remembered the Archbishop of Merangue, the literary man, the one who had given him a volume of Anatole France's *Le Jongleur de la Sainte Vierge and other stories* when he, the Cardinal, had had his tonsils removed.

'*Poetry of Pölätüomism,*' he repeated.

Never in his life had he written a poem, or composed a piece of music, or painted a picture. Never in his life had he juggled with balls. How could he know how to juggle with words?

For a fraction of a second he felt humiliated at comparing himself with a juggler, but, at the same time, he found that he liked the feeling of being humiliated and felt proud of it, and also of the fact that the pride he felt was so humble. He was still on his knees. His elbows rested on the desk. The dictaphone was switched off. A faint smell of violets was just distinguishable. It was calm. And in that calm the Cardinal's lips began to move while his ears listened to them with curious and gentle astonishment:

'~Mãscărŏnĭnŏpŏlĕvă
Cắscărŏnĭnŏpŏlĕvă
Lắscărŏnĭnŏpŏlĕvă'

He felt happy. He must ask the Archbishop of Merangue to dinner and recite the poem to him. He felt the blessedness of peace. He pressed the button, and the praying-desk began to move slowly and to pass from the class that contained all the praying-desks of the Universe into the class that contained all its beds.

1 2

Ever since he had begun to use the Rybka armchair as a bed, his dreams had been marked by an embarrassing particularity. That didn't worry him unduly at the beginning. But when one night his dream placed him under a transparent sheet of plate-glass on which the late elderly maiden lady he had met on 12 September 1862 at Messieurs de Goncourt's was now walking in circles and epicycloids so that he couldn't see her long-forgotten face because of the enormous round crinoline she wore for her only garment, Pölätüo decided to pay more attention to the problem. Did not Thomas Careña write ages ago: *'Should anyone utter heresies in his dreams, the inquisitors shall consider this a reason for investigating his conduct in life, for that is wont to return in sleep which occupies a man during the day.'*

'Father Douglas!' — Without moving his head, Pölätüo pointed his ringed finger at his secretary. 'I want you to do me a favour and fetch from the shelves of Original Sin a volume you'll find there between Ferenczi's *Pollution ohne orgastischen Traum und Orgasmus in Traum ohne Pollution* and Friedjung's *Traum eines sechsjährigen Mädchens?'*

But, when his secretary was already half-way up the ladder, he halted him: 'No, Father, you cannot climb on this errand unprepared as you are. You cannot go and fetch that book without first putting rubber gloves on your hands.' When Father Douglas took a step down and looked searchingly around, Pölätüo added: 'I mean: spiritual rubber gloves.'

Then he took a tiny sip of warm milk, and continued:

'It is a bad book, Father Douglas. And not scientific. When a scientist builds a system, he bases it on Knowledge gathered *In*directly, namely: through the intermediary of his senses. And what he does is legitimate. Because if he is right, his system is true. And, as the Church is based upon the Truth, the scientist's system cannot be dangerous to the Church, for one truth cannot be dangerous to Another, it complements It. Now, is that what the author of the book I've asked you to fetch does? No. *He* builds his system not on Indirect Knowledge, as it is supplied by senses, but on Direct Knowledge, as it is supplied by dreams. Yet a system based not on Indirect Knowledge but on Direct Knowledge is called not science but religion! However, as the only true religion is that of the Church, based on the only true Direct Knowledge, that revealed by God in Jesus Christ, his religion based on his Direct Knowledge as revealed to him in his Patients' Dreams is not necessarily true, and thus may become dangerous.'

He would have liked Father Douglas to have said something. Yet not a muscle moved on the secretary's face. Only his fingers played with a yellow Koh-i-Nor pencil which he held in his left hand and rolled between the index and thumb of the right.

'Father Douglas,' said Cardinal Pölätüo. 'We are compelled to ask you to do for us something in which you will not find much pleasure. You know, however, that even a dark and narrow gate may lead to a great light. May I have your pencil, Father?'

Father Douglas passed the pencil to him, and Cardinal Pölätüo put it on the shelf on the left arm of his chair. Then he rested his hands on his knees, and said:

'Now, the Pölätüomistic Principle of Indeterminacy says that if you accurately accomplish the act of reading such a book as this, your impartiality will be undetermined, while so long as you keep your impartiality determined, the act of understanding the book will remain unaccomplished. In other words, you can either read the book or be impartial, but you cannot do both, and that's because the very reading of it makes you prejudiced either in its favour or disfavour, and as a prejudiced person is not the same as an unprejudiced one, the person who has read the book is never the same as the person who was about to read it. Thus, Father, as it is fundamentally impossible for one and the same human being to do both, I propose that *you* read the book while *I* try to be impartial.'

'Yes, Eminence,' said Father Douglas.

The Cardinal smiled. The bunch of violets was there, in its usual place. A tiny control-lamp in the leg of the armchair showed that the device for generating the infra-red rays had begun to work. The curtains at the huge windows were soaked with the blue sky which flooded the garden outside. There was peace.

'You are embarking on a strange journey, Caro Douglas,' the Cardinal said. 'And the strangest thing is that the monsters who threaten you will appear not during your voyage but after you have come back to the Earth which, indeed, you will find an odd place to walk upon. What you now think innocent will then seem to you an incarnation of original sin. What you now think indifferent will become the Instrument of the Adversary. You will shiver when touching an ordinary pencil, you will think twice before you traverse the arched gate of any long passage, you will turn your face away at the sight of an innocent little girl eating a peeled banana fruit. The world will become a landscape filled with objects concave and convex, and serpents of Paradise will gorge themselves from the opened chalices of our little sisters the flowers in our garden. Einstein has changed the picture of the world by changing our innocent notion of time; Marx has changed the picture of the world by changing our innocent notion of change; now, that third Jew is changing the picture of the world by changing the innocence of our looking at its shapes!'

There was peace.

'"Behold,"' said the Cardinal, '"I send thee forth as a sheep in the midst of wolves: be thou therefore wise as a serpent, and harmless as a dove."'

He took another sip of milk from the thermostatic glass nestling in the arm of his chair, and continued:

'What we require of you, Father, is that you make for us an inventory of these shapes. "A shape one touches," says he "is never the shape one touches, but a symbol of another one does not." "A shape one sees in one's dream," says he "is never the shape one sees but a symbol of another one is dreaming of." You are requested to compile a catalogue of all the shapes mentioned by the author as those that were touched or seen, and of all the respective ones that were meant to be so. Then you will kindly arrange the data in alphabetical order and have three copies printed by brother Anthony for us.'

13

Cardinal Pölätüo had grave doubts about the wisdom of his action. Was it sagacious so to thrust the book into the hands of Father Douglas? It's true, Father Douglas was a perfect segretario and a splendid indexer. But he was also an Englishman. Which meant that if one day he came to the conclusion that he ought to pray standing on his head, he would have the arrogant innocence to find it easy to stand on his head, and, without asking the permission of his superior, he would do so. Knowing this, was it fair to endanger Father Douglas by making him read the book? The Cardinal scratched his knee nervously. Yes, the Institution of the Confessional should have made Father Douglas immune to the teachings of the book. And yet, on the other hand, had he not lived for thirteen years at Oxford, which is, as Mgr. K. says, the Paradise of Anglicanism? Do not all his Anglican roots lie there? Can we be sure that he has actually cut himself off from all those heretics and unbelievers among whom he was bred?

The Cardinal didn't mind unbelievers. Many accepted Suffering as part of their life's way to virtue, and he knew how difficult it was to choose the cross, even for one who was a Roman Catholic. So he admired the greatness of God who gave at least some of them such strength that, — without Christ, and believing in their souls' *Mor*tality, — they still didn't lodge their securities in things corporeal. He tried to imagine the world they must be constrained to think they lived in, and he shrivelled with awe. How could they bear the strain of existing at the mercy of Forces which to them must seem indifferent or inimical? How were they able to look at the sky if they saw nothing in it but space curved with time, and void of love? How could they look through a microscope if they saw through it nothing but a wild jungle of fighting cells, and no Purpose! Were they not aware that by rejecting God and thus taking the responsibility for the World off His shoulders they were placing it on their own? Heretics and dissidents didn't do that. They left the Responsibility with God, and all they found in themselves was an arrogance of revolt against the Authority. He despised them.

Yet, those whom he despised most were the Scientific Heretics. He was exasperated by the foolish naïveté of the editors of FISH, (to establish which he had sent Lady Eunice £37.10.0 in English money from his private purse,) when he saw in it essays on Eddington and Jeans, written by admirers of Jeans and Eddington. Surely, the fact that certain movements of electrons are not determined by any cause could not mean that science had discovered what by its nature must be not perceivable by science. Those certain movements either are or are not due to a supernatural agent. If they are not, there is no proof there of the existence of God. And if they are, it is not for science to pronounce on them.

'The Church Militant' he wrote to the editor of FISH, 'doesn't ask science to tint herself with Divinity. Science's business is to show *how* natural laws reflect in the brain of scientists, and not *by whom* they (both the laws and the brains) were given, or *why*. In particular, it is erroneous, if not a heresy indeed, to hold that miracles are scientifically possible. On the contrary, they are not so. Why!, it is only because they are impossible that they are possible, for only those that are impossible are miracles, and those that are possible are not.

'Thus, if it so happens (as, according to science, it may), that all the molecules of a human body suddenly chance to take an upward direction, and man is lifted from the earth, this will not be a miracle. Yet, when Jesus Christ was lifted bodily into heaven, this was a miracle. For this was due not to the chance governing the motion of the molecules of His body, but to the non-scientific reason that He wanted to go back to His Father.

'And, if it so happens (as, according to science it may), that an ovum starts to develop without any sperm stimulation, and a virgin gives birth to a babe, this will not be a miracle. Yet, when the Ever-Virgin Mary conceived, retaining her hymen intact, this was a miracle. For this occurred to her not because of an intracellular fertilisation, or of a pathological parthenogenesis, but in order that she should give birth to Jesus (Is.vii.14).

'Thus, as a fortuitous concourse of atoms is possible, it cannot be a miracle. A miracle, to be possible, must be a breach of those laws of nature in which a breach is impossible.

'Hence, we must be on our guard not only against those who, like Eddington and Jeans, expand the universe of science into what she is not, but also against those who, like Russell, so contract it to its roots that they arrive at the question: "Can a Law of Nature change?", and there remains in their hands nothing, no pen, no pencil, no broomstick, with which they could write: "No."

'Now, Can a Law of Nature change? We have already seen that a breach of law must be impossible for a miracle to be possible. Yet, what is a breach of law if it isn't a partial change of law, and what is any change of law if not the total breach of law? Thence, if a breach of law must be impossible for a miracle to be possible, then the total breach of law must be impossible for the total miracle to be possible. Now, is there a greater total miracle than the Day of Judgement and the End of the World, if due, not to atomic research (in which case it wouldn't be a miracle at all), but to the Will of God? Would you deny that it is, at least, *possible*? However, if this total miracle is to be possible, then, as we have already shown, the total breach of law must be impossible, which is only another way of saying that a Law of Nature cannot change, and any statement to the contrary is harmful and would be erroneous, if it were not, as we shall now demonstrate, meaningless.

'Supposing sugar refuses to dissolve tomorrow. If this is due to the Will of God Who wanted to show scientists that His miracles are possible, the scientists will not be able to find any cause for the sudden unsolubility of sugar.

If, on the other hand, it is not due to the Will of God, then, as all other constants are deducible from the fundamental constants quoted by Russell: $e, m, M, h, c, G, \lambda$, it will follow that a sudden change of sugar's solubility must be the result of some changes in the numerical value of $e, m, M, h, c, G, \lambda$. Yet, as these appear in the fundamental equations of physics, any change in their value must be followed by some changes in all brute fact, such as the structure not only of sugar but also of the instruments measuring the changes, and of the brains perceiving them. Now, Pölätüomism maintains that the changes in the instruments will be such that they will compensate for the changes in the fundamental constants, and therefore the instruments will be unable to detect them; which is only another way of saying that the changes in the value of $e, m, M, h, c, G, \lambda$, are not possible; which is only another way of saying that Laws of Nature cannot change; which is as it ought to be if a total miracle is to be possible.'

He pressed a button, and some Monteverdi appeared in the form of a sonorous, circular wave around his head, like a halo. It appeared literally all around his head, as the loudspeaker was placed just behind his tonsure, under the antimacassar in the upholstery at the top of the armchair. Monteverdi had always had a soothing effect on the Cardinal. He didn't know whether it was because one could listen to it without being aware that what one was listening to was a secular opera, or, on the contrary, because the opera *was* secular yet so gentle that it wouldn't be out of place to chant it in the Church of St. Mark's in Venice. He went all through:

'O ma lyre, quel honneur, ma lyre bien aimée! Tu as vaincu les dieux inexorables.
'O ma lyre, ta place est marquée dans le ciel. À ta voix les étoiles danseront...
'O ma lyre, c'est à toi que je dois le bonheur... la joie de revoir les yeux, les tendres yeux de ma bien aimée.'

— and he stretched out his arm to take hold of a paper from the shelf at his side. What he wanted to see was the statistics collected and classified by the St. Marguerite Research Committee of the Pontifical Academy of Science. But the paper was not there. He would have called Father Douglas to fetch it for him, but Father Douglas was now busy compiling the Dictionary of Traumatic Signs and Symbols, and the Cardinal didn't want to disturb him. After all, the correct figures of the Report didn't matter. What mattered was the fact they revealed. The fact that there was a proportionally greater number of Roman Catholics than of Unbelievers among those who had been convicted in criminal courts. The report was a nuisance. Mngr. Gavarni said: All statistics lie. Mngr. Zorge said: Frogs commit still less crimes than Unbelievers, so what? Mngr. Liutprand said: To commit a crime you must have guts, and Roman Catholics have guts. And a little Franciscan brother hanged himself in his cell.

As for Pölätüo, he had no doubts: That Earl of Unbelievers, Bertrand Russell, should have been led by his own logic to the conclusion that it was more advantageous to him to be bad than to be good. Therefore, if, in spite of that, he was good, did it not ensue that his logic was fallacious, and as such, should not be followed? Verily, he and the likes of him had no business to commit less crimes than Roman Catholics did. He had no reason not to kill. If Man was no longer the Lord of Creation for him, if there was no definite barrier between homo sapiens and animals, and between animals and plants, and between plants and crystals, did he not become a cannibal when he licked a simple crystal of common salt? And if he found it easy to lick salt, why didn't he kill his neighbours, whenever he wanted to, if there was no barrier between crystals and plants, and between plants and venison, and between venison and men? Indeed, his own logical reasoning pushed him into a position too foolish for Despair, but silly enough to make our age the age of Dissatisfaction. And that was precisely what must happen to any reasoning that was like a ship who had lost her anchor. She could attach her chain to a bigger chain hanging from a bigger boat, and the bigger boat could attach her chain to the chain of a boat still bigger, but finally, the biggest of the boats must have the first link the first major premise, of her chain attached to something that itself was a chain no more. And how could he achieve that, pray, if he rejected the Anchor and the Rock of Revelation, of which the Catholic Church alone is the guardian and infallible interpreter?

Impatiently, the Cardinal switched off Monteverdi, pushed another knob, and a spittoon of bottle-green glass moved slowly from its place in the armchair towards the Cardinal's chin.

Again: Let us take as fact that which is already made manifest, namely that Russell does not kill.

From the foregoing it is also clear that the Possibility of Acting on the Categorical Imperative of the Moral Law exists.

Now it has been shown (Kant) that such Possibility carries the practical implication that God exists.

Therefore: Is not Russell's own existence the proof of the existence of God?

How many times had he not tried to bring to the notice of unbelievers that claim which seemed so reasonable and so logical to him? Why did it not seem so to them, who claimed to be so reasonable and so logical themselves?

He felt uncomfortable and ill at ease. Though neither because of his thoughts, nor because of his armchair. He felt that something odd was going on, yet neither outside him, nor, strictly speaking, inside his body. He lurked in himself and watched. It was the tip of his tongue. It was moving slowly behind his upper teeth, and now the Cardinal knew that it was hopelessly searching there for the gap he had had between his canine and second pre-molar tooth. How long is the memory possessed by the tip of the tongue! There was no gap there at all. There had been no gap there for the last ten or twelve years, since he had had a gold tooth put in by a Harley Street dentist whom he went to see at the end of his short stay in England, where he had gone in order to tell Bertrand Russell that '4' is not a sufficient answer to the problem: '$2+2=?$'.

'My dear Bertie,' he had said.

14

'My dear Bertie,' he had said. '"4" is not a sufficient answer to the problem: "2+2=?" A sufficient answer should contain that Something, Locke Knows Not What, which makes you feel satisfied when, sitting at your desk, you put your forefinger to your forehead and give the answer: "4," but does not make you happy when the answer is "5," or "3$\frac{1}{16}$."'

His host had not budged when the Cardinal had stood up, gone to the shelf, taken two books, one thin, one very thick, and put them on the table, beside the white and blue Wedgwood tea-set.

With small silver sugar-tongs Pölätüo put two lumps into his cup and then continued:

'Even as a child, thus early, you knew that "two and two are four" felt quite different from such a proposition as "all swans are white." Yet, can you tell me *what* that Something is that makes it feel different?'

He paused, but it was clear that his ears were shut, he didn't wish to listen, his wish was to expound.

'What is that Something?' he repeated. 'What do we know about it? We know that it causes the difference. Yet, if it causes something, then it exists. Furthermore, if it exists, then either it is a physical fact or it is not. Now, if it is a physical fact, shouldn't there be a symbol for it among your physical fundamental constants?' — he had opened the thin book and moved his index finger along one of the lines:

$$e,\ m,\ M,\ h,\ c,\ G,\ \lambda$$

On the other hand, if it is not an empirical fact, should there not be a symbol for it among these logical constants?' — here he had opened the thick book, thick with:

$$\sim \quad \vee \quad \supset \quad \exists \quad = \quad 0 \quad s \quad (\quad) \quad ,$$

'Which of these symbols represents that Something? Which of them represents soul?' he had asked. And before the Earl of Unbelievers had had time to answer, he had continued:

'None! Of course! There is no room in your books for a theological fallacy. "4," you say, is just another name for "2+2." But what *is* a name? Are not names where men are? Consequently, if "4" is another name for "2+2" and names are where men are, then one cannot say that 2+2 would remain 4 in a world without men. Which means that the existence of men is necessary for 4 to be 2+2, which means that there is Something in *men* that makes 2+2 be 4. Now, what is it?'

His voice suddenly softened and became almost lyrical: 'Let me say this: even if I had learnt all your symbols by heart, it would still be impossible for me to foretell what kind of conclusion you will, or will not, be able to come to in the future. I may have all the pages of your symbols before me and still be unable to tell what you will do next. On the other hand, bring to my confessional the content of your heart, let me hear your soul, and I shall be more in a position to predict what you will do in a certain set of circumstances. Now, if science deals with predicting what's going to happen in a certain set of circumstances, then does it not follow that it would be more scientific to let me see your soul than to let me follow your logic?'

A young boy of about twelve who all that time had been sitting calmly in the corner of the room, now intervened suddenly:

'I say, Pölätüo, that's rot!'

'You make your statement in a very authoritative manner, my son,' Pölätüo said.

'My name is Ayer, and I'm not your son,' the boy said. With the thumb and index finger of his right hand he extracted, not without a certain charm, something from between his teeth, and then added:

'When I say "rot," I mean: "Meaningless." Russell cannot show you his soul.'

'Do you mean to say that he hasn't one?' Pölätüo asked.

'No,' the boy exclaimed. 'I mean that I do not see by what criterion it could possibly be decided whether he has or has not any such spiritual substance. Therefore the statements that he has, or has not, a soul are both equally meaningless. The noise: "soul" cannot be referred to anything observable. Therefore: a sentence that contains that noise is neither true nor false.'

The boy wore short white trousers, and there was a blot of black ink on one of his knees. He spat on it and tried to rub the stain off.

'You see, Pölätüo,' he continued, still occupied with his knee, 'I'm sorry for you, but your religion is full of such noises. Noises that don't refer to anything observable. Please don't take it personally, Pölätüo, but that's precisely why she cannot become a part of science.'

The Cardinal fixed his eyes on the boy, and his right hand made an almost unnoticeable sign of the cross.

'Why, of course!' he answered. 'Religion is not a part of Science. On the contrary, it is Science that is a part of Religion.'

'Come, come!' the boy said. 'Science can stand very well without Religion, while Religion falls down in the dust as Science takes from her one after another all questions that can be answered by using words which are capable of referring to what can be observed.'

'Exactly!' Pölätüo replied. 'That is exactly why I said that Science is a part of Religion, and not vice versa. Indeed, she, Science, can stand by herself, and be as grotesque as a solitary buttress in the centre of a desert would be. Whilst Religion, not supported by Science, would fall and be as tragic as the ruins of a gothic church not propped up by buttresses. Does Rome not affirm that there must be no discord between faith and reason, that the employment of reason, the gift of God, precedes the act of faith!'

'Blah! Blah! Blah!' the boy ejaculated. 'Now you start quoting authorities. It's no use talking to you! You'll never see it, Pölätüo! And that's because your inability to understand what I'm trying to convey is due not to your lacking intelligence, which is not the case, but to your having decided not to follow my way of thinking. That's not fair!'

'My son,' the Cardinal answered. 'We *have* been following your way of thinking, and we were doing so with great patience and humility. Though we have been sounding the very bed of the river on the surface of which, like a daddy-longlegs, you are strolling. You just be a good boy for a moment and listen. You maintain that Russell cannot show me his soul not because he hasn't one, but because the word "soul" cannot be given a meaning by reference to anything observable. But what do you mean by "observable"? Can the word *"observable"* be given a meaning by reference to anything observable? And to what must we refer the second word "observable" in the latter sentence to give a meaning to the first word "observable" in that sentence?'

He made himself more comfortable, and continued:

'Pölätüomism maintains: The word "onion" can be given a meaning by reference to something observable. But the word "observable" can only be given a meaning by reference to your activity. And here I score my first point: If the word "observable" can be given a meaning by reference to your activity, why, pray, cannot the word "soul" be given a meaning by reference to my activity?'

'Because your activities cannot be given a meaning by reference to anything that can be given a meaning by reference to those things by reference to which meanings are given to my activities,' the boy said. He had now taken a length of rope from the pocket of his short white trousers, a pencil, a nail, a handkerchief with a skull and crossbones inked on it, an empty lipstick-container, a box of matches, one threepenny bit, a soiled notebook, a magnetic needle, a magnifying glass, and a toy-pistol.

'Bang! Bang! Bang! Bang!' he started to shoot, and the smell of sulphur filled the room.

'He makes me angry!' he pointed his toy-pistol at the Cardinal. 'He makes me angry, and I don't like it. So I must get rid of it in some harmless way, mustn't I? That's what toy-pistols are for, aren't they? When I hear him say that Science is a part of Religion, it makes my finger press the trigger of my pistol!'

'Which doesn't wound the validity of our statement,' Pölätüo retorted. 'Science is that part of Religion which deals with the Universe as it enters our body through our external integument. Here I would extend the meaning of the term "integument" to the surface of your alimentary and respiratory canals, so that an aspirin tablet or a safety pin swallowed by you, and a dentist's finger manipulating in your mouth, could be regarded as being observable outside your body. They supply you with Indirect Knowledge of the Universe. But what about the toothache you feel *before* you go to the dentist? Is it not observable? I mean: not the tooth but the ache. And what about that something that makes you accept 4 as an answer to the question 2+2=?? and the feeling of bliss you experience when you find the answer? Is it not observable? I mean: the bliss, not its cause. And what about a feeling of Symmetry, aesthetic or otherwise, which some call a sense of justice and which Socrates called the harmonious balance between all the other virtues? Do they not supply you with Direct Knowledge about the Universe?'

'But if that's how you describe it, then your soul is a mere constellation of emotions!' the boy exclaimed.

'And what about an onion?' asked Pölätüo. 'Isn't an onion a mere constellation of sensations? And if an onion, being a mere constellation of sensations, can, nevertheless, be epistemologically regarded as possessing an actual objective reality existing outside the body, why, pray, cannot the soul, being a constellation of emotions, be likewise regarded as possessing an actual objective reality existing inside the body?'

'Wait a moment,' the boy interrupted. 'I don't say that an onion has an objective reality existing independent of experience. If the reality of an onion is somehow different from the experience of an onion, then the noise: "reality" is meaningless, because it pretends to refer to more than is observable. And if the reality of an onion and the experience of an onion is the same, why use two terms for one thing? I can talk meaningfully about an onion because I can eat it and experience it through my smell and taste; but I cannot talk meaningfully about a soul because I cannot do anything with it.'

'You can have it purged through pity and fear,' the Cardinal said.

'My dear Pölätüo,' the boy replied condescendingly. 'Now you fall so low as to quote Aristotle. I know where my nose is and I can refer the word "onion" to certain of my nose's experiences so that the word "onion" acquires a meaning. But, though I can find out where my tooth is, I don't know how to refer the word "soul" to its ache in order for the word "soul" to cease to be meaningless.'

'Merciful God!' Pölätüo exclaimed. 'But if you cannot refer the word "soul" to your suffering, then it is impossible for you to refer the word "meaning" to the soul, and thus every statement you pronounce must necessarily be meaningless. For, to what else can you refer the word "meaning" if not to this quality peculiar to man, wherein he differs from animals, that he alone is endowed with the perception to distinguish right from wrong, justice from injustice? And if you cannot refer the word "meaning" to the soul, because you cannot refer the word "soul" to an ache, or to the bliss of 2+2 being 4, or to the feeling of symmetry, in the same way as you refer the word "onion" to its smell or taste, then your problem is not a problem of knowledge, but that of your abilities!

'Now, my son, let us suppose that I have received an education in which my sense of smell has been neglected on purpose, and that I am practically anosmatic. The fact that I cannot refer the words "smell of onion" to anything observable by me will not make those words meaningless to you. Even I, noticing that they are meaningful to you, shall come to the conclusion that something is wrong with the reality of my sense of smell, and not with the reality of the onion.

'Thus, pray, why should the fact that you cannot refer the word "soul" to anything observable by you make that word "soul" meaningless to me? And, seeing that it is meaningful to me, why do you not come to the conclusion that something is wrong with the education of your Direct Senses, and not with the reality of the Soul?'

'Bless you,' the boy sneered. 'Now you say that I can't smell, and don't know it!'

'Your visible nose is sharp and observing,' the Cardinal said. 'But your invisible nose is asleep, atrophied through lack of exercise.'

'Could you produce any proof that there is anything to be atrophied at all?' the boy asked.

'The only proof I can think of is to wake it up.'

'Can you do that?' the boy was looking straight into the Cardinal's eyes.

'I can,' Pölätüo said. Slowly he approached the boy and, standing in front of him, asked: 'Please, move your legs so that the joints between their upper and lower parts rest upon the floor and support your body. Si! Bene...'

The boy was honest and sincere. And he wanted to give the Cardinal's experiment a fair trial.

'Shut your indirect, bodily eyes now...' said the Cardinal.

'I cudgel my brains to think of absurdities, but reality outdoes me every time,' said Russell.

The boy shut his eyes.

'And try to isolate yourself from Indirect, visible, Reality.'

The boy set his teeth.

'Now, my son,' the Cardinal said, 'In nomine Patris, et Filii, et Spiritus Sancti, repeat after me: "I believe in one God, the Father Almighty, maker of heaven and earth, and of all things visible, and invisible..."'

That was how Cardinal Pölätüo had lost his left upper first premolar. Though it wasn't true that the boy had jumped on him 'like a wild cat,' or 'like a devil incarnate,' with his fists clenched as some people who didn't witness the scene want to have it. No. He had opened his eyes and said: 'Take off your jacket, Pölätüo,' and he had taken off his own. 'If you don't take off your jacket, I'll fight you with it on!' the boy persisted. But Pölätüo had no jacket. And his tooth hadn't exactly fallen out but had got loosened, and he had had to have it extracted later on. Furthermore, it may be worth recording that it had been the same day some twenty miles from Richmond, at Lady Eunice's country house at Maidenhead, on the eve of the Oxford and Cambridge boat race, that he had had a vision:

two men a Cardinal and a Philosopher up to the very top of the mountain wherefrom with perfect clarity the lakes and the villages and some tatters of pearly mist in the vales between the green patches of the hills and kitchen-gardens and the horizon far away and beneath far beneath the level of the soles of their boots and the morning sun a white bright disk but edgeless half of its luminosity in the rest of the sky all over the rest of the sky and the very top of the mountain the reddish earth with dark-green clasps of shrubbery and clusters of grass-blades at the edges their green obstinate purpose the dark-green will solitary and unyielding above the lazy mass of green leaves and twigs and green leaves on the slope down to the thick greenness of the bottom of the mountain towards the fields and woods and villages and the Cardinal and the Philosopher one beside the other on the top of the mountain their eyes four conical volumes of vision down from above through fathoms of soft transparent aether and space upon the aches and ill ages and fieldmice half a right angle down and urinate; they urinate profusely without intermission and the fluid in two parallel curves crystal clear like spring water down on to the emerald and silver orchard of lakes and villages and woods beneath the pearly mist of the ocean of air and eight circular rainbows two in each eye. 'I called you "Bertie" because I had reasons for not knowing how to address him whose name may be spelt "Mephistopheles",' thus he, the Cardinal. No nightingales in the air, an ibis only, on foot, down the path, to the village. The Philosopher's thought wave of Marlowe of whom he likes Tamburlaine the Great better, and of Goethe, of whom he likes nothing; and of Valéry, whose Faust is too far away across the Channel. 'I was once held up by a similar perplexity:' he says — 'I had to write to the Aga Khan, but I did not know how to begin. I thought the correct way would be "Your Divinity!" but something — perhaps a subconscious memory of the First Commandment — made me shrink from this.' The two pellucid streams continue through the ample aether, the divine air, and down on to Wordsworthian fields. 'Most Philosophers are prudes,' he adds, 'and I doubt if they will take as much pleasure as we do in the vision of us peeing into the landscape. Some may think,' he adds again, 'that your vision represents our desire for Greatness.' 'Who?,' asks the Cardinal, — 'Moses?'. 'No I meant Freud, and I strongly advise you to steer clear of him.' 'Freud!' cries the Cardinal, 'but you cannot call him a philosopher! Not you! Not him! He is the Albert Memorial! He is Biedermeyer! He is the greatest fraud ever perpetrated on to the confession-starved British public. Escaping from Marx, they disembarked in Freud. Jesus stood on the cinderpath, but they passed Him by; because you told them that there is no refuge in Him.' He pauses a moment, and then adds: 'You are old-fashioned. You don't believe in God.' The Philosopher smiles gently: 'This reminds me,' he says, 'of a remark of my grandmother's. She knew the Miss Berrys, who were friends of Horace Walpole, and she said to me: "They were very old-fashioned. They used to swear a little." No,' he now goes back to the Cardinal's remark, — 'I do not think people have ceased to be religious. On the contrary, they are more religious than ever. I think the trend towards religion is an outcome of the Russian Revolution and the fear of Communism and Nazism. The same thing happened in England after the French Revolution. People will not cease to be religious until there is more security in the world. And I am in some doubt as to the pleasure that one should derive from the substitution of the Vatican for the Kremlin.' 'Pleasure?,' the Cardinal asks rising his brows, — 'but surely you believe that 2+2 are 4 not because the proposition is pleasant but because it is true!' His hands being engrossed in peeing, he cannot support his words by a gesture, he therefore turns his head a little sideways and bespeaks the Philosopher thus: 'If you believe that 2 and 2 are 4, then you believe. And if you believe, you are not precisely an Unbeliever. And if you are not an Unbeliever, why do you not believe in God?' One of the streams of translucent liquid soars to a greater height, as the Philosopher turns to the Cardinal and speaks to him thus: 'I find the word "God" very convenient and use it often in private, en pantoufles. But I do not see what can be gained by the substitution of the word "God" for the word "Truth." Besides,' he adds, — 'of course, if I wanted to be fussy, I could argue as to the way the word "believe" is to be used. I think that the way you use the word is the usual way. But mine, (as for instance when I say: "But you do believe that the sun will rise tomorrow morning,") I think, is common among philosophers.' Now the other stream of translucent scentless liquid jets higher, and the top part of the parabola it in fact is displays the precious brilliance of a million glittering gems, as the Cardinal lifts for a moment one of his ringed hands and, touching his pectoral cross, speaks to the Philosopher as follows: 'I wish to demonstrate that things are not what they seem to be. You say: "Granted science is true, how do we know it to be true?" and you look around questioningly; searching for what? I wish to demonstrate that it is *you* who cannot answer your own question about science without resort to Belief, it is *you,* for whom Belief is the ultimate answer, and it is *I* who expect Nature to provide me with the Evidence that would support the Truth which I already know, and therefore it is *I* for whom Science is the ultimate resort. And if knowledge is stronger than belief, then belief supported by knowledge is stronger than knowledge supported by belief.' He drops his hand back to where it was before, and the glittering brilliance in the sky jerks into a second of a joyous, spasmodic excitement, as he clears his throat and continues thus: 'Indeed, if you are an Unbeliever not because you do not recognise the Mystery of the World but, on the contrary, because you feel the Mystery is of such Greatness that no Religion is big enough to assuage your Thirst for Understanding, — you are a Roman Catholic without knowing it.' He has paused a moment and now continues: 'Again: if you are an Unbeliever not because you *believe,* which you do not, that a dislike of wanton cruelty is a matter of taste, like a dislike of tomatoes, but merely because you cannot meet the *arguments* against absolute ethical values, which you say you cannot, — you are a Roman Catholic without knowing it.' Now the other parabola jostles the first one in the sky, but it does not go upwards, it goes sideways, and the encounter of the two fountains seems to simmer with the drops of water which, in their rise and fall, reflect and refract and disperse the rays of the sun and shine like a hovering nest of diamonds, displaying the prolificness and pugnacity that fills the air with a chirping ballet of transfigured rainbow-coloured sparrows. Once more, however, the Philosopher finds his way to speak, to pee, and to smoke his pipe, all at the same time, and he reasons thus coolly with the Cardinal: 'It seems to me, Your Eminence, that you have not exactly understood what I meant. You seem to have assumed that "I do not believe p" is equivalent to "I believe not-p." This is not the case where there is doubt or suspense of judgment. I think my use of "arguments" and "believe" expressed exactly what I meant. I meant to say that there are reasons for thinking ethical values not absolute — i.e., that this conclusion follows from other things which appear tolerably certain. But it is not arguments that incline me towards the view that ethical values *are* absolute. *If* this view is correct, it can only be in virtue of some ethical premiss which is not itself induced, sorry, I mean: deduced from anything else. This is part of a general semantic principle, namely, that if a term is undefined it cannot occur significantly unless in virtue of one or more unproved propositions in which it occurs. The question whether ethical values are absolute is the same as the question whether there is any ethical term which cannot be defined.'

The Cardinal takes a very deep breath through his nostrils. 'I did not expect,' he says, 'my victory to be so easy.' 'Victory?' says the Philosopher, 'Oh, dear dear!', but the Cardinal's mind will not go away from the track now, and the stream of translucent liquid rises into the sky and falls on to the silver and emerald landscape steadily according to the laws of ballistics, as he speaks to the Philosopher as follows: 'What you have just said has been known to the Church for ages. That ethical values are absolute. And that they are so in virtue of some Ethical Premiss which is not itself deduced from anything else, but has to be believed in. However, I am sure you will not think it presumptuous of me if I ask you to imagine now that you live among people who *are* capable of understanding the truth, but are *not* capable of knowing and using such words as "general semantic principle," "significantly," "defined and undefined," "proved and unproved," "deduced and induced," "ethical terms, values, premisses, and propositions," "absolute," "tolerably certain," "suspense of judgment." What would you do if you wished to impart to them the truth that you possess? Would you not be obliged to begin with the vocabulary they already use? Would you not be forced to start by choosing some of the words they understand and giving them Special Significance? Would *you* not, in those particular circumstances, make father into Father, and son into Son, and the breath your disciples draw into their lungs — into Holy Ghost? Would you not try to extract Goodness from good meat and good soil, and Badness from decay and disease, and Soul from person? And Order from comfort, and Law from order, and Sin from transgression? And Immortality from insatiability, and Love from lust, and Mercy from equality in randomness? And Revelation from the signal of the bugle sounded at the break of day, or from a "Eureka!" exclaimed by an Archimedes in his bath-tub, or a Newton under his apple-tree? And having thus created a vocabulary of notions out of what used to be merely a vocabulary of things and events, can you now deny that it may be used to find and express the truth?' The sparkling mist is still there as before, but the circular rainbows grow pale and disappear as the two streams wane and go down the breeze. 'Now,' says the Cardinal, 'if things are the other way round, if one lives among men who will not admit such words as "God," and "Good," and "Evil," and "Soul," and "Revelation," should one not try to use the words they accept in their vocabulary, if one wishes to impart to them the knowledge contained in one's true Faith? Should one not try to express one's true Faith in none other than those words which have remained in Philosophy after you have extruded the notions of good and evil from her, and made her indistinguishable from logic? And is not to attempt this task the purpose and the mission of Pölätüomism?' The breeze has changed direction and died out. A few drops of water which had fallen on their boots still glitter. But the sky is now clean and blue. 'I find your fallacies delightful,' the Philosopher says, lighting his pipe again. 'I wish that real Cardinals were half as intelligent.' 'Real Cardinals?!' Pölätüo exclaims as he adjusts his black robe with red piping, (it had been a long time since he gave up wearing breeches) 'Am I not real?,' he wants to ask, but he cannot. The Philosopher is not there. The vision on the mountain is spent. There is the writing desk in Lady Eunice's country house at Maidenhead, the Boat Race tomorrow, the river Thames in the window, the fountain pen in his right hand, the nib still touching the surface of a white sheet of paper. 'Which reality is real?' he asks, — himself this time.

There is a thick black dot under the nib of his pen. His left hand is pleasantly cool as it presses his cheek which is still sore. But now his right hand suddenly jerks. And it may be worth recording that it was the same evening, and night, and the morning of the next day, that he had added to his *Philosophy of Pölätüomism* the now famous paper: 'On the Reality of Soul and on the Reality of Onion,' wherein he wrote:

15

ON THE REALITY OF SOUL AND ON THE REALITY OF ONION

'Is it right that we send our missionaries to the Papuas or Muzimbas who, after all, have some sort of Direct Knowledge, and not to the Logical Positivists who have none? Is a logical positivist, who sees nothing, less blind than are aborigines who see light in the wrong place? And, therefore, shouldn't a method that would deal with them be worked out for the use of our missionaries?

For the purpose of discussion with intellectual heathens, but not necessarily otherwise, Pölätüomism distinguishes two realities:

A. Indirect Reality (iR), or the reality of the onion; It consists of what we observe by means of the outer end of our senses, and the sum of our observations we shall call Indirect Knowledge.

B. Direct Reality (dR), or the reality of the soul. It consists of what we observe by means of the inner end of our senses, and the sum of our observations we shall call Direct Knowledge.

The Relation iR→dR is called by Pölätüomism:
Relativity of Reality (Я of R)
and we propose it as the subject of this chapter.

It has been, till now, more or less tacitly assumed
that
Reality (R) either is or is not.
We do not see why that should necessarily be so.
On the contrary,
Pölätüomism assumes
that:

§I. On the degree of Reality

1. *Reality is not governed by the All-or-None Law*
1a. *There is no reason why a thing must be either real or not real.*
1b. *There is no reason why things should not have different degrees of Reality.*
2. *The degree of reality of a thing depends either on the nature of the thing, or on the nature of the observer, or on the nature of language.*
2a. *It is by nature of the thing that the reality of a howling dog is greater than the reality of music, for the dog is an agglomeration of a greater number of sense stimuli than music. It is smellable, talkable to, biteable by, whereas music is only audible.*
2b. *It is by nature of the observer that the reality of an onion is greater for A who eats it than for B who looks at it from behind a window-pane, for A perceives it by many more senses than B does.*
2c. *It is by nature of language that the reality of an object can be of different degrees at the same time. When stripping an onion of the multitude of its skins, there is a moment when the onion ceases to be an onion and becomes skins-of-onion. At that stage its reality as Onion becomes smaller and smaller while its reality as Skins-of-Onion becomes greater and greater.*

§II. On the Relationship between two Realities

1. *The Relation between Indirect Reality and Direct Reality is:*

$$iR = \frac{P}{dR}$$

(where P stands for the Probability that a thing will happen to the observer), and it is called the Relativity of Reality (Я of R).

1a. Indeed, suppose somebody has raped a woman on the bank of the Mississippi; suppose a negro has already been lynched, and no more lynching is expected. Nevertheless, the reality of Lynch is greater for a black observer in Louisiana, than for a white poet laureate in Cambridge. Yet, —

1b. suppose it rains in Christendom, the reality of a Christian cold in the nose is greater if the observers happen to be Christians, it is less if somebody else is a Christian and it is less than any assignable magnitude or quantity if nobody is a Christian. Furthermore, —

1c. suppose we gradually and equally shorten all the four legs of a table. Its reality as a table lessens because the probability of our using it as a table lessens, but its reality as a bench may gradually increase because the probability of our using it as a bench increases.

2. As we intend to discuss here the reality of things actually happening to the observer, we can simplify the equation (§II.1.) by assuming the probability $P=1$.

2a. The Relation between the Indirect and Direct Reality of the things actually happening to the observer ($P=1$) is thus:

$$iR = \frac{1}{dR}$$

and it is called the Relativity of restricted Reality (Я of rR).

2b. It can be read: The reality of Onion increases as the reality of Soul decreases, or: The reality of Soul increases as the reality of Onion decreases.

3. Take two extreme cases: That of an animal; and That of a philosophical 'saint' Yogi. An animal's soul is sensitive and perishable, and for it Indirect Reality is all that exists ($iR \to \infty$). A philosophical 'saint' Yogi has united his individual Spiritual substance to that of the Universe, and for him Indirect Reality does not matter ($iR \to 0$). (That's why he can lie on a bed of nails.)

3a. Let us take the case of a 'saint' first. It would be a theoretical mistake to think that an increase in direct Reality alone causes an increase in true saintliness.

A Catholic saint, in contradistinction to a yogi, must be tried by both realities (dR and iR).

[Indeed, the Christian martyrs could not be said to have gained a promised hundred-fold reward in heaven, had the instrument used to mortify their flesh lost its indirect Reality, and become as harmless for their bodies as a bed of nails is for the body of a yogi.]

3b. Now, let us take the case of an animal. It would be a theoretical mistake to think that an animal, in having a perishable soul, resembles a logical positivist. An animal does not know that it does not have an immortal soul. A logical positivist does not know that he has one.

3c. In contradistinction to an animal, he (the logical positivist) maintains that both realities are not real, though one of them has meaning while the other is meaningless. Indeed, what forces him to reject Soul, is not so much the deficiency of his direct senses, as the quality of his logic, which would permit him to call a soul 'soul' if it had the characteristics of an onion, but forbids him to call a soul 'soul' because it has the characteristics of a soul.

3d. We have already seen that neither a yogi (*3a*) nor an animal (*3* and *3b*), nor a logical positivist (*3c*) can achieve the balance of the two Realities, iR and dR. The same is valid for a socialist. And, indeed, this is the true elucidation of the *Encyclical Quadragesimo Anno which says: 'no good Catholic can be a Socialist in the true sense.'* How could he, if a socialist is concerned with one reality while a Catholic must be concerned with both.

[It would be improper to augment unduly either of the two Realities. And if a bigoted woman were to try to repent a venial sin with the self-abasement and mortification appropriate to a mortal sin, she would distort the balance just as much in one direction (dR>iR) as by becoming a socialist she would distort it in another (iR>dR).]

4. The Roman Catholic balance of the two Realities is possible to achieve; it is commended; and it can be expressed by the equation: $iR=dR$

4a. but we already know from (*2a*) that:

$$iR = \frac{1}{d}R$$

4b. It follows that
　　$dR = 1/iR;$　　　　$dR^2 = I;$　　　　$dR = \pm\sqrt{I};$　　　　$dR = \pm I$
4c. Similarly
　　$iR = 1/dR;$　　　　$iR^2 = I;$　　　　$iR = \pm\sqrt{I};$　　　　$iR = \pm I$
4d. Therefore let both realities be greater than zero,
5. and the Equation Catholic for the Relativity of rReality assumes the form:

$$I = \frac{I}{I}$$

5a. (whose similarity to the shape of the Cross may or may not be accidental).

§III. On the Three Realities.

1. Indirect Reality is not made by anybody; nor is it created or begotten.
2. Direct Reality is from indirect Reality: not made, or created, but begotten.
3. Language Reality (lR) is from dR and iR: not made, not created, but proceeding from.

　　[NB. It will be noticed that the Equation for the Relativity of restricted (r) Reality does not contain a symbol for the Reality of Language (lR). This is as it should be, as the Reality of Language possesses a peculiar quality of assuming $lR = O$ when it is being added to something; while it assumes $lR = 1$ when something is multiplied or divided by it. Thus, whether we write $R = 1/iR + lR$ or $iR = 1/dR \cdot lR$, the final result will always be: $iR = 1/dR;$]

§IV. On the specific tactics to be used by Missionaries.

1. A missionary going to logical positivists ought to be fully prepared to use mathematical symbols in discussing the highest mystery of the faith.
1a. Do missionaries not learn savage tongues, and do they not translate into them the Holy names of the Trinity? Why should mathematical symbols be considered less worth using?
2. If God sacrificed His Son and His Son sacrificed Himself for the sake of

mankind, should we think They would mind if a missionary, for the specific purpose of converting a logical positivist, were to sacrifice the sound of Their names, by saying: iR, dR, and lR, instead of: Father (§III.1.), Son (§III.2.), and Holy Spirit (§III.3.), — if the Truth beneath the sound remains the same?

2a. THE QUESTION IS: *Whether the Truth remains exactly the same after the sound of the symbol has changed?*

THE ANSWER IS: *No, it does not remain exactly the same; it remains the same with a difference.*

2b. THE QUESTION IS: *What is that difference?*

THE ANSWER IS: *A Holy Name implies a Person; a Mathematical Symbol does not.*

2c. THE QUESTION IS: *Is that difference significant, and, if so, why?*

THE ANSWER IS: *The difference is significant: Person explains the nature of things; Nonperson — does not.*

2d. THE QUESTION IS: *Is every logical positivist capable of grasping the idea of Person?*

THE ANSWER IS: *Yes. If he be a mammal. God made every mammal infant helpless and dependent for the supply of its needs on its parent. Furthermore, God made their childish emotions of helplessness and dependence persist in grown up men. That's how He, in His Infinite Wisdom, provided men with what they can experience Him with. And that is how the Indirect Knowledge of the earthly father is trans-substantiated into the direct knowledge of the Heavenly Father. Therefore: if a logical positivist is a mammal, and capable of recollecting his childish experiences, then it must follow that he is also capable of grasping the idea of Person.*

2e. THE QUESTION IS: *In what sequence should a missionary proselytize a logical positivist? Should the latter be made first to recollect his childish experiences and thus grasp the idea of Person, and only then be taught the Equation; or should this order be reversed?*

THE ANSWER IS: *This order should be reversed. He should first be taught the Equation, then he should be made to see that, though it is true, yet, as it stands, it does not replace his feeling of not understanding the nature of things by a feeling of understanding the nature of things, that it does not fill his loneliness. But that it would do so if he were to accept the Elements of the Equation as representing Persons.*

3. *In Brief: To understand the nature of things, a logical positivist must be made to understand Persons. Before he understands Persons, he must be made to understand the Equation. Before he understands the Equation, he must be made to understand the Elements of the Equation, lR, dR, and iR.*

3a. *He understands the symbol 'lR' (Language Reality), though only as something which can be referred to iR (indirect Reality).*

3b. *He understands the Symbol 'iR,' though only as something to which lR can be referred.*

3c. *But he claims not to understand the symbol 'dR' (direct Reality), as he has never experienced any dR to which he could refer it.*
Thus,

4. *— the first task of a missionary going to a logical positivist is to make him experience dR.*

4½ NOW THE QUESTION IS: *What can be done to make him experience dR?*

4¼ BEFORE WE CAN ANSWER THIS QUESTION, *let us investigate a contrary case, that of the philosophical 'saint' yogi (§II.3) who doesn't experience any thing apart from direct Reality, ignoring the iR of his bed of nails.*

4¼a THE QUESTION IS: *What can be done to make him (yogi) perceive indirect Reality?*
THE ANSWER IS: *One should try to augment the degree of reality of his bed of nails.*

4¼b THE QUESTION IS: *Can that be done by augmenting the number of nails he is lying on?*
THE ANSWER IS: *No. Augmenting the number of nails would diminish the pressure of each nail exerted on his epidermis and thus the degree of reality of the bed of nails would fall instead of rise.*

4¼c THE QUESTION IS: *Can it be done by reducing the number of nails he is lying on?*
THE ANSWER IS: *No. As soon as we reduce the number of nails so that they start piercing his external integument, his sense of touch will give place*

to his sense of pain, the function of which is to cleanse his heart in the springs of pure contrition and thus supply him not with Indirect but again with Direct Knowledge of the Universe.

4¼d THE QUESTION IS: *How to raise the degree of reality of the bed of nails?*
THE ANSWER IS: *Pölätüomism maintains that the reality of a thing increases not so much with the increase of the intensity of the stimulus it supplies, as with the number of senses through which it is being perceived (§I.2b).*

4¼e THE QUESTION IS: *How to make a yogi perceive the bed of nails through a greater number of senses?*
THE ANSWER IS: *By augmenting the number of characteristics which could be perceived by his senses (§I.2a).*

4¼f Thus, if we want a yogi to perceive the Reality of Onion, we should make his bed of nails smell, dance, be savoury, experienceable sexually, furnished with oral commentary, and it should stand in front of a mirror in which the yogi could perceive it by means of his sight. It is the independence of various observations which ensures the real (non-ad-hoc) character of the Reality of Onion.

4¼g Now, if a yogi can be persuaded to notice the Reality of Onion by our augmenting the number of senses involved in his perceiving it, then, surely, — the logical positivist can be persuaded to notice the Reality of Soul by our reducing the number of senses involved in his perceiving an onion.

4¼h THE QUESTION IS: *How to reduce the number of senses involved in perceiving an onion?*
THE ANSWER IS: *An Onion possesses the greatest indirect Reality when it sings, smells, moves, is looked at, savoured, experienced sexually, and accompanied by an oral commentary. Now, by reducing these qualities one after another we can cause a decrease of the indirect Reality of the onion, and therefore an increase of its direct Reality (§II.2a).*

4¼i We have already learned (§I.2b) that the indirect Reality of an onion is less when the onion is placed behind a window-pane. It is still less when it is not an actual onion but its cinematographic representation, and it diminishes further as we proceed from sound films to silent films, from the screen to a *photograph, and from the photograph to a hand-made picture.*

Now, we shall not be arguing here whether the reality of the onion printed on an envelope in which gardeners sell seeds is or is not less than the reality of a photograph. Neither shall we argue whether the reality of a still-life painted by a Dutch old master is or is not less than the reality of the said envelope; nor, whether that of an impressionistic onion is or is not less than the old master's. What it seems legitimate to say, however, is that the indirect Reality of a Cubist Onion is much less than any of the above mentioned, and that as we proceed to so called 'Abstract' Onions their indirect Reality begins to approach the minimum, *in consequence of which, according to the equation for the χ of rR, its direct Reality will be rising towards the* maximum.

4¾h *And thus we have arrived at a point where we are prepared to answer* THE QUESTION RAISED IN 4½.

5. THE ANSWER IS: *The first task of the missionary going to Logical Positivists is to treat them intensely with Abstract Painting, so that they experience the direct Reality which is necessary for understanding the Equation, which is necessary for understanding Persons, which is necessary for understanding the Nature of Things, which they must do before the claims of the Church Catholic are brought to their notice by the missionary so that they may die in communion with the See of Rome, as extra Ecclesiam Catholicam nulla datur salus.'*

1 6

'A sales representative, Robert George Foster, aged 47, of Park Avenue, Driftfield, broke down at Hull today when he described how, waking at 5 a.m. with a pain in his neck, he groped in the dark and grasped the eight-inch long blade of a sheath knife which an intruder was holding over him. The horn-handled knife was an exhibit in the case in which William Trevor Lynch, of Keighley, and James Nigel Saunders, of Blacon, Cheshire, both aged 20, were jointly accused of robbery with violence at Hull and Lynch with the further charge of wounding Mr. Foster with intent to do grievous bodily harm.

'Describing Mr. Foster's injuries Mr. Croft, for the prosecution, said the gash two inches and a half long cut the external jugular vein and missed the carotid artery by a fraction. "If the knife had gone a fraction of an inch deeper Mr. Foster might have bled to death and Lynch would have been guilty of capital murder whether he intended to kill Mr. Foster or not," Mr. Croft added.'

The golden tooth had been in the Cardinal's jaw for the last ten or twelve years, yet the memory of the gap he had had between his canine and second premolar was still there in the tip of his tongue. He pressed the button and the spittoon of bottle-green glass slid back into its nest in the armchair. '... *nulla datur salus.*' He put away a copy of the London *Times,* looked again through the pages of the last Chapter, and a new idea possessed him:

'But if…' he began to arrange the words in his mind so that they would not only express but order the thoughts now crowding into it. 'But if that which is experienced by *more* senses is *more* real, if I must have evidence of more senses than one to ratify and confirm a thing's reality, then what will happen to the reality of God?

'I feel pain, therefore there is a sharp knife. Or neuritis.

'I feel elated, therefore there is God.

'But an apple that is identifiable optically only, (and not in any other way) is not an apple but a Picture of an Apple. Is a Pain a picture of a Knife?

'To locate, to identify a knife, to know that it is Knife (and not neuritis) that is waking me at 5 a.m. with a pain in my neck, I need the corroboration of other witnesses, of other senses, besides my feeling of pain. I need to hear the intruder, I need to smell his breath, I need to see the knife's blade and its horn handle. Yet, whom do I call as witnesses to corroborate the testimony of my feeling of Elation, and thus help me to locate and identify Him?'

Pölätüo half-closed his eyes.

And then he said with deep emotion:

'"I charge you, O daughters of Jerusalem, if ye find my beloved, that ye tell him, that I am sick of Love."

'Yet, who *are* the other witnesses besides my feeling of Love?'

And in the light diffracted by the snow-white eyelashes of his half-closed eyes, he descried a host of people in white cassocks and frocks, who were all Abstract painters and were rushing to convert some Logical Positivists. They were rushing and yet, at the same time, they were standing in front of their Easels, and covering white squares of canvas with white squares of paint. And all the canvases (not the painters) were shouting, one louder than the other, one and the same thing, over and over again. And the thing they were shouting was: 'Pölätüo is sick of Love.' 'Pölätüo is sick of love.'

And Pölätüo said:

'Yea, Ye are the Witnesses of Elation. But where are the others?'

And the painters disappeared, and Euclid and Euler and Cantor, and Thomas Aquinas and Russell and a great multitude of black-jacketed men took their place. And the first said: 'The sum of the three angles of a plane triangle is a straight angle.' And the second said:

'$\frac{a+b^n}{n} = x$ donc Dieu existe, répondez!' And the third said: 'an infinite collection is one which has parts containing as many terms as the whole collection contains.' And Thomas Aquinas said: 'I have discovered the Impossibility of Infinite Regress and called and identified it as God, therefore God exists.' And Russell said: 'He is ignorant of mathematics. There is no good reason why a regress should be rejected. The series of rationals greater than zero up to and including one is infinite, and yet has no first member.'

And Pölätüo said: 'You are not Witnesses you are Judges. And what I am asking for is evidence of His reality and not proof of His existence.'

And the Mathematicians and Reasoners disappeared, but the space in front of his half-closed eyes filled again with a procession of multiheaded mankind. And the first multiheaded man said: 'I was the first scientists to put forward a hypothesis in which it was suggested that the world was created. Which was not such an obvious thought at the time the covenant of God with the Hebrews was set forth in the Bible, as it seems to have become later. And this hypothesis has not yet been falsified, not really. And I was the first scientists to make a hypothesis about the manner of the creation of the earth, and of the sun, moon, and stars, and of fish and fowl, of beasts and cattle, and of man, in this sequence, and whatever we may say of it today, when translating it into modern language, it was I, first, who enquired. Though it was not I who codified it into a Dogma.'

And another multiheaded man came forward from the middle of the procession and said: 'I am the scientists of the Turning Point. I was the first ones who, for the verification of their hypothesis, looked not into the codified accounts made by their predecessors but into the book of Nature spread around.

'You condemned me to the stake. If you were the Possessor of the Truth, you had no reason to do so.

'Because the Nature of Truth is such that everything that contradicts it is not truth; and everything that doesn't, is.

'And the findings of science are true, unless they are contradicted by other findings of science;

'Therefore: scientific truths that are not contradicted by other scientific truths, do not contradict the Truth;

'Therefore: if you are the Possessor of the Truth, you must not condemn to the stake, but welcome the Witnesses who come to you from Scientific Laboratories, whatever they bring in their hands, whether viruses, atoms, or inertiae. Whether conditioned reflexes or social justice. Their discoveries are Revelations, and their writing letters to the Editor of "Nature" is a religious activity.'

Jonathan entered, carrying a glass of warm homogenized milk to put into the thermostatic compartment of the armchair, and the procession of mankind dispersed.

Cardinal Pölätüo divided a page in two, and wrote as follows:

St. Thomas Aquinas	Pölätüomism
The Christian thinker must not divide his allegiance between the philosophers & Christianity but discover the meaning of reason	*The Christian thinker must not divide his allegiance between the scientists & Christianity but discover the meaning of research*
the conditions of true thinking	*the conditions of true observation*
learn to be a philosopher	*learn to be a scientist*
discover the philosopher within the Christian man in order to achieve the harmony	*discover the scientist within the Christian man in order to achieve the harmony*
between Reason & Revelation.	*between Reality & Revelation.*

'Reason, Reality, Revelation,' Pölätüo said, and felt desperately dissatisfied.

Through the white eye-lashes of his half-closed eyes, he now descried *Three* little Black-and-Tan Manchester Terriers, chasing each other's tails in a circle.

Part Three

A Selection of Letters

Written by Cardinal Pölätüo

to his Biographer

I

Palazzo d'Ormespant,
Verumontanum,
Roma

Dear Son,

You ask us who were the Abstract Painters we mentioned in our Speculation on the Reality of Onion and on the Reality of Soul. We saw them in our dream and cannot be very certain as to their names. There was, however, one who stood among them but was different. His picture was a picture of reality. It represented a joyful French monk and a succulent leg of English beef. 'Are you a Karl Marx?' we asked the painter. 'I am not,' he answered. 'My name is William Hogarth, and I am a painter of Reality.' 'And what is Reality?' we asked him. His answer was what we least anticipated, and at the time we did not realise that it was the answer to our question. 'A line of beauty,' he said. 'Such a line must express symmetry, variety, uniformity, simplicity, intricacy, and quantity. And a painting, whether it is a painting of a leg of beef or of the line itself, becomes beautiful as and because it exhibits this line.'

We didn't tell you about this sequel to our vision before, Dear Son, because we did not wish to complicate any further the difficult problems which our confrontation of the Onion with the Soul has given birth to.

We must put this letter aside now, Jonathan is rushing across the room like a hare and the humming of his old hoover has become the high-pitched squeak of unoiled door-hinges.

> Ever yours,
> Pölätüo,
> Card.

II

> Palazzo d'Ormespant,
> Verumontanum,
> Roma

Dear Son,

    I'm sorry if I gave you the impression that something had happened to our dear Jonathan. No, nothing has happened to Jonathan, and nothing to his old hoover! It is the growing slowness of my life that makes them appear so quick. My pulse beats forty times a minute. I open my eyes in the morning and before I have time to notice my presence in this world, the sun sets and the day is gone. To my entourage I must look like a very old tortoise; they — to me, — as if the projecting machine has gone mad, and forced personages on a screen to run about at twice their normal speed.

    Undoubtedly, I am the oldest man in the world. Has God forgotten about me? No. Rather, I think, I have not yet accomplished some special task He has for me, and He, in His infinite patience, still expects me to perform what, unknown to me, must be the purpose of my existence. What is it? If only I knew what it is, what bliss it would be to fulfill it and be allowed to leave this mortal world for ever.

    As you may know, Thomas Aquinas died when he was engaged in interpreting the beauty of Solomon's Song.

I wonder... I wonder...

> Yours ever,
> Pölätüo,
> Card.

III

Palazzo d'Ormespant,
Verumontanum,
Roma.

Dear Son,

Some very bad news is unfortunately all I can send you this time. Not unexpectedly, it is about Father Douglas. Had it happened when I was younger, I would either have been filled with remorse or laughed heartily. Now, I am only sad. Father Douglas finished the Dictionary of Dreams. I am finding that it has been done in a very scholarly manner and even with some kind of gusto. Yet Father Douglas himself disappeared. Without leaving a word. I looked through the Dictionary, and I can't say I don't see why he has done so.

Even though I warned him before I put this heavy weight on to his narrow shoulders, I feel somewhat responsible for him and I would like to know what sort of course he will take. My information is that he fled to London. If Destiny wills that your paths should cross, please tell him that my blessing follows him and please let me have some news about him.

Yours ever,
Pölätüo,
Card.

IV

Palazzo d'Ormespant,
Verumontanum,
Roma.

Dear Son,

I too attempted to translate the beauty of the Song of Songs. Yet, unlike Thomas Aquinas, I am still alive; I must conjecture, therefore, that my effort, and expectation, and desire, were misdirected. Posterity may think they were foolish. It would take too long to tell how the idea, or shall I call it temptation, came to me to use Father Douglas's Dictionary for the interpretation of the Song. A most arduous task. And not at once did I realise the depthless futility of it.

My pulse today is 38, but Dr. G. says not to worry. What an expression!

Yours ever,
Pölätüo,
Card.

V *Palazzo d'Ormespant,*
Verumontanum,
Roma.

Dear Son,

No, no, no! Why repeat the most fraudulent piece of nonsense that has ever infested your universities? Namely: that there is an unpassable gap between empirical statements and ethical statements; in other words: that it is illegitimate to reason from 'IS' to 'OUGHT.' What a splendid fallacy! Of course, it is improper to reason from 'is' to 'ought.' The proper reasoning ought to be and is from 'OUGHT' to 'IS.' And this, of logical necessity, applies to both empirical and ethical statements:

A released stone <u>ought</u> to fall in order to <u>be</u> a stone within the meaning of the accepted Gravitational System of Co-ordinates; —

A man <u>ought</u> to love his neighbour in order to <u>be</u> a man within the meaning of the Christian System of Co-ordinates*; —

And it is neither oughtness nor beingness but a Gravitational System of Co-ordinates (any gravitational system), and the Christian System of Co-ordinates (the Catholic system), that the Church claims to be absolute.

Now, which of the two systems of co-ordinates is prior in importance, a Gravitational or the Catholic?

Consider the flight of an arrow. The day when some men discovered that its velocity does NOT *depend on its destination and that the arrow will pierce a good man with the same force as a bad man, — that day the very heart was carved out of the philosophy of Secular Humanism cum Naïve Rationalism.*

The fact that the goodness of the target cannot be inferred from the velocity of the arrow has slain the philosophy of all Natural Moralists. And it was in the funeral oration for them that their logicians invented that unbridgeable gap between empirical and moral statements.

---

* ('Se d'alcuno s'intende, o legge, che, senza alcuno suo commodo, o interesse, ami più il male, che il bene, si deve chiamare bestia, e non uomo, poichè manca dell' appetito naturale,' said the lieutenant-general of the papal army, Guicciardini).

Let us examine the problem coolly. Let us imagine that the arrow DOES *stop in its flight whenever a St. Sebastian happens to be its target. Do you see the* LOG-ICAL *impossibility of such an arrangement? Don't you see that if arrows were to stop in their flight when St. Sebastians are targets, it would be impossible for St. Sebastians to become martyrs? Therefore, if St. Sebastian is a martyr, as he undoubtedly is, and if the word 'martyr' implies 'being pierced by an arrow,' as it undoubtedly does, then the indiscriminate flight of the arrow is a* LOGICAL *necessity. And, as St. Sebastian's martyrdom takes place within the Ethical (Christian) System of Co-ordinates, and the indiscriminate flight of the arrow — within the physical (gravitational) System of Co-ordinates, then Is not the latter the logical necessity of the former, and the former, therefore, prior in importance? And, furthermore, if one is a logical necessity issuing from the other, as we have just demonstrated that it is, then Does not the famous Gap invented by your clever philosophers vanish?*

Indeed, where your philosophers err is where they assume that an 'OUGHT' *('you ought to love your neighbour') presupposes the existence of men, while an* 'IS' *('the sun is in the sky,' 'the arrow is in flight') does not presuppose the existence of men. This is an error. Both do:*

By the Grace of God, the World is divided into Things by our Minds, and to talk about entities qua entities as existing in a mindless world is beyond my comprehension: because it is our Mind which, by the Grace of God and by the Mercies of Jesus Christ, contains in itself the Systems of Co-ordinates which decide not only what to distinguish within the world as the Sun, or Inertia, or a Neighbour, or Love; but also what to call 'absolute,' and 'objective,' and 'superhuman,' and 'eternal.' Because none of these things can be understood apart from a system of co-ordinates.

It is, therefore, defenceless of your philosophers to maintain that ethical values are absolute because there are some ethical terms which cannot be defined. What they do not see, like a fish that does not see the water in which it swims, is Systems of Co-ordinates*. Indeed, ethical terms are as well defined within the

---

**Berkeley said: 'Let us imagine two globes and that besides them nothing else material exists, then the motion in a circle of these two globes round their common centre cannot be imagined. But sup-*

Ethical system of co-ordinates as physical terms are within the Physical. Your philosophers forget that a stone is not a stone in order to fall, but that it falls in order to be a stone. And that a Christian is not a Christian in order to do good, but that he does good in order to be a Christian.

Yours ever,
Pölätüo,
Card.

P.S.: *Whatever the soul is, what it does is at least accompanied by some changes in the body.*

Therefore: patterns that occur in the body (say: electron patterns in the brain) refer to both what is called physical & spiritual, or existential & ethical worlds.

Therefore: a list of patterns can be thought as a vocabulary suitable for describing both worlds. Therefore: there exists at least one one-language in which both worlds can be described.

Therefore: the divergence, or the Gap between the two is what we have, fallaciously, arrived at, and not what was there primarily at the point of departure.

---

pose that the heaven of fixed stars was suddenly created and we shall be in a position to imagine the motion of the globes by their relative position to the different parts of the heaven.' This, we maintain, applies to all relationships. The minimum number of terms in any relationship is 3. A relation aRb is a relation between 3 terms. The third is hidden in R. Theology knew it long ago. She discovered it in the Trinity, which, for the present purpose, can be defined as that minimum number of terms which can make a monotheistic system consistent within itself.

VI

Palazzo d'Ormespant,
Verumontanum,
Roma.

Dear Son,

I am delighted to hear that you enjoyed reading the copy of the Dictionary I sent you.* I studied it again myself and dared to compare it with the content of my own dreams. With some surprise, I found that instead of dreaming symbols I usually dream what we may call 'real things.' E.g. I don't remember ever having seen an umbrella in my dreams, but I certainly HAVE *seen that which is symbolised by umbrellas. At first this discovery made me rejoice, as I thought it proved my lack of hypocrisy and a certain courage to see things uncensured. Then, however, I recollected the author's thesis that wish-fulfilment is the basis of all dreams and, I confess, it disconcerted me for a moment; that's to say, until dear Father Slonimski suggested that, as I don't dream in symbols, the Dictionary should be reversed for me, and my seeing in a dream e.g. a male organ, or a beautiful bosom, should be interpreted as a wish to buy an umbrella or a kilogram of apples, which are very innocent wishes and can easily be satisfied. Every morning, for the last fortnight, I have been supplying Jonathan with a special shopping list, and my antechamber is already half filled with a quantity of most useless objects. Today I acquired a dinner table, which reminded me of my poem (which you seemed to like) and of my wish to invite the Archbishop of Merangue to dinner. I shall do so very soon.*

I am astounded by your news about Father Douglas. A successful psychoanalyst! What a career for an unfrocked priest!

Yours ever,
Pölätüo,
Card.

---

* (see: Appendix)

VII

Palazzo d'Ormespant,
Verumontanum,
Roma.

Dear Son,

The news about poor Father Douglas affected me more deeply than I at first thought possible (considering that my pulse slows down to 37 these days). I wonder whether the most evil thing in the world today is not exactly that art of psycho-assaying by which Father Douglas has become seduced, the art of levelling down our spiritual substances by reconciling them not with God but with the platitudinousness of the world as it is made by men, the same men who then ask Father Douglas to reconcile them with what they themselves have created. What a vicious circle!

Yet this melancholy day has not been without its bright moments; since Father Douglas left me, Princess Zuppa (whom I believe you have met) comes more often to visit me and to supervise my new secretary. Today, when taking her leave, she knelt and kissed my ring, leaving the pink impression of her lipstick on my hand, as she usually does. At the same time, however, my other hand of its own accord gently touched her body. It was a moment of an absolute and pure beauty; a moment which gave birth to an awareness of the physical existence of the universe, the awareness of such overwhelming innocence that it exorcised the shadows thrown on my thoughts by the news of poor Father Douglas's psychoanalytic exertments, and quickened my pulse to 39. When Princess Zuppa left, Jonathan wiped off what I believe was the 'rose-nacré' lipstick butterfly on my hand by means of cotton-wool soaked in eau-de-cologne. It seems that as my sense of smell becomes paler, the remembrance of some fragrance smelt in the past becomes stronger and, what happens to me now is that when I look at a rose, I see the one in front of me and feel the fragrance of a rose I admired before the Boer War. So it is now with the smell of eau-de-cologne. I feel it only very faintly in my nostrils, yet it invokes an inner fragrance which I am sure I am experiencing more strongly now than I did on the original occasion. I feel it at this very moment, yet my memory fails me. I see a dove-grey sheet of note-paper. Yet nothing is written on it.

Caro figlio, my pulse quickened to 39, and the day which was so melancholy at the start, has become crowded with events of some brightness. I have finally fixed the day for the Archbishop of Merangue's dinner (next Friday) and so I summoned my cook and read him a chapter on cooking fish from Brillat-Savarin, — 'Physiologie du Goût.' It gave me intense pleasure — the few pages of beautiful prose in their original French. Viz: 'Méditation: § vi Du poisson 40. — Réflexion philosophique 42.'

Yours ever,
Pölätüo,
Card.

VIII

Palazzo d'Ormespant,
Verumontanum,
Roma.

Dear Son,

Your further news about Father Douglas's activities has filled our heart with sadness. He has, you say, restrung his aesculapian lyre by putting a range of Christian catholic symbols in place of Freudian symbols and is now using the former to cure his clientèle of their higher-income group illnesses. Let me explain why this news is so painful for me.

'Existence,' dolce figlio, is an unnecessary metaphysical adjunct to some sets of qualities which alone are sufficient to make a thing real for us. And if things which we ordinarily call bread and wine do in special circumstances, at least for some of us, display the qualities of the Very Body and Blood, they are the real Body and Blood. And if they are the real Body and Blood, it is erroneous to say that they are symbols. Because a symbol is never the thing it stands for. Were it the thing it stands for, it would be the thing not the symbol that stands for it. Therefore they are not symbols. And if He displays the qualities of the Lily of the Valleys, then He is the Lily of the Valleys and the Lily of the Valleys is not a symbol. Nor was the Assumption of the Blessed Mary, Ever-Virgin, Mother of God, Symbolic — it was Corporeal, which is very well known to Father Douglas, as he was here with me at the Feast of All Saints 1950, when the doctrine was defined, and he knows that on whosoever presumes to contradict the definition, the verdict is: Let him be anathema. Therefore, what Father Douglas is doing is playing not with christian symbols, which would be blasphemy, but with christian realities which is sacrilege.

(We must do something about it.)

> Yours ever,
> Pölätüo,
> Card.

IX

> Palazzo d'Ormespant,
> Verumontanum,
> Roma.

Dear Son,

Thank you for your description of Prof. Ryle's cake. No, I should not think that his way of dividing it among children would affect Thomas Aquinas's Impossibility of Infinite Regress, and it certainly does not reflect on the five loaves and two fishes which Christ divided between a great but finite number of 5,000 men who were all filled.

You can, dear Son, break an army of soldiers into brigades, a brigade in regiments, a regiment into battalions, a battalion into companies, and so on till you come to a single soldier, and this soldier will still be a military unit. Now, our proposition is that you can divide the soldier in practice, but not in theory. You can cut him in two physically, to do so LOGICALLY, however, is absolutely impossible. Because, in whichever way you cut the soldier, across, or lengthwise, or from front to back, none of the two units into which you divide him will be a MILITARY unit. And similarly, when your Scientists break or smash a molecule of cake, or bread, or fish, — what the obstinacy of your philosophers continues to divide is no longer cake or bread or fish.

Now, dear Son, Pölätüomism suggests that what is good for fish, and bread, and cake, and the army, is also good for Time and Space. There is no logical necessity for their being continuous. We suggest that there is a smallest unit of space, and a smallest unit of time. And that even if you succeed in breaking them into bits in your laboratories, the bits are no more bits of space or bits of time than a bit of a soldier is a soldier. Therefore, the smallest unit of space and the smallest unit of time are each logically indivisible, even if they were divisible physically. Pölätüomism suggests that the size of the smallest unit of space is 10^{-32} of a cm. and the smallest unit of time is 10^{-32} of a second. This may not be exactly so, but it is the scientists' business to find the exact figures, not ours.

Now, what we have just said about the smallest units applies to the largest units as well. It is possible to imagine an elephant twice its normal size both physically and logically. Perhaps it may be possible to have it 10 times as tall. But to enlarge it 1000 times is logically impossible, because its weight would be 1,000,000,000 times as great, while its knees would be only 1,000,000 times stronger, and such an animal would have to change its anatomical shape to survive physically, and so it would no longer be an elephant; therefore, as he would no longer be an 'ELEPHANT,' it is logically impossible to have an elephant over a certain weight, even if physically it were possible to continue enlarging the animal.

Now, Pölätüomism suggests that what is good for an elephant is also good for Space and Time. There is no logical necessity for the universe to be Infinite. We suggest therefore that there is a biggest unit of Space and a biggest unit of Time, the biggest in the sense that if you endeavour to magnify it further the result will cease to be a unit of Space, or a unit of Time, just as the hyper-elephant ceases to be an elephant and becomes, — what?

Now, be reassured, dear Son, we do not intend to say that it becomes God, as some contributors to 'Fish' might venture to suggest. What we do state is merely that the above conception of the universe enables 1° Achilles to catch the Tortoise, 2° an arrow to fly, and 3° St. Thomas Aquinas to assert that FINITE Regress is a logical necessity, which assertion is the basis of his impeccable demonstration of the existence of God.

Yours ever,
Pölätüo,
Card.

X   *Palazzo d'Ormespant,*
Verumontanum,
Roma.

Dear Son,

You would not be reading this letter if it had not been for Dr. Goldfinger. (I think you have met him; he is Princess Zuppa's friend, the one she rescued during one of the recent wars from the cruel fate which threatened his race.) Now, if it hadn't been for him you wouldn't be reading this letter, because this letter wouldn't have been written. However, it is not for saving my life that I am grateful to him (and to Jonathan, with his usual presence of mind), but for saving me from dying a sudden death at the very moment when some perplexing information about my half-forgotten past came to my knowledge and disturbed the serenity of my thoughts. Yet let me start from the beginning.

You know how much I had been looking forward to dining with my good friend the Archbishop of Merangue. He came last Friday as arranged and we were most delighted to see each other. As he is (in my eyes) a comparatively young man, (born at the very end of the last century), and his life moves much more speedily than mine, we agreed at the very outset of our meeting to adjust the pace of our speech: I promised to speak as fast as I could and he as slowly as possible without inconveniencing himself unduly, and consequently, thanks to this little stratagem, our conversation proved to be most enjoyable to us both.

I told him what my views on poetry are. Poetry, I said, is a most repulsive profession; in which physiological and psychological tricks are craftily and fraudulently used to make us swallow and absorb such concepts as, if served prosaically, AU NATUREL, *would not be considered good enough by even the most stupid of human intellects. I was* NOT *talking of the Sacred Scriptures. The view that prophecies and miracles set forth and narrated therein are the fictions of poets was justly condemned in the* SYLLABUS OF ERRORS, *appended to an Encyclical* QUANTA CURA, *on the feast of the immaculate Conception 1864. I was talking about* POETRY. *To be more explicit: it was poets who invented the concept of beauty and embedded it in our civilisation. When God created light He saw that it was* GOOD, *it isn't said that He saw that it was* BEAUTIFUL. *It was poets who associated the notion of beauty they invented, with the holy concept of goodness, which association is contrary to what we learn from observation and causes much discomfort to every parish-priest, tempting him to infer the goodness or badness of his parishioners from the fairness or ugliness of their bodily appearance. Again: it was poets who accustomed us to associate the brightness and light of the sky with holiness and Heaven, which metaphor has caused us many theological problems. It was their adolescent imagination which took Pythagoras literally and painted a cosmos made of crystal spheres, whose subsequent breakage caused the first rift between the Church and the astronomers. 'Behold,' I said to my guest, the Archbishop, 'organised Christianity laid the foundations for present day civilisation, yet it was poetry which supplied it with those most unscientifically-baked bricks and metaphorical mortar which will continue to cause us much trouble. The advent of organised christianity killed poetry and kept it en-graved for a thousand years. But its seeds were left in the very masonry of our Vernacular and from these seeds, hélas, the Weed came into being again and grew right through the cracked body of our Edifice.'*

We were eating oysters (which both Brillat-Savarin and the Church classify as FISH*), when my dear friend the Archbishop said: 'You have just spread before me the peacock fan of your arguments against poetry. Yet, I understand that you yourself have written a poem and intend to recite it to me. How will you explain the contradiction?'*

To which I answered: 'There are three poets to which my diatribe does not apply. The first is Dante. Because the essential substance of his poetry is prose, and the poetic form — its mortal body. The second, for a similar reason, is a communist martyr, Majakovsky. Because with him too prose is the imperishable soul of his poems. It is IT *that determines the mortal layout of their shape. And the third, am I. Because my little poem is pure form. There is nothing in it. Not a thought. It is like an empty slipper, left by his Holiness on the footstool.'*

I moistened my lips with the remaining drop of Sauternes, and recited my little poem which you know:

*'Mascaróninopólevá
Cáscaróninopólevá
Láscaronínopólevá.'*

At this moment they brought *un brochet de rivière piqué, farci et baigné d'une crème d'écrevisses, secundum artem,* and laid it on the table between us.

'Beautiful,' said the Archbishop, though I was not quite certain whether what he said referred to the poem or the fish.

It was after this that the terrible thing happened. The Archbishop put his elbows on the table, hands upwards, as if he were measuring the length of a fish between his outstretched palms. He looked inspired. His wide-open eyes looked like two blue gates to Paradise when he took a deep breath, and said:

> 'Que ton coeur soit l'appât et le ciel, la piscine!
> Car, pécheur, quel poisson d'eau douce ou bien marine
> Égale-t-il, et par la forme et la saveur,
> Ce beau poisson divin qu'est JESUS, Mon Sauveur?'

I was savouring the beauty of these lines when I suddenly noticed that the Archbishop's face had grown very red.

'By whom is the verse?' I asked innocently.

His face now grew all pallid and wan.

'Guillaume Apollinaire,' he said.

When I heard this name I suddenly realised that I had never read anything by Apollinaire. This thought perplexed me in the extreme. The piece of Fish was already in my mouth. And there was a bone in the piece of fish. And the bone stuck in my throat.

You'll understand that I was not in a position to observe the sequence of events, which I reconstructed afterwards as follows: Both the Archbishop and Jonathan showed great presence of mind. The former hurried on his poor lame legs to my private Chapel to fetch the Holy Ointments, the latter rushed to fetch Doctor Goldfinger, who quite miraculously was just visiting our dear Princess Zuppa at her residence across the Via.

It seems that Dr. Goldfinger arrived before the Archbishop. Without any instruments, he put his long fingers very courageously into our orifice and took the bone out of our throat.

As to my dear friend the Archbishop of Merangue, he confessed to me afterwards that when he entered the chapel he stopped for a second to look at the floor.

He was certain it had been no more than two seconds, yet these two, and certainly no more than three seconds weighed upon his heart. It was the mosaic picture on the floor that stopped him. Which is strange, because the picture has been there for years now. I commissioned it, I remember, from a painter called Mondrian, a long time ago, when I was engaged in composing a set of tactical rules especially devised for the use of some missionaries, who were setting out to convert certain stubborn logical positivist aggregations. 'What do you want me to do?' the painter asked. 'I want you to make an abstract picture,' I said. 'What do you want me to abstract?' was his question, and I saw it was good. 'I want you to abstract this,' I said, and I recited:

> *'Filiae Jerusalem dicite dilecto meo,*
> *quia prae amore morior.'*

'What do you want me to abstract it from?' was his next question, and I saw it was very good. 'From the universe,' I answered. Upon which he set to work.

The floor of my chapel is white. And the whiteness of it is divided by two vertical black lines and four horizontal black lines, and it possesses in itself a large yellow square and a small blue rectangle. I like it: I like it because nothing in it represents anything, because nothing in it is a symbol of anything; it is what it is and nevertheless, whenever I look at it, whenever I walk upon it, it sings: 'I charge you, O daughters of Jerusalem, if ye find my beloved, that ye tell him, that I am sick of love.'

(I said Mass for Father Douglas this morning.)

Yours ever,
Pölätüo,
Card.

CODA

In the year 2022, the Post Office Express Delivery Services (Extra-European System) operate by television which is three-dimensional and works on the following principles.
1. systematic analysis of the object into protons, neutrons, and electrons (disintegrating);
2. sending the signals to the receiver;
3. synthesis of the 'same' object from different protons, neutrons, and electrons (integrating).

A letter is disintegrated in the sending station, and integrated (from 'raw' protons, neutrons, and electrons) by the receiver.

The pope dies. For the election of the new Pontiff, Pölätüo is urgently needed in New Vatican (Florida, U.S.A.). He decides to go there 'by mail.' To get disintegrated in Rome and integrated in U.S.A.

Before the actual operation (which must take no more than one 10^{-32} of a second), the telephonist in Rome calls her counterpart in New York, — Stand by! — . By a coincidence, instead of one in New York, 12 telephonists in different parts of America receive the call and stand by; and the Cardinal, 'broadcast' from one station in Rome, is 'received' by 12 stations in the U.S.A., and 12 identical (?) cardinals make their way from different states in the U.S.A. to New Vatican, Florida.

How many souls have they?
How many votes have they?

How do the new acquired characteristics begin to differentiate them?

New possibilities of asexual reproduction: you choose the type of homo you need (Army, clergy, &c) and multiply it by the intermediacy of the Post Office (Duplicate Copies) Supplementary Services.

You disintegrate a person and keep a record of the process. At any time in the future, you can pass it through the receiver and have the person again as he/she was 10, 100, or 1000 years before.

(— in that case — what happens to Original Sin?).

New possibilities of immorality?

New possibilities of immortality?

HERE BEGINNETH

The Dictionary of Traumatic Signs

COMPILED & ALPHABETICALLY ARRANGED

FOR H.E. CARDINAL PÖLÄTÜO

BY FR DOUGLAS

FROM THE MATERIAL GATHERED BY

PROF. SIGM. FREUD, M.D., LL.D., VIENNA,

IN HIS 'INTERPRETATION OF DREAMS'

& 'INTRODUCTORY LECTURES'

'Pluck up thy spirits, man, and be not
afraid to do shine office, my neck
is very short. Take heed
therefore thou shoot
not awry
for saving thine honesty.'

ABBREVIATIONS USED IN THE DICTIONARY:

esp.	especially
f.	female
m.	male
s.	symbol
sx	sex
sxl	sexual
sxlly	sexually
sxs	sexes
wf.	wife
y.	young

(if f.) if you (the dreamer) are a female
(if m.) if you (the dreamer) are a male
(usually) words in brackets describe how often interpretation is valid, or some special circumstances, e.g.:
(if an orphan) if you (the dreamer) are an orphan
(smtms) sometimes
Cf: compare
see: cross reference
inR: in Reality (in real life, not in the dream)
mng: the meaning is:
sngl: single
wsh: wish
wshflflmnt: wish-fulfilment
*glosses on the dream

A

aeroplane: 1. m. organ; 2. ability of penis to raise itself upright; *Cf:* FLYING.

affectionately behave to the husband of your lover: 1. *wsh:* to kill him to win his wife; 2. *wsh:* to kill your father to have sxl intercourse with your mother. *Cf:* MOTHER, HAVING SXL INTERCOURSE WITH.

alone (without your 'little one', *which see,)* **through the streets, going:** having no man, no sxl relations.

angel, to be an: *see:* FLYING (*if* f.) 4.

animals: *see:* SMALL ANIMALS; *see:* WILD ANIMALS.

another person: your own beloved ego in a disguised form; *Cf:* PERSON WHO ATE THE JOINT &c.

anxiety in flying, falling, vertigo & the like: a transformed recollection of pleasurable sensations of games of movement; *see also:* FLYING.

Apollo, candles of,: *see:* CANDLE, INTO A CANDLESTICK TO PUT A.

apples: 1. a beautiful bosom; *hence (possibly):* your wet-nurse; *hence (possibly):* her bosom; *hence (possibly):* an inn (for children); *Cf:* NURSE; *Cf:* INN; *or:* 2. the larger hemispheres of the human body.

aprons (sack-like) tied round the loins of two vagrants going along with a policeman: (*if* f., *if your husband is a policeman*): the two halves of the scrotum.

arrange flowers: *see:* TABLE WITH FLOWERS IN THE &c.

arrest for infanticide: *inR:* you had performed coitus interruptus clumsily; *wsh:* that you have not begotten a child.

ashamed for being naked; partially clothed &c: *see:* NAKED, OR &c.

asparagus: m. member.

B

bad tone, having a,: *see:* PIANO.

balconies: *see:* HOUSE.

baldness: castration.

balloon: ability of penis to raise itself upright; *Cf:* FLYING.

balloon, captive, & rather limp, attached to a small vestibule (*which see*)**, in front of rotunda** (*which see*)**:** (*if* m.) your penis; you have been worried about its flaccidity.

basket: *see:* MARKET-BASKET.

beat a little child: *see:* CHILD.

beating a... rock &c: *see:* RIDING WHIP.

bed & board (mensa et thorus): *see:* BOARD.

bedroom: wife (*supposing one to be in the house*).

bedwetting: *see:* URINATION.

beheading: castration; *Cf:* HAIR-CUTTING.

bird, to be a little: (*if* f.): to long, ('If only I were a little bird!').

birthday, making preparations for,: (*possibly*): birth of a child; (*or*): being prepared for a birth=having coitus with.

blinding: castration; *see:* EYE 2.

blossoming bough, holding a,: sxl innocence; **if studded with red blossoms which begin to fall:** menstruation; *also:* joy at having succeeded in passing through life unsullied, & its opposite: being guilty of various sins against sxl purity (in childhood).

blossoms & flowers: f. sxl organs, *esp.* in virginity.

blouse, milk-stains on the front of your,: *see:* MILK-STAINS &c.

board: (*often*): bed; 'bed & board'; *hence:* eating: (*often*): sxl representation-complex.

boards: women.

books: *see:* PAPER.

bottles: f. genitalia.

box: *(sometimes)* chest; *hence:* two small hemispheres of the f. body. *Cf:* PIANO.

box, child in the: *see:* CHILD IN THE BOX.

box, which has a bad tone, a disgusting old,: *see:* PIANO 3.

boxes, of all sorts & sizes: f. genitalia *(in general, but Cf:* CUPBOARD; STOVE).

branch: *(usually):* m. organ.

branch, pulling of a: *(v. typical):* onanism.

branch, to take a chopped-off: *(if* f.): to masturbate.

branch, asking whether you may take one,: *(if* f.): asking whether it is permissible to masturbate.

breaking into a house: *see:* HOUSE.

breathlessness: *see:* HEIGHT REACHING WITH &C.

brother: *(if* m.): a representative of all rivals for woman's favours; *see also:* LITTLE BROTHER.

brothers: s. of the larger hemispheres.

brothers & sisters growing wings,: *see:* FLYING UP & BEING GONE.

burglars: *see:* ROBBERS.

C

candle, into a candlestick to put a,: 1. masturbation; 2. *a broken candle:* impotence on the man's part.

carnal: *see:* CARNATIONS.

carnation (flesh-colour): *see:* CARNATIONS.

carnations *(or pinks):* *('carnal'* + *'carnation'* e.g. *flesh-colour,* + *incarnation):* m.s.; phallic significance; *(if expensive, Cf:* FLOWERS, EXPENSIVE &C. 2.).

carry a woman up &c.,: *see:* CLIMBING (TO CARRY &C.).

carrying a shabby travelling-bag with a label: 'For ladies only': homosexual relations with a lady friend.

cat: genital s.

'categorizing' *(word): (may mean):* urinating.

'category' *(word): (may mean):* f. genitals.

caves: f. genitalia.

chapel: = CHURCH, *which see.*

cheeks: *(smtms):* buttocks; *(for further details) see:* LIPS; *see also:* NOSE.

chest: *see:* BOXES OF ALL SORTS.

child: *(v. often):* genitals, ('little man', 'little woman', 'little thing'); ***to beat a little child*** *(often):* masturbation; ***to play with a little child:*** ditto.

child in the box: child in the mother's womb; but *see:* DAUGHTER LYING DEAD IN A BOX.

church: vagina; **steps leading up to it:** s. of coitus.

cigarette: s. of penis.

climbing: sxl intercourse.

climbing, difficult at first, & easier at the top of the hill: *(if* f.): to be at first respectable, but to lapse subsequently into the demimonde & form relations with highly-placed lovers; *Cf:* DOWNHILL FASTER & FASTER.

climbing down from a height over a curiously shaped trellis: *wshflflmnt:* to be of exalted origin; proper *mng:* to be of humble origin; *Cf:* climbing, (TO CARRY A WOMAN UP &C.; *Cf:* DOWNHILL FASTER & FASTER.

climbing over walls: *see:* SMOOTH WALLS OVER WHICH &C.

climbing, (to carry a woman up), easy at first, & difficult at the top of the stairs: *(admonishment?):* not to lavish an earnest affection upon girls of humble origin & dubious antecedents.

cloak: *(usually):* m. *(though sometimes without special reference to organs of sx); see also:* HATS & CLOAKS.

clothed, partially: *see:* NAKED, OR &c.
clothes: nakedness; human form.
clover-leaf, *(if 3 leaves): see:* THREE.
coal: secret love.
coffer: *see:* BOXES OF ALL SORTS.
commercial dishonesty: secret practice of masturbation.
company, large: a secret.
compartments: *see:* ROOMS, GOING THROUGH &c.
cupboard: uterus rather than other genital organs.
customs official: your psychoanalyst.

D

Daddy carrying his head on a plate: castration.
dagger: m. member.
dancing: sxl intercourse.
dark place: *see:* *THEN COMES A DARK PLACE &c.
daughter lying dead in a box: *(if inR unhappy to find oneself pregnant) wsh:* that the child might die before birth *(though it may be an old wish, no more recognisable). Cf:* DEATH OF A BELOVED RELATIVE, 2.
death of a beloved relative: 1. *(if dreamer remains unmoved): flflmnt* of another *wsh* of some kind, *(Cf:* DEATH OF A NEPHEW); 2. *(if painful affect is felt): wsh,* current or bygone, that the person in question might die, *(Cf:* DAUGHTER LYING DEAD IN A BOX). (However, one should never adduce your grief as proof that you wish him/her dead *now;* one is satisfied with concluding that you wshd him/her dead at some time or other during your childhood).
death of a nephew: *(if inR you have ever seen a person you are in love with beside the coffin of another relative): wsh:* to see again the person you are in love with. *Cf:* DEATH OF A BELOVED RELATIVE, I.
death of the father: 1. *(if you are* f.): you are an exceptional case: you should have dreamt of the death of your mother, a woman generally does; *Cf:* DEATH OF THE MOTHER 1 & 2. 2. *(if you are* m.): as a boy you regarded your father as your rival in love by whose removal you could but profit, in order to sleep with your dear, beautiful mamma in his absence; you thought that, like Kronos, he devoured his children, as the wild boar devours the litter of the sow; you wished to emasculate him *(Cf:* HAIR-CUTTING), like Zeus who emasculated his father and took his place as ruler.
death of the mother: 1. *(if you are* m.): you are an exceptional case: you should have dreamt of the death of your father, a man generally does; *Cf:* DEATH OF THE FATHER 1 & 2. 2. *(if you are* f.): as a girl you regarded your mother as your rival in love by whose removal you could but profit; you harbour a childhood *wsh:* 'Now mummy can go away; then daddy must marry me, & I will be his wife'.
death of your elder brother/sister: *(he/she ill-treated you, slandered you, robbed you of your toys; you were consumed with helpless fury against him/her, envied & feared him/her; your first impulse towards liberty & your first revolt against injustice was directed against him/her):* you harbour, in your unconscious, hostile wishes, survivals from the time when as a child you felt your wants acutely, and strove remorselessly to satisfy them, esp. against your competitors (him/her); these *wshs* have just realised themselves in your dream.

death of your younger brother/sister: *(as a child you realised that your happiness might be prejudiced by the arrival of the new-comers):* you harbour a childhood *wsh:* 'The stork had better take him/her back again'; or that your mother 'should drop him/her into the bath while bathing him/her, in order that he/she might die'.

decorate flowers *(which see)* **with green** *(which see)* **crinkled paper** *(which see)* **to hide some gaps** *(which see)* **in the flowers:** *(if* f.): your thoughts of shame & frankness: you make yourself beautiful for him, you admit your physical defects, are ashamed of them, *wsh:* to correct them.

deep shaft in which there is a window, to be in a, : recollection of the intra-uterine life; *Cf:* FIELD BEING &C.

déjà vu *('I have been here before'):* (always): the genitals of your mother: of no other place can it be asserted with such certainty that one 'has been here before'.

dense forest on top of the mountain *(which see)* **behind a church** *(which see):* crines pubis.

dental dream: *see:* TEETH, EXTRACTION OF.

depart, to: death.

*****desired solution reversed in a dream, a:** *wsh:* that the psychoanalyst should be wrong.

dig for hidden treasure: *see:* TREASURE, BURYING A.

disgusting old box: *see:* PIANO.

door: bodily aperture; genital opening; *see also:* WINDOWS & DOORS.

door, open: *see:* OPEN.

double form; to see any common symbol for the penis in a,: insurance against castration; *Cf:* LIZARD.

downhill faster & faster: *(if* f.): have relations with highly-placed lovers but to lapse subsequently into the demi-monde; *Cf:* CLIMBING, DIFFICULT AT FIRST &C.

downstairs, to be: to lose your social position, *or (by inversion):* to gain your social position; *Cf:* UPSTAIRS, TO BE.

down the ladder (=up the ladder)**:** sxl intercourse.

drawer: f. genital.

E

ear: f. genital orifice.

eat: *see:* PERSON WHO ATE THE JOINT &C., *see:* TWO PEARS, EATING ONE OF THE.; *see:* BOARD.

either - or: *(mng):* both.

elongation, all objects capable of,: m. organ.

enemy country, to see one's troops in: *wsh:* for a successful war with the country; *(in general you ought to be satisfied with this dream-wsh-flftmnt; if you are a general, however, you may also try to attain the actual goal inR.) Cf:* RIDING WHIP: BEATING A SMOOTH &C. 2.

entrance to a room: *see:* ROOM.

examination: don't be afraid, this time, too, nothing will happen to you; *but see:* MATRICULATION.

exhibitionism, infantile delight in,: *see:* NAKED OR &C.

exit from a room: *see:* ROOM.

extraction of teeth: *see:* TEETH, EXTRACTON OF.

eye: 1. *(occasionally):* f. genital orifice; 2. disguised Oedipus s.; *see:* BLINDING; *Cf:* MOTHER, HAVING SXL INTERCOURSE WITH &C.

F

facades of houses across which you let yourself down: *see:* SMOOTH WALLS OVER WHICH YOU CLIMB.

face: *(smtms):* genitals; *(for further details) see:* CHEEKS.

falling: *(if f.):* 1. you *wsh:* to give way to an erotic temptation; *(you wish to be picked up & fondled; — and taken into your bed);* 2. *(almost always):* sxl significance: 'a fallen woman'; *Cf:* FLYING; **anxiety in falling:** *see:* ANXIETY IN FLYING &c.

falling out: *(certainly):* castration as a punishment for onanism.

family, the whole: same significance as STRANGERS, A NUMBER OF, *which see.*

father, death of the,: *see:* DEATH OF THE FATHER.

field being deeply tilled by an implement, & seen from a shaft or tunnel through a window: in your phantasy you have profited by the intra-uterine opportunity of spying upon an act of coition between your parents.

fire: *see:* SWIMMING, 1.

fire-arms: penis.

fireplace: the womb of the woman.

fish: genitals.

flame: m. organ.

flowers: 1. the virginal female (*Cf:* LILIES-OF-THE-VALLEY); 2. m.s. (*Cf:* CARNATIONS); 3. violent defloration (*Cf:* VIOLETS); **expensive flowers, flowers for which one has to pay:** 1. *(if lilies-of-the-valley):* you expect your husband to appreciate the value of your virginity; 2. *(if carnations):* a sxl present & a return present which may have a financial meaning; 3. *(if violets):* you have to pay for them with your life by becoming a wife & a mother; *see also:* TABLE WITH FLOWERS IN THE &c.

flying: *(if f.):* 1. *(if short of stature):* wshflflmnt: your head towers into the air; 2. *(if fearing intercourse with human beings):* wshflflmnt: your feet are raised above the ground; 3. longing (*Cf:* BIRD, TO BE A LITTLE); 4. *(if nobody called you his angel by day):* wshflflmut: you are an angel at night; 5. you wish to be a man *(see below);* *(if* m.): 1. erection *(apparent suspension of the laws of gravity, 'winged phalli',* Cf: BALLOON; *Cf:* AEROPLANE); 2. to copulate.

flying up & being gone, brothers & sisters growing wings,: your childish egoism regarded your brothers & sisters as rivals; *wsh:* the death of all your brothers & sisters; *Cf:* DEATH OF A BELOVED RELATIVE.

foot: *(smtms):* m. member.

forest: *see:* DENSE FOREST.

'For ladies only': *see:* CARRYING A SHABBY &c.

fountains: *(inR):* a disturbance of your bladder, *(regression to the infantile form of urethral erotism).*

front of the blouse: *see:* MILK-STAINS ON THE FRONT OF &c.

fruit: 1. breasts *(& NOT a child);* or: 2. the larger hemispheres of the f. body.

funeral of an old woman: *(sometimes):* a veiled version of DEATH OF THE MOTHER *which see.*

G

gaps: *see* *THEN THERE ARE SOME GAPS IN THE DREAM.

garden: f. genitalia, *(Garden of the maiden in the 'Song of Songs').*

gliding: *(v. typical):* onanism.
going through the streets alone: *see:* ALONE (WITHOUT YOUR &C.)
gold: *(intestinal stimulus): see:* FOUNTAINS; *see:* TREASURE.
gold crown *(just put in — fell out):* commendation of material advantages of masturbation as against the economically less advantageous object-love.
glued to the stairs after hurrying upstairs, being, : *(may be an exhibition-dream): see:* NAKED, OR &C.
'Go & hang yourself!', saying: *wsh:* 'an erection at any cost'.
going up or down: *see:* LADDER, *see:* STAIRS.
great man of high authority, a, : your father.
greed for money: *see:* MONEY, GREED FOR.
green *(colour):* 1. hope; 2. pregnancy.
gun: *(v. appropriately on account of its shape):* penis.

H

hair-cutting: castration; *Cf:* EXTRACTION OF TEETH.
hair, *on face:* genitals; **on cheeks:** buttocks; **on lips:** labia minora; **on nose:** penis.
hammer: *(undoubtedly):* m. sxl s.
hand: *(smtms):* m. member.
hanging down, an object which is, : *see:* TIE.
hat: s. of man; *(usually):* m. genitals; *(occasionally):* f. genitals; **woman's hat:** *(if f.):* whole m. genital organ; *its raised middle piece:* penis; *its two downward-hanging side pieces, one lower than the other:* your husband's splendid testicles; *hat with an obliquely-standing feather in the middle:* impotent man.
head-covering: *see:* HAT.
hearth: the womb of the woman.
height, descending from a, : exalted origin.

height reaching with rhythmical intervals & increasing breathlessness, & coming down again in a few rapid jumps: *see:* STAIRS.
*****Here something is missing:** the principal characteristics of the f. genitals. *Cf:* *THEN THERE ARE SOME GAPS &C.
*****Here the dream was wiped out:** infantile reminiscence of listening to someone cleaning himself after defaecation.
hidden treasure: faeces; *see:* TREASURE.
hollow objects: *(always):* f. genitals; *(never:* m.); *Cf:* WEAPONS &C.
horse-shoe: f. genital opening.
house: 1. typical s. of the human form as a whole; 2. *(when the walls are smooth):* a man; 3. *(when there are ledges & balconies which can be caught hold of):* a woman.
houses, facades of: *see* FACADES OF HOUSES ACROSS WHICH &C.
husband: *see:* AFFECTIONATELY &C.
husband & father (confused): *(may mean an equivalent of):* 'the maidservant is expecting a child'.

I

inability to do something *(in your dream):* you express negation; you say 'No' to your own will.
incarnation: *see:* CARNATIONS.
income tax questioned: *wsh* to be known as a person with a large income.
infanticide: *see:* ARREST FOR &C.
infantile delight in exhibitionism: *see:* NAKED OR &C.
inn: *(smtms):* the bosom of the nurse; *Cf:* NURSE; *Cf:* APPLES.
*****innocent dreams, conspicuously:** *(commonly embody):* crude erotic wishes.
intercourse with one's mother, having sxl, : *see:* MOTHER, HAVING SXL &C.

interest in another person: *(invariably):* the wishes of your own ego; *see:* PERSON WHO ATE THE JOINT &C.

interruption: *see:* *THEN COMES A DARK PLACE &C.

Italy, to: *(if you are a German):* gen-italien.

J

jars: f. genitalia.
jewel: beloved person.
jewel-case: f. genital organ.
jumps: *see:* HEIGHT REACHING WITH &C.

K

King & Queen: *(in most cases):* your own parents.

King of Italy, to talk angrily of the, when walking towards the top of the hill: *(in some cases):* to resent the intrusion of people of low rank into aristocratic society; *Cf:* CLIMBING (TO CARRY &C.)

key: m. member; *see:* LOCK.
knife: m. member.

L

ladder, act of mounting: *(indubitably):* sxl intercourse.

lance: penis; *see:* RIDING-WHIP.

landscapes, *(esp. with bridges or wooded mountains):* genitals; *(with rocks, woods & water):* topography of f. sxl organs. *see:* MOUNTAIN, ROCK, WOODS, CHURCH &C.; — *déjà vu: see:* DÉJÀ VU.

large company: a secret.

left-hand direction: road to crime: homosexuality, incest, perversion; *Cf:* RIGHT-HAND DIRECTION.

lilies-of-the-valley: *(if* f.*)*: the preciousness of your virginity; *(if expensive, see:* FLOWERS, EXPENSIVE &C. 1.)

lily: chastity; *(Cf:* LILIES-OF-THE-VALLEY)

limpidity of a balloon: flaccidity of your penis.

linen: *(in general):* f. s.

lips (which enclose the orifice of the mouth): labia minora; *Cf:* FACE.

little child ('little one'): sxl organ in general; *little daughter:* f. sxl organ; *little son; little brother:* m. sxl organ.

little one: see above.

little sausage: little boy's genitals; *(Cf:* PURSE).

little trunk, a: *see:* TRUNK SO FULL &C.

lizard *(whose tail, if pulled off, is regenerated by a new growth):* wsh: insurance against castration; *Cf:* DOUBLE FORM; TO SEE &C.

**locality-*déjà vu: see:* DÉJÀ VU.

lock: f. organ; *see:* KEY.

locked room: *see:* ROOM.

long, stiff objects & weapons: *(always):* m.; (never f., *unless* you are a woman who wishes to be a man).

luggage: 1. the burden of sin; 2. your own genitals.

M

machinery, all kinds of,: mechanism of the m. sxl apparatus.

manual occupations, certain,: sxl intercourse.

maps: human body, genitals, &c.

market-basket: 1. snub, refusal; 2. to be married beneath your station; 3. the mark of a servant.

material *(of different kind):* s. of WOMAN; *Cf:* WOOD; PAPER.

matriculation *(examination):* (invariably or

frequently): sxl experiences & sxl maturity.

meal eaten by an anonymous person, an abundant,: you are the person.

meatshop, a closed: *(if you are a German):* neglect of man's clothing; *(if you are English): see:* 'YOUR FLY IS UNDONE'.

menses, having: *(if* y. wf.) *mng:* menses have stopped *inR; wsh:* to enjoy your freedom a little longer, before the discomforts of maternity begin.

milk-stains on the front of your blouse: *mng:* pregnancy *inR*, and not the first one; *wsh:* to have more nourishment for the second child than you had for the first.

missing, something is: *see:* *HERE SOMETHING IS MISSING.

miss a train: reassure yourself, you are not going to die; *Cf:* TRAIN, TRAVELLING BY; *Cf:* DEPART; *Cf:* EXAMINATION.

money, greed for: *(often):* the uncleanliness of childhood, filth, having soiled the bed.

moon: the place from which one is born; bottom; — **reflected in water:** *see:* WATER, FLING YOURSELF INTO &c.

moss: crines pubis.

mother, death of the,: *see:* DEATH OF THE MOTHER.

mother, having sxl intercourse with your,: *(as undisguised Oedipus dream): if you are Julius Caesar:* you will take possession of the earth; *if you are a Tarquinius:* you will become the ruler of Rome; *if you are Hippias:* you will return home & regain power; *in general:* you manifest in life confidence in yourself & unshakeable optimism which compel actual success; *(Cf:* RIDING-WHIP 2. *if you are a Bismarck).* Also: as the key to the tragedy & the complement to the dream of the DEATH OF THE FATHER, *which see. Cf:* AFFECTIONATELY BEHAVE TO THE HUSBAND OF ONE'S LOVER 2; *Cf:* EYE 2.

mountain: m. organ.

mountain behind a church *(which see); Also:* **mountain overgrown on both sides with grass & bushes which grow denser & denser:** Mons Veneris; *see also:* DENSE FOREST.

mounting, act of: *(indubitably):* sxl intercourse.

mouse: *(because of hairiness):* genitals.

mouth: f. genital orifice.

mucus: semen; *(smtms also):* urine; tears.

multiple form; to see any common symbol for the penis in a,: insurance against castration; *Cf:* LIZARD.

*multiplication of an object *(representing temporal repetition): see:* TWO PEARS... EATING ONE *('once')* DESIRING THE OTHER *('again').*

mushroom *(esp. 'Phallus impudicus'): (undoubtedly):* penis.

mussels: *(unmistakably):* f. s.

N

naked, or partially clothed, or feeling ashamed for your clothing (being in a chemise; petticoat; without your sabre; having no collar; &c); *'exhibition dreams': wshflflmnt:* you *wsh* to be taken back to the age of childhood (paradise) in which the sense of shame is unknown, prior to the moment when shame & fear awaken, expulsion follows, & sxl life & cultural development begin. *See also:* STRANGERS, A NUMBER OF.

nail-file: *(undoubtedly):* m. sxl s.

narrow space, traversing a,: *see:* TRAVERSING A NARROW SPACE.

narrow steep passage: vagina.

necktie: *(if* m.): penis; *(you probably possess a whole collection of neckties inR); wsh:* to possess a collection of penes & be able to

select them at pleasure.
nightly visitors: *see:* ROBBERS.
*****non-fulfilment of your wish:** the fulfilment of another, *e.g.:* that the theory of wish-fulfilment should go wrong.
nose (esp. in the presence of hair): penis.
number of strangers, a: *see:* STRANGERS, A NUMBER OF.
nurse: *(smtms):* abandoned mistress.

O

object capable of elongation: m. organ.
obstacles: *see:* INABLITY TO DO SOMETHING.
old woman, funeral of an,: *(sometimes):* a veiled version of DEATH OF THE MOTHER which see.
open room: *see:* ROOM.
opening of locked doors: commonest of sxl s.
open, to find the door: to find a f. no longer a virgin.
oven: 1. a woman; 2. mother's womb.

P

palaces, two stately: *see:* TWO STATELY PALACES.
pale moon: white bottom; *Cf:* MOON.
paper (& *objects made of p.*): s. of woman.
partially clothed: *see:* NAKED, OR &C.
passage, narrow steep: vagina.
peaches: 1. the breasts; *or;* 2. the larger hemispheres of the human body.
pears: *see:* TWO PEARS &C.
pencil: *(undoubtedly):* m. sxl s.; *pencils which slide in & out of a sheath: see:* ELONGATION.
penholder: *(undoubtedly):* m. sxl s.
penetration into narrow spaces: commonest of sxl s.
person a,: m. organ. *Cf:* ANOTHER PERSON.
person who ate the joint, you did not see the,: you are the person; *Cf:* ANOTHER PERSON.
piano: 1. chest; *hence* 2. two small hemispheres of the f. body; 3. *if having bad tone:* two large hemispheres of the f. body. See also: SCALE.
piano, playing the,: *see:* PLAY, ANY KIND OF; *see:* PRACTISING &C.
picture: woman; *big p.:* grown-up woman; *small. p.:* little girl; *cheap p.:* prostitute; *your signature on the little p.:* parent complex; *p. of a deeply tilled field: see:* FIELD.
pike: m. member.
pillars: legs; ('Song of Songs').
pinks: *see:* CARNATIONS.
pistols (v. appropriately on account of their shape): penis.
pits: f. genitalia.
plans: human body, genitals, &c.
play, any kind of, (incl. playing the piano): gratification derived from a person's own genitals.
play with a little child: *see:* CHILD.
ploughshare: m. organ.
pocket: *see:* BOXES OF ALL SORTS.
pole: penis.
policeman in helmet: phallus.
posts: legs.
practising Études of Moscheles & Clementi's 'Gradus ad Parnassum': moderate masturbation would probably be less harmful to you than your enforced abstinence.
present of flowers: *(if* f.): rich love-life in exchange for virginity; *Cf:* FLOWERS, EXPENSIVE &C.
President, the: *(in U.S.A.):* your father; *Cf:* KING & QUEEN.
pulley lamps: *see:* ELONGATION.

pulling off a big piece of some material: 1. commercial dishonesty; 2. masturbation.

pulling of a branch: *(v. typical):* onanism.

'pull one out'; 'to pull one off': the act of masturbation; *Cf:* BRANCH PULLING &C.; *Cf:* TEETH, EXTRACTION OF; *Cf:* TWO TEETH &C.

pullover: *(if in summer):* a thin condom; *(if in winter):* a thick condom.

purse: a little girl's genitals.

pursuit by a man armed with a knife or rifle: *see:* KNIVES; *see also:* ROBBERS.

Q

Queen of Sweden, behind closed shutters, with the candles of Apollo, When the,: *see:* APOLLO, CANDLES OF.

R

rain: urination=s. of fertilisation.

receptacles, objects capable of acting as,: f. genitalia.

red flowers on a branch: innocence & menstruation.

relatives: *(generally):* genitals.

reptiles & fishes: m. sxl s.

revolver: *(v. appropriately on account of its shape):* penis.

rhythmical activities: sxl intercourse.

rhythmical intervals &c: see: HEIGHT REACHING WITH &C.

riding: sxl intercourse.

riding-whip: m. member; *its extensibility:* phallic symbol, erection; *if 'endlessly long':* infantile attitude; *taking it in your hand:* masturbation *(which may refer not to the present but to your far distant childish impulses);* **if it is the left** *(which see)* **hand:** your childish masturbation was practice in defiance of prohibition; *beating a smooth wall (which see) of rock with it & disclosing a broad road:* 1. longing for erotic conquests; 2. *(if you are a Bismarck):* thoughts of a serious nature, & quite remote from the sxl, *as e.g.:* ENEMY COUNTRY, TO SEE ONE'S TROOPS IN.

right-hand direction: way to righteousness: marriage, relations with a prostitute, &c. *(according to your own moral standards); see also:* LEFT-HAND DIRECTION.

robbers: *(in anxiety dreams):* your father *(who, perhaps, used to wake you in order to set you on the chamber, so that you might not wet the bed; or to lift the coverlet in order to see how you were holding your hands while sleeping).*

rock: m. organ; *(but Cf:* LANDSCAPE WITH ROCKS).

rod: phallus; *the production of fluid by striking with it:* infantile masturbation-phantasy; *Cf:* RIDING-WHIP &C.

room: s. for 'woman'; *Cf:* HOUSE.

room divided in two, one,: *see:* TWO ROOMS WHICH WERE &C.

rooms, going through a number of: marriage *(the expression of monogamy according to the rule of opposites).*

rotunda: buttocks; *see also:* VESTIBULE IN FRONT OF &C.

run over, being: sxl intercourse.

S

sabre: penis.

secretions: *see:* MUCUS; TEARS; URINE; SEMEN.

semen: *(may mean):* mucus; tears; urine *(hence:* greatness); *(though it is not clear why this important secretion, s., shld be replaced by an indifferent one).*

sxl intercourse with one's mother, having,: see: MOTHER, HAVING SXL &C.

shaft, the walls of which are softly upholstered: vagina; **going down the shaft:** coition in the vagina; see also: DEEP SHAFT IN WHICH THERE IS A WINDOW, TO BE IN A.

ship: f. genitals; Cf: RECEPTACLES, BOXES.

ship, sailing on the sea: to urinate.

shoes: f. genital organs.

shooting: s. of coitus.

silk handkerchiefs, being bound with: identification with a homosxl.

sisters: s. of the breasts.

sliding: (v. typical): onanism.

slippers: f. genital organs.

small animals: little children, (e.g. undesired sisters or brothers).

'smooth' walls: men; Cf: HOUSE.

smooth walls over which you climb: erect human bodies, (reminiscence of climbing up your parents? nurses?)

snail: (unmistakably): f. s.

snake: the most important s. of the m. member.

snake as a necktie: (if m.): penis; (esp.: if it is turning towards a girl).

space, object enclosing a,: f genitalia.

springs: (inR): a disturbance of your bladder, (regression to the infantile form of urethral erotism).

stabbing: s. of coitus.

stains: see: MILK-STAINS &C.

stairs (or anything like them): definite s. of coitus; Cf: HEIGHT REACHING WITH RHYTHMICAL &C.

steep inclines: sxl act.

steep narrow passage: see: NARROW STEEP PASSAGE.

steep places, act of mounting: (indubitably): sxl intercourse.

steps leading up to the church: see: CHURCH.

stick: m. member; see: RIDING-WHIP.

stove: uterus rather than other genital organs.

strange person: see: PERSON WHO ATE THE JOINT &C.

stranger, a: somebody on to whom an embarrassing situation can be displaced.

strangers, a number of: 1. (as a counter-wish): a secret; 2. the substitute for those persons who were the object for your sxl interest in childhood and are usually omitted from all reproductions, in dreams, in hysteria or in obsessional neurosis; 3. (if in connection with exposure, in which case see: NAKED, OR &C.): counter-wsh to that single intimately-known person for whom exposure was intended.

stream of urine, the: see: URINE 3.

streets, going through the,: see: ALONE (WITHOUT YOUR &C.).

suite of rooms: (v. often) a woman. **walking through a suit of rooms:** a brothel; a harem; marriage (contrast); Cf: ROOM.

sweetmeats: (frequently): sxl pleasures.

swimming: 1. repeating a child's pleasure of wetting the bed; 2. full bladder; 3. dwellingplace of the unborn.

sword: (unmistakably): s. for the m. organ.

T

table (whether bare or covered): women.

table, being flat like a,: virginity.

table, with flowers in the centre, arranging: (if f.): yourself and your genitals; wsh: to be married. (Cf: FLOWERS).

talk angrily &c: see: KING OF ITALY &C.

tears: semen; (smtms also): urine; mucus. Also: grief.

teeth, extraction of,: (if m.): (without doubt

nothing other than): masturbatory desires of puberty; *(certainly):* castration as a punishment for onanism; *(if f.):* parturition, birth, (removing a part from the whole body); *see also:* TWO TEETH &C. *Cf:* HAIR-CUTTING, & GOLD CROWN.

*****Then comes a dark place, an interruption:** f. genitals.

*****Then there are some gaps in the dream:** the genital apertures of women. *Cf:* *HERE SOMETHING IS MISSING.

thickets: pubic hair (both sxs).

three, the sacred number,: s. of the whole m. genitalia, of which more conspicuous &, to both sxs, more interesting part is the penis, *which see under various long & upstanding objects, such as:* UMBRELLA; POLE; TREE.

tie: *see:* NECKTIE.

till a field deeply: *see:* FIELD BEING &C.

tools: *see:* MACHINERY ALL KINDS OF.

tooth-ache: *(always):* onanism & fear of punishment.

train is about to start & you cannot reach it: *see:* INABILITY TO DO SOMETHING.

train, travelling by: dying; *Cf:* MISS A TRAIN.

transplant branches in your own garden: *see:* BRANCH; *see:* GARDEN.

traversing a narrow space: intra-uterine life; sojourn in the mother's womb; act of birth; (for phantasies & unconscious thoughts relating to life in the womb, *see:* FIELD BEING &C; *see:* WATER).

travelling-bag to carry: *see:* CARRYING A SHABBY &C.

travelling by train: dying; *Cf:* MISS A TRAIN.

treasure: beloved person; (*Cf:* JEWEL; JEWEL-CASE; GOLD); *burying a treasure: (inR):* an intestinal disorder, (regression to the infantile form of intestinal erotism); *Cf:* FOUNTAINS.

tree-trunk: m. member.

trinity of three persons *(e.g.: a watchman accompanied by two tramps):* whole m. organ; *see also:* THREE, THE SACRED NUMBER.

trunks: f. s.; *two black trunks:* two dark women.

trunk so full of books as to have difficulty in closing it, to fill a little, : *see:* CHILD IN THE BOX; for *wsh see:* DAUGHTER LYING DEAD IN A BOX.

two pears *(pommes ou poires):* breasts of the mother who nursed you; *two pears on a windowsill: see above* + WINDOW-SILL; *eating one of the two pears:* mng: 'Mother, you suckled me *once* for much longer than the customary term'; *desiring the other pear:* mng: 'Mother, give (show) me the breast *again* at which I once used to drink'.

two rooms which were previously one: child's view of f. genitals & anus as a sngl opening.

two sisters: breasts; *shake hands with two sisters: wsh:* to grasp b.

two stately palaces: two stately buttocks of the f. body; *being led along a road to a small house between them:* attempted coition from behind.

two teeth, put hand in mouth & draw out,: *(if* m., y., homosxl): to masturbate twice in succession.

two vagrants: *see:* APRONS (SACK-LIKE) &c.

tunnel, (*see also:* DEEP SHAFT) **through which trains go in & out in opposite directions; travel in uncomfortable position in a,:** with some difficulty, you succeed in changing from masturbation to sxl intercourse.

U

umbrella: m. member; *its opening:* erection.
underlinen: *(in general):* f. s.
uniforms: nakedness; human form.
up or down, going: *see:* LADDER, *see:* STAIRS.
upstairs and downstairs, being busy; *'above' and 'beneath':* fancies or memories of a sxl content; suppressed cravings; Lesbian practice.
upstairs, to be: to gain your social position, or *(by inversion):* to lose your social position; *Cf:* DOWNSTAIRS, TO BE.
up the ladder (= down the ladder): sxl intercourse.
urination: 1. desire for greatness; 2. s. of fertilization; 3. sxl ejaculation.
urine: 1. semen; 2. mucus, tears; 3. greatness *(if there is the stream of u. that washes everything clean).*

V

vegetable, longish: *see:* ASPARAGUS.
velvet: crines pubis.
vermin, to be infected with: *(often):* pregnancy.
vessels of all kinds: f. organ.
vestibule in front of rotunda, a small,: scrotum; *see also:* BALLOON, CAPTIVE, ATTACHED TO A &C.
victory & conquest: *(often):* longing for erotic conquests; *(yet Cf:* ENEMY COUNTRY, TO SEE &C.).
violence, experiencing some,: sxl intercourse.
violets: violence of defloration, *(if expensive, Cf:* FLOWERS, EXPENSIVE &C. 3.).

W

walls over which &c.: *see:* SMOOTH WALLS OVER WHICH &C.
walls, 'smooth',: *see:* SMOOTH WALLS; *see:* HOUSE.
water: *(invariably):* birth; *falling into, or clambering out of —, saving someone from, or being saved:* the relation between mother & child, giving birth or being born; *staying long in the —:* intra-uterine life, sojourn in the mother's womb, act of birth; (hence: 1. dread of being buried alive; 2. belief in a life after death = projection into the future of this mysterious life before birth); *entry of a child into —:* delivery of a child from the uterine waters; *bobbing up and down of a child's head in —:* recollection of the sensation of quickening experienced in your pregnancy; *flinging yourself into the dark water at a place where the pale moon (which see) is reflected in it:* 1. *wsh:* to be born again; 2. *wsh:* to become a mother; 3. *wsh:* to continue psycho-analytic treatment at the summer resort.
watering-can: m. organ.
water-pipe: the urinary system.
water-tap: m. organ.
weapons, elongated &/or sharp, all,: m. member; *— pointed:* ditto. *(never:* f.).
weapons, being threatened with,: sxl intercourse.
wet: *(smtms):* dry.
wet, getting,: enuresis = coitus = pregnancy.
whip: *see:* RIDING-WHIP.
wild animals: human beings whose senses are excited; *hence:* evil impulses *or* passions.
window: *see:* FIELD.

window-sill: projection of the bosom; *Cf:* HOUSE, 3.
windows & doors: the openings of the body.
wings growing,: *see:* FLYING UP & BEING GONE &c.
wiped out: *see:* *HERE THE DREAM WAS WIPED OUT.
woman carrying a man: being carried by the nurse; *Cf:* NURSE; *Cf:* CLIMBING, (TO CARRY A WOMAN UP &c.).
woman, funeral of an old,: *(sometimes):* a veiled version of DEATH OF THE MOTHER *which see.*

woman's hat: *see:* HAT, WOMAN'S.
wood: feminine matter; *objects made of w.:* s. of woman.
woods: pubic hair *(both sxs).*
work hard: *see:* TILL A FIELD DEEPLY.
writing-table drawer: f. genital.

Y

'your fly is undone': *(if in your childhood you were the victim of sxl attempts)* you wsh them to be repeated.

It was said of St. Francis of Assisi
that he can be dismissed
'as a harmless enthusiast, pious & sincere,
but hardly of sane mind,
who was much rather accessory to the intellectual
than to the moral
degradation of mankind'.

Envoy

Venice, 10 June, 1961.

Dear Pölätüo, Dear Princess Zuppa,

    I am still under the spell of the most wonderful time you gave me under the roof of d'Ormespant and wish to thank you both for your unforgettable hospitality. I am especially grateful for the placet (I realise its private, personal and not in the least official character) you, Y. E., have given my book. How magnanimous your non obstat *is*, one understands only when one remembers that it covers also those episodes which you most certainly would rather have exposed in a somewhat different light than that in which my book presents them. But, as you said quoting John xix.22,: *What I have written I have written.*

    Ever since my wife made me a present of a typewriter that possessed the letters ä, ö, ü, I have been dreaming of writing your biography. I wrote the first page in French, and discarded it. Then I wrote the first version of the first part in the language of Madame Kostrowicki's ancestors, the language most fit for the purpose. This was published in 1945 by my friend Antoni Slonimski in 'Nowa Polska', a literary magazine he edited at the time in London, and thousands of Roman Catholics read the story of your Life with great joy and, so far as I can ascertain, without detriment to their faith. Then, however, my friend Anthony Froshaug persuaded me to render that first version of the first part into English, co-operated with me to that end, and by so doing became, perhaps unconsciously, responsible for my subsequent finishing of the whole book in that language, so that there is a chance now that a few stern Protestants and other Infidels may also happen to read it and wonder what it is all about. And I can only hope, or should I say: pray, that their sense of humour is not very far removed from yours, which I admired so much as I watched you laugh when Princess Zuppa read to you some parts of the Life, including the beginning where, in a light vein, I speculated on the subject of your past, and the Coda, where I did so about your future.

Well, twenty years (since I first met you) have fled, your portrait is painted, no conclusions are drawn, or have been intended. My paper and the thought of your patience both remind me to close.

Kissing your ring, and Princess Zuppa's hands, I assure you that whatever are the ways of my lay reason's thinkings, it will respect and esteem your blessing as much as my heart will rejoice in it.

All your friends ask me to send you their love with mine,

Your biographer.

H.E. Cardinal Pölätüo,
Palazzo d'Ormespant,
Verumontanum,
Roma.

BIOGRAPHER'S NOTE:

Official biographers of Guillaume Apollinaire give the date of the birth of his mother as 1858; this would imply that in 1862, when the Cardinal met the elderly maiden-lady at the Goncourts, (see: Part One, Chapter One), the Countess was 4 years old which is nonsense.

The confusion has arisen in the following way: Knowing that the Countess was 21 when she conceived Guillaume, they count that she was about 22 when he was born. As he was born in 1880, arithmetic gives them 1858 as the date of birth of his mother. But we know that she was carrying the child not for 9 months but for 18 years, which makes her 39 in 1880, and 21 in this crucial year of 1862.

Palazzo d'Ormespant,
Verumontanum,
Roma.

To the Editor   *16th May 1959*
The Times,
Printing House Square,
London E.C. 4

Sir,

  Prompted by Dr. J.O. Wisdom's appreciation of Mr. Themerson's work entitled 'factor T' (see: British Journal for the Philosophy of Science, *May, 1958), we have had this little booklet read to us, and having noticed that our name is mentioned in it on more than one occasion, which will surprise nobody who knows that Mr. Themerson, for the last seventeen years, has been engaged in writing both our biography and a disquisition on our philosophy, we feel it desirable that certain twists of thought be disentangled so that neither the biographer nor ourselves be made to suffer the unfairness of censure for the idiosyncrasies of the other.*

  Let us at once say this: Voices have recently been heard insinuating that the author of the little booklet, by the very fact of writing what he wrote in it on ethical and religious subjects, has shown himself unworthy of becoming the historian of our life and the exponent of our philosophical teaching. These harsh voices are disagreeable to our ears and we belie their rash message. We have no quarrel with the opinions expressed by Mr. Themerson. On the contrary, we endorse them.

Though, as will be shewn presently, we go a step further than he has so far ventured or adventured, and we draw our own and inevitable conclusions.

Mr. Themerson's dissertation consists of three parts. The third seems to be composed in a form which looks like verse to the eye, and, though there are no rhymes in it, we shall say no more about it.

The second part of the dissertation deals, putting it summarily, with the usage and abusage of the word 'belief'. In contradistinction to what some authorities expect from us, we wholly approve the author's endeavour to arrest the recklessness with which the word 'believe' is used by philosophers, and, though we would have placed the emphasis differently, we join him in his appeal for a divorce between this word ('believe') and such words as: 'to accept, to consider, to be certain, confident, convinced, to have no doubt, to know, to be positive, to reckon, to rest assured, to be satisfied, to be sure, to think' &c.

Yet, what we are mainly concerned with here is Part One where the tree of Ethics is tapped to give out the bitter sap of what the author names factor T. *This factor, to quote Dr. J.O. Wisdom, 'is the tragedy that results from Needs plus Dislike of what is needed — when it is vitally necessary to do what one vitally dislikes.' Again, we see nothing blasphemous in this effort which aims at finding the origin of the Spiritual in the Flesh; on the contrary, we approve it. And not only do we approve it but, more, as we have already announced, we regret that the author did not go still further in his search for the Material beginning of the Moral but, having stopped half-way, satisfied himself with using such general notions as Needs and Dislike. Thus earning for himself the doubtful compliment of having built 'a fundamental theory of psychology having affinities with Freud and Plato' (l. c.). This we regret. Because whoever introduces notions which may be said to have affinities with Freud and Plato, is like a heretic who introduces new additional deities. And as new deities are of necessity false deities, and false deities belong to the class of things that are not known, then Appealing to them for the elucidation of an unknown problem is* ignotum per ignotius, *unless they are subsequently reduced to some terms that denote physical processes,* id est: *such processes as were created by the Almighty.*

We do not contradict Mr. Themerson when he says that the Tragic Conflict between the Dislike to kill and the Necessity of doing so created Ethics and

Religions. This granted, we expect him to go further and demonstrate that what he calls 'Dislike' and 'Necessity' is essentially physical in its nature, that it belongs to the material universe, and thus, together with the rest of the world, belongs to the Reality of the Arsenal wherein the Omnipotence of God is stored. If he does not do this, then his Dislike and Necessity become two new spiritual entities, and the prospect of adding them to the Trinity will offend both the Faith and the Principle of Entia non sunt multiplicanda praeter necessitatem.

As he has not shewn any tendency to move in that necessary direction, we have decided to do so ourselves:

* * *

Now, let us imagine a kind of Henri Poincaré Island in which man's only food is a kind of Hieronymus Bosch Skunk. No other means of satisfying your hunger are given to you; if you do not want to die, you must hunt for a skunk. Whose nature it is to surround himself, when attacked, with a scent which is not to your liking. Your profound dislike of this smell is something you were born with, and you have to be really hungry to make yourself overcome it. This is an abominable situation. Abominable, but reasonably clear. There is no mystery in it, so far. You feel your hunger, and you feel the smell, there is a straight fight between the two feelings, both equally understandable. Now, however, try to imagine that there exists a skunk which produces a new and peculiar kind of smell. A smell-less smell. It still evokes in you the same pattern of behaviour as before, and yet you do not feel it in your nostrils. You do not feel it at all. And when you observe yourself and notice that you are behaving as if the skunk stank, and he doesn't, it does fill you with Great Wonderment. And you invent some Tremendous Rigmarole to explain this state of affairs, because you cannot know that your body has been entered by a molecule of what was no longer a smell but was still keylike enough to open the door of that particular kind of behaviour.

At this stage of our deliberation, we were fortunate enough to open a copy of Nature (3, January, 1959) on a page where the discovery of a completely new word was reported. It has always been our opinion that the discoveries of new words are the most important events in the history of scientific thought. The discovery of a new fact, or a new gadget, just adds new data to the equipment you are burdened with in your mortal life; it is when you hear of the discovery of a new word that you feel the history of mankind making a step forward into the future. The word we have in mind this time was discovered jointly, on 12 November 1958, by Mr. P. Karlson of the Max-Planck-Institute for Biochemistry, Munich, and Mr. M. Lüscher of the Zoological Institute, University of Bern, and it is spelled: PHEROMONES.

Their report runs as follows:

'During the past few decades, investigations have been made into various active substances which, though they resemble hormones in some respects, cannot be included among them. For example, the sexual attractants of butterflies are, like hormones, produced and secreted by special glands; minute amounts cause a specific reaction in the receptor organ (the antenna of the male), which eventually leads to a state of copulative readiness. Unlike hormones, however, the substance is not secreted into the blood but outside the body; it does not serve humoral correlation within the organism but communication between individuals...

We propose, (therefore), the designation "pheromone" for this group of active substances. The name is derived from the Greek pherein, *to transfer*; hormon, *to excite*. Pheromones are defined as substances which are secreted to the outside by an individual and received by a second individual of the same species, in which they release a specific reaction, for the example, a definite behaviour or a developmental process...'

As the present fashion in scientific research tells us that we gain knowledge not by reading 'the book of Nature' or by following 'a principle of induction', but by inventing a hypothesis and letting others try to falsify it, we feel it will be legitimate for us to put forward what follows:

We assume the existence of pheromone d and of hormone n.
Pheromone d *is produced and expelled into the surroundings by an animal whenever he finds himself in distress, fear, or in* articulo mortis. *Assimilated by an*

animal belonging to a not very far removed species, it evokes in him a pattern of behaviour which may be described as 'moving away from the source of stimulation'.

Hormone n *is produced by an animal when he is in need of* e.g. *food, and it is injected into his own bloodstream, thus evoking in him a pattern of behaviour which may be described as 'killing for food'.*

There is a constant keeping of balance between hormones n *and pheromones* d, *and it assures the survival of the species. If there had ever appeared a species of carnivorous creatures completely lacking in hormone* n, *it must have starved itself to death in the first generation. If there had ever appeared a species completely lacking in pheromone* d, *it must have become extinct, as its members, not restrained by the action of* d, *would have eaten the offshoots of their own family before these had time to mature to give rise to the new generation.*

And thus the tragic factor T, *or the conflict that results from Needs plus Dislike of what is needed — when it is vitally necessary to do what one vitally dislikes,* can *be reduced to the interaction that takes place between pheromone* d *and hormone* n.

Q.E.D.

Now, here is hypothetical case-history:

1. *There is a prey in front of us. The prey is frightened. But we are not hungry.* d>n. *We do not kill.*
2. *After a time the situation changes: We have become hungry. But the prey is gone.* n, d=0. *We ask ourselves: Why did we not kill when the prey was there? The question puzzles us. If the prey were a stinking skunk, we would have remembered its odour and it would serve us for an answer. But it was not a skunk. There was no sensation of smell there at all. It was a pheromone. And thus, all that our Memory can tell us is that there was something* (Md, *not seen, not heard, not smellable) which ('mysteriously?') stopped us from killing the prey. An X!*
3. *So now we again lie in wait for the prey to come. We are hungry. And the prey comes.* n>d. *We kill. And yet, even if we are a tiger we still make noises and faces, and display other signs indicating that we have to*

overcome some resistance when in the act of killing. In this case, it is a physiological resistance: our hormone n *has to overcome the pheromone* d.

4. *However, we have now killed and eaten. We are hungry no more. Yet we remember the time when we were hungry. And if the next opportunity to kill now arises, we find ourselves under a number of stresses. Physiologically: we are not hungry now,* n<d, *and we should refrain from killing. Psychologically, however, the Memory of the time when we suffered hunger may be strong,* Mn>d, *so strong that we may find ourselves in the process of killing and storing food for the future.*

5. *Thus we have two manners of killing and two manners of not killing. Physiological manner of killing and not killing (based on* n *and* d*), and psychological manner of killing and not killing (based on* Mn *and* Md*).*

6. *If we have been chosed to be what zoologists call 'thinking animals', we have the power to observe our own behaviour and we try to explain it. We understand the necessity of killing. Both on the physiological and on the psychological level. We are also capable of inventing some explanation of not killing, on the psychological level. But* not *killing on the physiological level defeats us. Why shouldn't we? What is it that makes us not? We don't know anything about the existence of pheromone* d. *And we say: there is an* X. *And we say: when we need food,* X *does not forbid us to kill, but when we are not hungry,* X *does. And we ask: Who is* X? *And we go back to the point of departure and answer:* X *is one who forbids us this and that in these and those circumstances, but commands us to do that and this in those and these circumstances; and thus we arrive at a series of explanations and rules which become the basis and the beginning of ethical and religious orders.*

Therefore, and in contradistinction to what some authorities maintain, we fail to see any blasphemy in this bringing down of ethical and religious manifestations to Mr. Themerson's tragic conflict between Needs and Dislikes, provided it is further reduced (as it has just been done by us) to the conflict between pheromones and hormones. Verily: we commend it:

Because: if God wishes so, is it not His Right to take out from His Arsenal His hormones and pheromones and use them upon men so that they are forced to ask question: Who is X?, and thus prepare themselves for His being revealed to them?

Indeed, there is nothing in Mr. Themerson's paper that would be odious to the teaching of the Church; and, if it is moved that it be placed on the Index librorum prohibitorum, *we shall object to such tendencies very forcibly.*

Pölätüo

Card.

P.S.: Cooking destroys pheromone d.